People in Glass Houses

Titles by Jayne Ann Krentz writing as Jayne Castle

THE GUINEVERE JONES SERIES

Specials

Anthologies

Titles written by Jayne Ann Krentz and Jayne Castle

Titles by Jayne Ann Krentz writing as Amanda Quick

The Bride Wore White
When She Dreams
The Lady Has a Past
Close Up
Tightrope
The Other Lady Vanishes
The Girl Who Knew Too Much
'Til Death Do Us Part
Garden of Lies
Otherwise Engaged
The Mystery Woman
Crystal Gardens
Quicksilver
Burning Lamp

The Perfect Poison
The Third Circle
The River Knows
Second Sight
Lie by Moonlight
The Paid Companion
Wait Until Midnight
Late for the Wedding
Don't Look Back
Slightly Shady
Wicked Widow
I Thee Wed
With This Ring
Affair

Mischief
Mystique
Mistress
Deception
Desire
Dangerous
Reckless
Ravished
Rendezvous
Scandal
Surrender
Seduction

Titles by Jayne Ann Krentz

THE LOST NIGHT FILES TRILOGY

The Night Island
Sleep No More

THE FOGG LAKE TRILOGY

Lightning in a Mirror
All the Colors of Night
The Vanishing

Untouchable
Promise Not to Tell
When All the Girls Have Gone
Secret Sisters
Trust No One
River Road
Dream Eyes
Copper Beach
In Too Deep
Fired Up
Running Hot
Sizzle and Burn
White Lies

All Night Long
Falling Awake
Truth or Dare
Light in Shadow
Summer in Eclipse Bay
Together in Eclipse Bay
Smoke in Mirrors
Lost & Found
Dawn in Eclipse Bay
Soft Focus
Eclipse Bay
Eye of the Beholder
Flash

Sharp Edges
Deep Waters
Absolutely, Positively
Trust Me
Grand Passion
Hidden Talents
Wildest Hearts
Family Man
Perfect Partners
Sweet Fortune
Silver Linings
The Golden Chance

PEOPLE IN GLASS HOUSES

Jayne Castle

BERKLEY
NEW YORK

BERKLEY
An imprint of Penguin Random House LLC
penguinrandomhouse.com

Library of Congress Cataloging-in-Publication Data

Names: Castle, Jayne, author.
Title: People in glass houses / Jayne Castle.
Description: New York: Berkley, 2024. | Series: A Harmony novel
Identifiers: LCCN 2023046050 (print) | LCCN 2023046051 (ebook) |
ISBN 9780593639887 (hardcover) | ISBN 9780593639900 (ebook)
Subjects: LCGFT: Science fiction. | Paranormal fiction. | Novels.
Classification: LCC PS3561.R44 P46 2024 (print) |
LCC PS3561.R44 (ebook) | DDC 813/.54—dc23/eng/20231220
LC record available at https://lccn.loc.gov/2023046050
LC ebook record available at https://lccn.loc.gov/2023046051

Printed in the United States of America
1st Printing

Book design by Kristin del Rosario

For Newton:
influencer extraordinaire

A NOTE FROM JAYNE

Welcome to my Jayne Castle world—Harmony. If you're new to this series, let me give you a quick tour.

Here's how it went down: Late in the twenty-first century a vast energy curtain opened in the vicinity of Earth. It made interstellar travel not only possible but practical. In typical human fashion, thousands of eager colonists packed up their stuff and headed out to create new homes on the unexplored planets that were suddenly within reach. Harmony was one of those worlds.

The First Generation colonists who settled Harmony brought with them all the comforts of home—sophisticated technology, centuries of art and literature, and the latest fashions. Trade through the Curtain flourished and allowed people to stay in touch with families back on Earth. It also made it easy to keep the computers and other high-tech gadgets functioning in a psi-heavy atmosphere. Humans had no trouble adapting to the strong paranormal forces on the planet, but that kind of energy was murder on Old World tech.

Things went swell—for a while.

One day, without warning, the Curtain closed, vanishing as mysteriously as it had appeared. Cut off from Earth, no longer able to obtain the equipment and supplies needed to keep their modern, sophisticated lifestyle going, the colonists were abruptly thrown back to a far more rustic existence. Forget the latest fashions; just staying alive suddenly became a major problem.

But on Harmony, people did one of the things humans do well—they hunkered down, struggled, and survived. It's now been two hundred years since the closing of the Curtain. It wasn't easy, but the descendants of the First Generation colonists have succeeded in fighting their way back from the brink of disaster to a level of civilization that is roughly equivalent to the first half of the twenty-first century on Earth—with a few twists due to the aforementioned paranormal environment.

The four original colonies have grown into four large city-states united under the umbrella of a federal government. With no enemy nations to worry about, there is no standing army. But every society requires some form of policing. On Harmony those tasks are performed by three different agencies. Aboveground, the various police departments and the Federal Bureau of Psi Investigation (FBPI) take the lead. But in the ancient Alien ruins belowground, law enforcement and general security are handled by the powerful Ghost Hunters Guild.

Vast stretches of Harmony have yet to be explored and mapped, both aboveground and down below in the amazing, mysterious maze of green quartz tunnels that were constructed by the long-vanished Aliens who first colonized Harmony. No one knows why they disappeared, but they left the lights on, literally. The ruins belowground as well as on the surface were abandoned centuries ago, but they are still luminous (mostly), thanks to the paranormal radiation infused into the acid-green quartz used to construct them.

Interestingly, a wide variety of psychic powers have appeared in the population. Evidently the high levels of paranormal radiation in the environment are bringing out the latent paranormal talents in the descendants of the colonists.

Harmony holds many mysteries, wonders, and dangers. But, as usual, the real trouble is caused by humans.

PEOPLE IN
GLASS
HOUSES

CHAPTER ONE

THE PAST . . .

"Higher," Molly shouted, thrilling to the reckless sense of freedom she got on the swings. "I can almost see the sign."

Leona obliged, pushing harder on the playground swing. The billboard on the other side of the brick wall came into view. It had been erected a few months earlier and had not yet had time to fade in the desert sun. GRIFFIN INVESTIGATIONS. WANT ANSWERS? WE'LL GET THEM FOR YOU. CALL NOW. NO WAITING. Beneath the words was a phone number printed in giant red letters. Molly and Leona had both spent so much time on the swings they had memorized it.

Molly's full name was Molly No Middle Initial No Last Name. She was six and a half years old. Her sister's name was Leona No Middle Initial No Last Name. Leona was also six and a half years old. Ms. Inskip, the director of the Inskip School for Orphan Girls, had explained that although they had been left on the doorstep of the school together when they were infants, Molly and Leona were not biological sisters. Molly and

Leona had decided to ignore her. After a while Ms. Inskip had given up trying to explain the facts of DNA.

A few months earlier, Molly had found a couple small chunks of untuned amber in the orphanage garden. During arts and crafts class, she and Leona had figured out how to tie lengths of ribbon around the amber to create necklaces. They wore the pendants night and day, symbols of their sisterhood.

Molly and Leona had grown up together within the confines of the school. It was not a bad place like the orphanages in some of the stories they read. Ms. Inskip was stern but not mean. For the most part she hired trained, caring teachers and staff.

As the years went by, Molly and Leona had watched as the other girls who wound up in the orphanage were adopted. But no one had ever wanted the sisters with no last names. Ms. Inskip had told them that they were very special and that someday special parents would come to adopt them. They had stopped believing her.

"Can you see it yet?" Leona demanded, giving the swing another strong shove.

"*Want answers?*" Molly sang out. "*We'll get them for you. Call now. No waiting.*" She rattled off the phone number.

"My turn," Leona announced.

Molly wanted to argue, but there were rules. They had agreed that when the sign came into view it was time to take turns on the swing. Besides, Ms. Inskip would soon call them back inside. The director believed in an orderly routine. She claimed it was the best way to ensure that the orphaned girls in her care developed what she called *the life skills needed to take their place as respectable, responsible adults in society.*

What Molly and Leona were gradually figuring out was that becoming a respectable, responsible adult in a society in which family and family connections were everything was not easy for orphans—and even more difficult for those whose last name was No Last Name.

A complete absence of basic personal information—no birth certificates, no sad notes from desperate unwed mothers, no ancestry records—was an extremely rare circumstance, but Ms. Inskip insisted that was the case for Molly and Leona.

Molly reluctantly jumped off the swing. Leona took her place.

"Make it go really high," Leona ordered. She was inclined to tell others what to do and how to do it whether or not they wanted the instructions.

Molly pushed until Leona was flying high enough to read the Griffin Investigations sign. She was about to demand another turn on the swings when a man's arm wrapped around her from behind, squeezing her so hard she couldn't breathe. A big hand clamped across her mouth. Remembering Ms. Inskip's rules for dealing with *Stranger Danger*, she struggled wildly. But in the next instant she felt a sharp sting on her upper shoulder. She got dizzy.

She was dimly aware that the stranger was carrying her out through the open gate. She wondered briefly how he had managed to steal the key from Ms. Inskip, and then she fell into darkness.

The last thing she heard before she went unconscious was Leona's scream.

Chapter Two

THE PAST . . .

She woke up in a radiant green chamber. There was a high, arched doorway but no windows. She was a fan of the rez-screen series *Jake Carlisle, Underworld Explorer,* so she recognized the setting immediately. She was in the maze of ancient underground tunnels that crisscrossed the planet.

Two metal tables sat in the center of the room. There were a notebook and a small pile of yellow crystals on one of the tables. The other table was covered with glass tubes and jars, some of which contained strangely colored liquids. The items reminded Molly of a scene in the video Ms. Inskip had made the girls watch the previous week, *Do I Want to Be a Scientist When I Grow Up?* She remembered that chambers like the one she was in were called laboratories.

Leona had been fascinated with the video. Molly had been bored.

At the thought of Leona, she reached up to take comfort from the amber pendant. But it was gone. She realized she must have lost it in the struggle with the stranger.

Out of nowhere, terror swept over her, closing her throat and making it almost impossible to breathe. There was no sign of the man who had taken her, but she was sure he was not far away. She was afraid to move, because every instinct warned her that doing so might draw his attention.

After a while she realized she could not stay motionless forever. She had to pee and then she had to escape. She scrambled to her feet, never taking her eyes off the doorway. When the stranger did not appear, she started to move out into the hall to search for a bathroom.

Without warning the doorway began to shiver with shadows. Another wave of fear lanced through her. Somehow she knew she must not touch the strange darkness that whispered in the opening.

Unable to come up with an alternative, she retreated to a corner to take care of the immediate problem.

When she was finished, she went back to the doorway again, hoping the scary shadows were gone. She was not sure what she would do if she did get out of the horrible chamber. Like every other kid on Harmony, she and the girls at the orphanage had been warned repeatedly about the risks of going down into the maze of ancient green quartz tunnels that crisscrossed the planet. Children who went into the Underworld alone never returned to the surface, according to Ms. Inskip. But anything was better than staying in the laboratory waiting for the stranger to come back.

She moved as cautiously as she could, trying to sneak up on the shadows, but when she was a couple of steps away, they flared in the doorway, blocking her path.

She looked around the small space. There was nowhere to hide. She stood in the center of the room, tears leaking from her eyes, unable to think of anything else to do.

She cried until she could not cry any more, and then she hunkered down against a wall, drew up her knees, and hugged her legs close, trying to make herself as small as possible.

She had no idea how much time passed before the first dust bunny showed up in the doorway. He stood on his hind paws and chortled. He looked just like the pictures of Newton, the Clever Dust Bunny, the hero of her favorite series of children's books. He was a scruffy ball of gray fur with two small ears and six paws. He watched her with his bright blue eyes. She knew he had a second set that he used for hunting, but they were closed.

It was such a relief to see a nonthreatening creature that she almost cried again.

"Hi," she whispered.

The dust bunny fluttered through the doorway, unconcerned about the dark shadows, and halted in front of her. She patted him gently on top of his furry head.

"You should leave before the stranger comes," Molly said. "He'll probably hurt you."

The dust bunny made encouraging noises and zipped back and forth between her and the doorway. She shook her head.

"I can't leave," she said. "The shadows won't let me."

The dust bunny abandoned the attempt to coax her out of the chamber. He gave a farewell chortle and disappeared out into the hall. She wanted to cry again but she couldn't. It was as if she could not feel anything at all now.

After a while she went to the table that held the yellow crystals. Curious, she picked one up. It felt good in her hand. She dropped it into the pocket of her blue Inskip School uniform. Then she chose a second stone for Leona and put it in her other pocket.

The dust bunny returned some time later. At first she thought she was dreaming. In her many lectures on the risks of wandering into the tunnels, Ms. Inskip had talked about something called *hallucinations*. She had explained that they were among the many terrible things that happened to little girls who took a notion to explore the Underworld. She had explained that experiencing *hallucinations* was a lot like falling into a bad dream while you were awake.

The dust bunny chortled and bustled through the doorway, once again ignoring the shadows. Molly decided she did not care if he was a hallucination.

"Thanks for coming back," she whispered. "I'm glad to see you again, but it isn't safe here. You should go."

The dust bunny ignored the advice and bounced a little, clearly excited about something. She picked him up and hugged him close, taking comfort from his furry presence. But he immediately wriggled free and fluttered back toward the doorway. He chortled down the hallway.

A moment later she realized he had not returned alone. A half dozen dust bunnies scampered through the doorway and chortled at the sight of her. It was as if they had just played a game and won. They were beside themselves with glee.

Before Molly could understand what was going on, two women appeared in the opening. They had flamers in their hands and knives on their belts. Both wore small day packs, the kind adults carried when they went into the Underworld, but aside from the weapons and the packs, neither of them was dressed like Jake Carlisle, Underworld Explorer.

The shorter one had shoulder-length, silver-blond hair. She wore tight faded jeans, a crisp white shirt, a wide leather belt studded with amber, and boots. The taller woman had on a blue pantsuit and low-heeled dress shoes. There was a pretty scarf around her throat. Her dark hair was pinned up in a knot.

Both women wore matching wedding rings.

"Told you the dust bunnies were not playing a game," the one with blond hair said. "Hang on while I de-rez the shadow trap."

A moment later the strange darkness that had barred the doorway disappeared. The dust bunnies chortled approval.

Molly gazed at the two women. A part of her was thrilled, but she was also worried about hallucinations. "Are you angels?"

The one with blond hair chuckled as she strode through the opening. "Sorry, no. Charlotte and I were out partying at a bar the night the angel recruiter came around looking for talent."

"What?" Molly said.

"Never mind, honey," Charlotte said. "Eugenie here likes to make dumbass jokes at inappropriate times."

"Ms. Inskip doesn't like it if we say *dumbass*," Molly said.

"Screw Ms. Inskip," Eugenie said cheerfully. She surveyed the room. "On second thought, forget that idea. What the hell is this place?"

"It's a laboratory," Molly announced. "I saw one in the career video."

"Good observation," Charlotte said.

She went to the smaller table and scooped up the notebook.

"Here's the deal, kid," Eugenie said. "We're no angels but we're the next best thing. We're the team from Griffin Investigations."

Molly was dazzled. *"Want answers? We'll get them for you,'"* she recited. *"'Call now. No waiting.'"*

Charlotte glanced at Eugenie. "And you said those signs were a waste of money." She turned back to Molly. "Your sister, Leona, called us. When we showed up at the Inskip School, she told us what had happened and gave us your necklace. Helen Inskip claimed you'd been adopted, but we didn't believe her for a second, did we, Eugenie?"

"Nope." Eugenie snorted. "It was pretty clear Inskip was lying. But we'll let the authorities deal with her. Right now our job is to get out of here."

The dust bunnies chortled and took off through the doorway.

"I guess they figured their work here was done," Charlotte said.

"Ours isn't," Eugenie said. "You take Molly. I'll handle security."

"Right." Charlotte stuffed the notebook into her pack. Flamer in one hand, she extended the other hand to Molly. "Ready to leave?"

"Yes, please," Molly said.

When Charlotte's fingers closed around her small hand, she knew everything was going to be all right. Eugenie went out into the hall, checked both ways, and then beckoned.

"All clear," she announced.

Molly was so happy to be out of the green chamber she almost cried again. But she managed to avoid embarrassing herself in front of the brave team from Griffin Investigations.

Eugenie led the way. When they reached an intersection, she motioned for Charlotte and Molly to wait.

She moved out into the intersection.

"Well, shit," she said.

Molly started to say that Ms. Inskip did not approve of the word *shit*, but there was not time, because Eugenie was diving back into the corridor where Charlotte and Molly waited. A bolt of fire flashed in the intersection. Thanks to two seasons of *Jake Carlisle, Underworld Explorer*, Molly knew that she had just seen a blast from a flamer.

"How many?" Charlotte asked.

"I only saw one. Not a pro. Bad beard. Bad hair. Bad glasses. He's wearing a white lab coat."

"That fits with the lab stuff we just saw," Charlotte said. "He may have security working with him."

"I don't think so. Pros would have done a better job of guarding the kid."

An outraged male voice thundered in the other hallway.

"You can't take the child. She is a subject in a very important research project. She will be returned to the school unharmed when I have completed the exam."

"This case just keeps getting weirder and weirder," Charlotte said.

"The situation seems pretty straightforward to me." Eugenie crouched at the entrance to the intersection and raised her voice. "You're guilty of kidnapping. There are witnesses. I'm making a citizen's arrest."

"You stupid woman, you cannot interfere with my work. You don't know what you're doing."

Two more bolts of flame flashed across the intersection. Eugenie leaned around the corner, fired once, and ducked back into the hallway.

Molly heard a muffled thud.

Eugenie risked a quick glance and then got to her feet. "He's down. Stay here. I'll take a look."

She reappeared a short time later. "He's alive but unconscious. I took his nav amber. He won't be going anywhere even if he wakes up before the Guild gets down here to make the arrest."

"Good," Charlotte said. "Let's get out of here."

The next several minutes were a chaotic blur. Molly glimpsed a man in a lab coat lying on the quartz floor. The next thing she knew, she and the team from Griffin Investigations were climbing a green quartz staircase. At the top Eugenie opened a steel vault door. They entered a dark basement, climbed a few more steps, and emerged inside an old house.

There were two vehicles in the backyard—a dirty white van and a plain gray compact.

The three of them piled into the compact. Eugenie got behind the wheel and drove around the house, heading for the street.

"Why don't you have a bigger car?" Molly asked. "Like the kind Jake Carlisle, Underworld Explorer, drives?"

"Big SUVs like that monster vehicle Jake Carlisle drives on the rez-screen series tend to be noticed," Eugenie said. "Private investigators like to drive cars that don't stand out."

"Oh," Molly said. She pondered that information for a moment, decided not to show her disappointment, and moved on to the next question. "How did you find me?"

"We used the Inskip School's security camera footage to ID the owner of the van that took off with you in it," Charlotte said. "I dug up the address online. His name is Nigel Willard."

"Creeps like Willard tend to keep their activities close to home," Eugenie added. "Probably a control thing. Sure enough, we found the van in his backyard and his hole-in-the-wall entrance to the tunnels in his basement."

"Willard is not what you'd call a professional criminal," Charlotte added. "*Deranged, disorganized,* and *delusional* would be better descriptors. We were on our way to you when the dust bunnies found us. Which reminds me—I've got something that belongs to you."

She reached into the pocket of her suit jacket and took out a familiar amber necklace. "Leona gave this to us. She said it would help us find you."

Molly took the amber and clutched it very tightly. Then she remembered her manners.

"Thank you for rescuing me," she said.

Eugenie met her eyes in the rearview mirror. "You're welcome, honey."

"Are you going to take me back to the Inskip School?" Molly asked.

Charlotte turned in the passenger seat. Her eyes were very intent. "Do you want to go back?"

"No, but I have to go back because Leona is there," Molly explained. "When we're older we're going to leave, though."

"Where will you go?" Charlotte asked, sounding genuinely curious.

"We don't know yet," Molly admitted. "Somewhere."

There was another silence. Eugenie and Charlotte exchanged glances.

Charlotte turned back to Molly. "One thing is certain. You won't be staying at the Inskip School for Girls."

"Why not?" Molly asked.

"That orphanage won't be in business after today. The authorities

11

will shut it down. Do you think you and Leona might like to come home with Eugenie and me until you decide what you want to do?"

"Are you going to adopt us?" Molly said, hardly daring to believe. "That would be awesome."

"Uh," Eugenie said. She flicked a sidelong glance at Charlotte. "Well, we haven't had a chance to discuss anything as serious as—" She broke off because she got tangled up in a cough.

"That would depend on whether you and Leona wanted to be adopted by Eugenie and me," Charlotte said.

"We will," Molly said. "This is so high-rez. Wait until I tell Leona we're going to get a real last name."

Chapter Three

PRESENT DAY . . .

The Funhouse was at its most dangerous after dark.

Joshua Knight went up the stairs to the third floor and opened the door of the old séance room. It was coming up on midnight. The lights had gone out, as usual, an hour earlier. He carried one of the old-fashioned amber lanterns to compensate.

The yellow glare of the lantern revealed the table and chairs in the center of the small room. Another lantern sat on the table, unlit. Presumably, the previous owner of the house, a medium, had used it for atmosphere when she held séances.

The uncovered mirrors on the walls seethed with hallucinations and visions. One of the looking glasses was draped in heavy black silk. He had found it that way when he moved in nearly three weeks ago. It hadn't taken long to figure out why it had been covered.

It was not the only draped mirror in the mansion.

The covered mirrors were the most dangerous, but he took care not to focus for long on the uncovered mirrors, either. He was able to handle the energy in them, but he did not like what he saw in the glass.

He could have draped all of the mirrors in black silk—that probably would have been the wisest course of action, given his shattered senses. But that would have defeated his purpose for moving into the house. He needed answers, and his only hope of finding them lay within the walls of the mansion.

In addition to his burned-out talent, the doctors at Amber Dawn Para-Psychiatric Hospital had diagnosed him as paranoid and delusional. Yet another humiliation for the Knight family.

Fortunately his parents and siblings lived a thousand miles away in Resonance City. He had told them that he had gone into seclusion and was receiving therapy in a private clinic. They chose to believe him. It was easier for all of them that way, so much less stressful than dealing face-to-face with the member of the family who had sullied the proud reputation of a clan of explorers; a reputation established by four generations of Knights.

There were no answers to be found in the séance room. He turned and went out into the hall. The lantern light sparked on the mirrors that covered the walls. The looking glasses whispered to him, urging him to peer into them. They promised astonishing wonders, but he knew they lied. Unlike the medium, he did not believe that there were ghosts trapped in the glasses, but the mirrors were, nevertheless, dangerous.

He went down the stairs. The lights were off on the ground floor as well as everywhere else, but the first wisps of blue fog were starting to rise up from the basement. The mist came in every night. The stuff was infused with enough paranormal radiance to illuminate the old-fashioned furnishings and faded carpet. Unfortunately, it also generated hallucinations. The only way to keep them at bay was with the amber lantern.

He reached the ground floor and made his way through the living room, weaving a path between countless end tables and display stands.

The tables and stands were cluttered with vases, ornaments, lamps, and figurines—all made of crystal. Mirrors hung on the walls on this floor, too. The largest ones were draped in black silk.

On the far side of the living room, he went down a short hall and opened the mag-steel vault door at the end. A river of glowing fog poured through the opening. The door kept out a lot of the mist, but there were small, hidden leaks throughout the house. He had located and blocked a few, but not enough to stop the nightly invasion.

He paused for a moment, readying his badly weakened senses for the descent into the sea of nightmarish fog. When he was ready, he went down the old concrete steps and into the radiant mist that seethed in the basement. In the nearly three weeks he had been living in the house, he had learned that the stuff dissipated just before dawn, only to return the following night. The fog was as relentless as the tides. Lately, it had grown stronger and heavier. If the trend persisted, it would soon engulf the whole house every night.

The lantern helped, but it was not a complete shield. In the old days—pre–Hollister Expedition disaster—he would have had very little trouble quashing the disturbing images. Now it took the lantern and some serious effort. He told himself the nightly exercise was building up his psychic stamina.

During the daylight hours he convinced himself that he was getting stronger. But every night when he went down into the basement, the doubts roared back.

He reached the bottom of the steps. Holding the lantern aloft, he walked through the glowing fog and stopped in front of another mag-steel vault door. He rezzed the lock. There was a muffled clang as the bolt slid aside.

He wrapped one hand around the steel handle, pulled the door open, and looked into the sea of darkness on the other side.

Every other sector of the ancient catacombs that had been discovered to date glowed with the acid-green energy of the nearly indestructible quartz the Aliens had favored for construction material. But the Funhouse had been built above a tunnel filled with a strange darkness that could not be penetrated by flashlights, amber lanterns, or flamers. The darkness did not extinguish light but somehow absorbed it, rendering it useless for visual navigation.

He was limited to fire and basic amber-powered technology. More sophisticated devices, such as cell phones and quartz-powered light sources, did not function in the currents of paranormal energy that flowed throughout the Underworld.

The tuned amber used to navigate the rest of the catacombs went dead in the tunnel of night. To cross the threshold was to step into a wildly disorienting storm of energy that blinded all of his senses. He knew that because on two occasions he had tried to force his way into the darkness. He was well aware that he had been lucky to survive.

Each attempt to find a means of navigating the dark tunnel had resulted in failure. Yet less than a month ago he had survived the Hollister Expedition disaster and somehow managed to walk through the tunnel of night. Not only that, he had found the basement door of the Funhouse, gotten it open, and made his way to the surface.

Afterward he had hiked through the desert night, following the river, until he had reached the small, rural community of Outpost. He had collapsed in front of the general store. When he woke up, the only things that he remembered clearly were the dark mansion and the mirrors.

He had voluntarily committed himself to the para-psychiatric hospital, but once he was inside, the doctors had confined him to a locked ward on the grounds that he might be a danger to himself and others. A week later he had escaped the hospital and returned to the house of mirrors.

The mansion was as off-the-grid as it was possible to get without losing all connection to the basic amenities of civilization. The two things he required—groceries and a public library that had rez-net service—

were available a few miles away in Outpost. In the two and a half weeks he had been in residence in the Funhouse, he had made the trip twice to stock up on High-Rez Energy Bars, heavily caffeinated Hot Quartz Cola, and a few basics for easy-to-prepare meals. He had also picked up a couple of boxes of wine for medicinal purposes.

He had used the forays to drop in to the library to check the online media for news of the Hollister Expedition disaster. On his last trip he had learned the search had been called off. The members of the expedition had been declared lost and presumed dead.

He went back up the steps and into the living room. He paused to close the basement door and then he headed for the stairs. He desperately needed sleep. He was halfway across the cluttered space when he made the mistake of glancing into the mirror over the sofa. For a beat he was unable to look away, once again forced to acknowledge the full horror of what was happening.

Back at the start, when he had looked into the mirrors, he had seen the man the press had portrayed—a washed-up Underworld navigator who had abandoned the team he had been assigned to protect. A man hiding from his employer, the media, his family, and the rest of the world.

A man who had brought the hammer of dishonor down on his family. A man who had escaped a para-psych clinic and set up housekeeping in the middle of nowhere. A man who walked the halls of the mansion from hell most nights because nightmares haunted his sleep.

Those early reflections had been depressing, but at least he knew them to be real.

The far more troubling visions had begun appearing a week ago. The dreamscapes came straight out of his nightmares. That was bad enough.

The truly terrifying thing was that he could no longer see his own reflection in the mirrors. It was as if he had disappeared.

Chapter Four

"Is this going to be seriously creepy?" the client asked.

His name was Rick, he was fourteen years old, and he had been on the streets since arriving in Illusion Town two months earlier. That was the only information he had provided to the staff at the Lost Lane Youth Shelter.

According to Margaret Barnes, the night manager, Rick had checked in shortly before six that evening, as usual. He'd had dinner and played some video games with the other kids before going to bed around midnight. The nightmares had struck at one a.m.

Margaret and her assistant had found Rick fighting a desperate battle with an unseen demon on the floor beside the bunk bed. Margaret had immediately diagnosed the cause—Emergent Senses Dream Disorder. ESDD.

The condition was not uncommon in the teen years when the paranormal senses began to develop. Most parents knew to anticipate the problem and how to get professional help if needed. But young people living on the streets—and there were some, even in a culture that was founded on the importance of Covenant Marriages and family connections—lacked access to proper therapy. The result was that they became frightened and anxious. That often led to dangerous attempts to self-medicate.

Molly was the volunteer dream therapist on call that night. The rez-rock ringtone of her phone had pulled her out of a fractured sleep and an ominous dream of her own. She had welcomed the distraction. Now she and Rick were sitting in a couple of plastic chairs in the otherwise empty cafeteria.

"It will seem weird to have me show up in your dreams," she said. "But after you get used to the feeling, you'll be more comfortable with the process. Remember, this is a form of lucid dreaming. You'll be in a kind of trance, but you'll also be awake and aware that you're dreaming."

"Okay, I guess."

"Don't worry, as soon as you are in control of the dream, I'll let you take over and then I'll step out."

What she did not add was that the last thing she wanted to do was hang around in his dreamscape. The dream-walking experience was usually more disturbing and disorienting for her than it was for her clients, although she tried to hide that detail. The worst part was that scraps of Rick's nightmare were likely to show up in her own dreams when she finally returned to her apartment tonight—assuming she could sleep.

Maybe she wouldn't bother going back to bed. It wasn't as if she had been sleeping much lately. She knew the moms were not sleeping, either. Leona's disappearance into the Underworld had traumatized all of them. The authorities had called off the search for the Hollister Expedition, but the Griffin family refused to give up.

Eugenie and Charlotte spent their days and most of their nights working the computers and phones, running down leads, searching for the one person who might be able to help them find Leona and the team: the missing navigator. Joshua Knight was the only member of the expedition who had made it back to the surface. He had vanished, too, first into the locked ward of a para-psychiatric hospital and then into thin air.

The speculation in the media had ranged from bizarre conspiracy theories to the possibility that Knight had been driven insane by whatever had happened down in the tunnels. Many were convinced that, unable to live with the shame he had brought upon himself and his family, he had walked into the catacombs minus the tuned amber needed to navigate the heavy psi environment. If that was true, there was no point looking for him. He had effectively taken his own life.

"I'm ready to try anything that will stop the nightmares," Rick said.

"I understand, believe me." Molly smiled. "It was like that for me, too, when I came into my talent."

But she'd had the moms to comfort and support her while she wrestled with the dream demons the year her psychic senses emerged. All Rick had was a part-time volunteer therapist at a youth shelter. The good news for him was that she had a talent for dream-walking.

It was not an ability she wanted to turn into a full-time career. Dream-walking didn't provide the rush of delight and satisfaction she got from her work as a crystal artist. Tuning crystals that could sing to the senses was her true passion.

Nevertheless, she saw her therapy work as a personal mission. Helping young street people like Rick learn how to handle their psychic senses was her way of giving back.

"How does this work?" Rick asked.

"I can't make the bad dreams go away," Molly said. "What I'm going to do is show you how to rewrite the script of a nightmare so that you are in charge. Are you ready?"

"I guess."

She reached into the black satchel she had brought with her and briefly considered the assortment of transparent viewing crystals inside. Each crystal was round, six inches in diameter, framed in a thin metal band, and fitted with an amber handle. The crystals resembled magnifying glasses, but they had not been ground for magnification. Instead, she had tuned them in ways that allowed her to step into someone else's dreamscape with the least amount of psychic dissonance for both her and the client.

She selected the viewing crystal she thought would work best with Rick and took it out of the satchel. Gripping the amber handle, she reached for Rick's hand.

She steadied her nerves and focused her senses.

"Now, let's walk through your nightmare," she said.

Cautiously she generated a little pulse of psychic energy. The storm of Rick's ominous dreamscape appeared in the crystal.

"Wow," Rick whispered, fascinated. "That is so high-rez. It's like I'm watching a movie of my dream."

That was why her version of dream-walking worked. It allowed the client to take a step back and view the nightmare from outside the dreamscape. Unfortunately, she got to see it, too.

"How come I can't see myself?" Rick asked.

She smiled. "Good question. Do you ever see yourself in your dreams?"

He gave that some thought. "Huh. No, I don't think so."

"That's because you *experience* a dream. It's like walking down a street. You see the shops and cars and people around you, but you don't see yourself."

"Got it."

"But here's the weird part," she continued. "I am about to enter your dream, and you *will* see me."

"Okay. Let's do this."

Easy for him to say, she thought. Rick was standing safely outside his dreamscape—a viewer, not a participant. That allowed him to detach emotionally to a great extent. She was the one who had to walk through his nightmare.

Chapter Five

He had a legal name, but in his business, professionals with a lot of street cred earned sobriquets. He was the finest cat burglar in Illusion Town, a local legend the press had named Mr. Invisible.

He could not really make himself disappear, but he had a psychic talent for breaking and entering that was almost as good as a magic cloak.

He had never encountered a lock he could not get past or a safe he could not crack. The amber mechanism that had secured the alley door of the shop was of respectable quality, but it had required less than thirty seconds to crack it. A hooded jacket had been all it took to evade the camera.

If the rest of the security in the shop was the same grade of technology, he would be on his way in a few minutes. Later there would be plenty of time to change back into his civilian clothes and hit the card tables at the Lucky Quartz casino. He could already envision the headlines in the morning papers. *Guild Wedding Crystals Stolen. Mr. Invisible?*

He gave himself a moment to absorb the energy in the atmosphere. The place had a pleasant buzz—the shop sold art crystals, after all—but he did not detect the unique vibe of serious, quartz-based tech that indicated a high-end security system. Understandable. Singing Crystals was a small business that had been open for only a few months. It was operating on a shoestring. What money was available no doubt went into the raw materials. Quality crystal suitable for artistic tuning was expensive.

He had cased the shop a day ago, pretending to be a browsing customer. It hadn't taken long to realize that there was no safe, hidden or otherwise, on the ground floor. Vaults and safes absorbed a lot of the emotions of the people who relied on them to protect their valuables.

His intuition combined with past experience assured him that the objects he was after were probably stored in the personal quarters of the owner's apartment on the upper floor. And the owner had conveniently left the shop for some unknown reason a short time ago. Things could not get any easier.

He glided up the stairs. Maybe he would leave a note advising the artist to invest in better security. The thought amused him. Too bad he was not here to steal some of the flowers on the sales floor tonight. He knew a fence across town in the Shadow Zone who would pay big bucks for beautifully tuned crystals, no questions asked.

He stopped on the landing and surveyed the entryway in front of the apartment door. An amber wall sconce glowed warmly, illuminating the tasteful arrangement of three crystal flowers in a glass vase on a red lacquer table. The tuning was subtle, but exquisite. The effect on his senses was similar to the lift he got when he heard his favorite music or drank a fine wine.

He hesitated. He knew true artistry when he came across it. Even a couple of the tuned flowers would constitute a good night's haul.

Some other time, he promised himself. He was a professional. Business first. Tonight he was here to steal the crystals that had been tuned to create the traditional energy circle at the wedding of the new Guild boss, Gabriel Jones, and his bride, Lucy Bell. Time to focus.

He examined the lock on the apartment door. Another bit of standard-issue hardware. He reached for his lock pick but froze when the flowers in the vase beside the door started to glow.

"Fuck."

So much for concluding that all the security was unsophisticated. The crystals in the shop downstairs were vulnerable, but the apartment had a very exotic alarm system, one that he could not disarm. He recognized a signature tuning job when he ran into one. The only person who could get past it without triggering the alarm was the individual whose personal psychic signature had been locked into the crystals.

He was getting paid a lot to grab the energy crystals, but not enough to risk getting caught. He had survived as long as he had in a high-risk, high-reward line of work precisely because he knew when to walk away from a job. He would inform the broker that he had been unable to complete the project tonight. The client would then have two options—instruct the broker to commission a second attempt or cancel altogether.

With a sigh of regret, Mr. Invisible headed back downstairs. When he reached the ground floor he stopped, enthralled by the delightful energy that whispered from the sales floor. It would be a shame to walk away empty-handed tonight.

He went around the sales counter and stopped at a display of crystal orchids. After a moment's consideration he selected two delicate sculptures. Each radiated a gentle energy that sang to his senses. He would keep them for his personal collection.

Flowers in hand, he turned to leave through the same door he had used to enter the shop. Shock jolted through him when he saw the shadowy figure looming in the doorway.

He dropped the flowers and reached for the flamer. It was set to stun for the same reason he never carried a mag-rez pistol. Going down on a burglary charge was one thing. Murder was something else altogether.

He never got a chance to rez the trigger. The mag-rez bullet slammed into him, propelling him backward. He was briefly aware of a terrible chill, heard crystal flowers shatter on the floor as his flailing arm swept them off the shelves, and then the darkness took him.

CHAPTER SIX

Twenty minutes after the therapy session started, Molly left Rick sleeping peacefully in his bunk bed. She said good night to Margaret, snagged a personal-sized bag of Original Zesty Flavor Zing Chips from the basket at the end of the cafeteria counter, and walked outside into the night. She hoped the dust bunny would be waiting for her again.

He was.

He chortled and bounced out of the green shadows to greet her. Only two of his four eyes were open. Evidently he did not need his second set, the amber pair, to navigate the night.

"Hi, there," Molly said. "Don't worry, I've got the goods."

She tossed the bag of Zing Chips toward him. With an adroit move he caught it with two of his six paws. But instead of dashing off with it as he had done on the previous two occasions, he stood on his hind paws and offered her a small object.

She smiled. "For me? Really, you shouldn't have."

She crouched in front of him and took the chunk of unpolished, untuned rose crystal.

"This is lovely," she said, getting to her feet. "Thank you."

The dust bunny ignored her. He was intent on opening the bag of Zing Chips. He took his time about it, as if he were unwrapping a special gift.

She closed her fingers around the rough stone and rezzed her talent a little. The powerful vibe thrilled her senses. All she had to do was unlock it and make it sing with positive energy.

"This is a very high-quality stone," she said.

The dust bunny chortled. He had the bag open now. He reached inside with one paw and carefully selected a chip.

Molly smiled. "You know, if we're going to keep seeing each other like this, we should probably exchange names. I'm Molly. You look a lot like Newton, the Clever Dust Bunny. I loved those books. What do you think of that name?"

The dust bunny chortled and munched another chip.

"Newton it is," Molly said.

She took a small flamer out of her satchel and started walking the two blocks to her apartment. The weapon was set to stun, but she did not expect any trouble on the short walk home. She had grown up in the Dark Zone and knew its twisty streets and narrow lanes and alleys well. This particular neighborhood was quiet and safe. It was also well lit, thanks to the close proximity of the ancient Dead City wall. The green quartz that the Aliens had used to construct their aboveground metropolises gave off an eerie green energy after dark that illuminated the zone in green shadows.

The city of Illusion Town, built on gambling and the often-shady businesses that went with it, was composed of eight districts called zones. Each zone was built against one side of the eight massive walls that enclosed the ancient ruins of the Dead City.

At night the glowing green energy of the quartz illuminated the nearby neighborhoods. The towering hotel-casinos in some of the districts added their own radiance. The result was that the city in the desert always lit up the night. That worked nicely with the image of a never-ending party that the board of tourism liked to sell.

Newton scampered alongside her. She appreciated the escort service.

He looked cute and cuddly, but everyone knew dust bunnies could be dangerous. As the saying went, *By the time you see the teeth, it's too late.* They were not known to attack humans unless seriously provoked, but she had no idea if Newton would protect her if she ran into a bad guy on the walk home. He had no reason to do so—unless he felt compelled to defend his source of Zing Chips.

She stopped at the glass-paned front door of her shop. In spite of the stress of the past few weeks, she experienced a familiar little rush of pride and satisfaction at the sight of the gilt signage:

SINGING CRYSTALS

Unique Crystal Arrangements for Every Occasion

Energy Circles Our Specialty

"After years of screwing up, I finally found my calling," she said to Newton. "I love my work."

A crystal artist could make any crystal object resonate, but many chose to work with crystals that had been cut into the shapes of flowers. It was a competitive market but a stable one. People wanted crystal floral arrangements for the same reasons they had historically sought botanical flower arrangements. Real flowers were still popular, but when it came to special occasions—weddings, birthdays, anniversaries, graduations—

they wanted objects that would last. Well-tuned crystals could endure, providing positive energy for a lifetime.

Crystal artwork provided the creative outlet she had not realized she had been searching for until a year and a half ago. She would never forget the day she had discovered her passion.

Fresh off being fired from the latest in a long string of boring, unsatisfying jobs tuning navigation amber, she had entered a crystal shop in search of another position. The charming, good-looking man behind the counter had asked her to tune a crystal flower for him. When she finished, he hired her on the spot. *You've got the talent*, Reed Latimer said. *You just need some training and experience.*

She started work at Resonant Crystals the following day. One month later she had launched an affair with the attractive man who had hired her. A month after that, the job and the affair had both come to a flaming conclusion. She had two rules when it came to relationships. Reed Latimer had broken rule number one.

The romance had gone bad, but she knew she owed Reed for recognizing her talent and teaching her the finer points of the crystal arrangements business. He had introduced her to the career of her dreams.

She rezzed the lock and opened the door of the shop. "Thanks for seeing me home, Newton. I have to tell you that you are the most gentlemanly date I've had in a long time. Enjoy the rest of your night."

Newton growled.

Startled, Molly glanced down. The dust bunny was not in sleeked-out, all-teeth-showing combat mode, but it was clear he was on high alert. His second pair of eyes, the amber ones he used for hunting, were open.

"What's wrong?" she whispered.

Then it hit her. The energy laid down by death was unmistakable. Icy frissons pulsed across the back of her neck. Frozen with shock, she could not even scream. The only thing that kept her from outright panic was the realization that Newton was neither attacking nor retreating. Rather, he was alerting.

Her intuition told her that the dust bunny's reaction indicated there was no immediate threat. She managed to rez a light switch.

The dead man was on the floor. Two beautifully tuned orchids lay in pieces beside him. There was a great deal of blood.

CHAPTER SEVEN

Body Found in Crystal Arranger's Shop
Bad Omen for Big Wedding?

The body of an unidentified man was discovered early this morning on the premises of Singing Crystals, a business that specializes in art crystals. Singing Crystals has been in the news recently because it received the contract for the upcoming wedding of Gabriel Jones, the CEO of the Illusion Town Ghost Hunters Guild, and Lucy Bell.

According to the police report, Molly Griffin, the proprietor of Singing Crystals, discovered the body of the intruder shortly after two this morning. Ms. Griffin, who lives above the small business, told police she had been out late and that she had discovered the dead man upon returning home.

Speculation concerning whether or not the negative energy laid down at the scene of the murder was infused into the crystals prepared for the Jones and Bell nuptials is swirling ...

"Shit." Molly tossed the early edition of the *Curtain* onto the sales counter. "I was afraid of this. We're doomed."

"It'll be okay, boss," Clement Mitchell said. He was at the far end of the shop, sweeping up the last of the shattered crystal flowers that littered the floor. "Everyone knows gossip travels quickly in this town and then it goes away just as fast."

"Not fast enough to save Singing Crystals," Molly said.

Newton popped out from under a display cabinet. He waved a chunk of broken crystal that he had discovered and chortled.

"Easy for you to say," Molly muttered. "You're a dust bunny. You don't have to worry about the reputation of your business."

"Trust me, this is a one-edition story," Clement said. "By the midday edition the media will be back to covering the plans for the big Guild wedding."

"Sure," Molly said. "But the coverage will be all about the bride pulling the contract for the energy circle from Singing Crystals and giving it to another shop. Probably Resonant Crystals. By the end of the week you and I will both be lucky to get jobs polishing amber in a third-rate tuning shop."

Newton was not concerned by the report in the paper, but the anxiety and frustration in her voice clearly worried him. Clutching the broken crystal in one of his six paws, he fluttered across the floor and vaulted up onto the counter. He chortled again and offered the chunk of crystal as a gift.

"Thanks," she said.

She was not in the mood to be comforted—she would rather have throttled the reporter who had written the story for the *Curtain*—but she took the crystal and patted Newton on the head, because he was impossible to resist when he was in full-adorable mode.

"Is that all there is to the story in the *Curtain*?" Clement asked.

Molly groaned. "Of course not."

She picked up the paper and read the next paragraph to him.

. . . Detective Mercer stated that the deceased appeared to have broken into the shop with the intent of stealing some of the crystals and was shot with a mag-rez pistol. The possibility that Ms. Griffin, the owner of Singing Crystals, walked in on a burglary in process and killed the intruder has been considered and discarded, according to the detective.

Clement whistled. "Sounds like you had a close call. I never realized you were a suspect."

"Of course I was," Molly said. "The person who finds the body is always the number one suspect."

"How do you know that?"

"I watch *Psychic Forensic Investigations* like everyone else."

"Oh, yeah, right." Clement went back to sweeping up shards of crystals. "So what convinced the cops that you didn't kill the thief?"

"A bunch of clues, including the energy prints on the back door of the shop and the video from the security camera. Also, the timing doesn't fit. I was still at the youth shelter when the intruder was killed. Detective Mercer says it's clear there was someone else at the scene. His theory is that the thief had a partner who turned on him."

"Luckily the killer didn't get your beautiful energy circle crystals."

"For all the good that's going to do," Molly said. She read more of the story.

Reed Latimer, owner of Resonant Crystals and an expert in art crystal arrangements, was asked for a comment. He reminded this reporter of the old saying "Negative energy crystals at the wedding mean bad energy in the marriage."

Mr. Latimer pointed out that when it comes to wedding crystals there is nothing more negative than stones that have been associated with death . . .

"That does it." Molly folded the paper and hurled it into the trash bin under the counter. "I refuse to read any more of that crap. I might as well file for bankruptcy this afternoon."

"Don't give up," Clement said. "You don't know for sure that you're going to be ruined by this."

"Yes, I do know that I'll be ruined," she shot back. "A lot of people, especially wedding planners and brides, are very superstitious when it comes to crystal arrangements. I'm surprised Mr. Claude hasn't called already to tell me I've been fired. This is just the excuse he's been hoping for."

Mr. Claude was one of the most sought-after event planners in Illusion Town. He had a reputation for staging spectacular celebrations that would have been deemed outrageously theatrical and downright tacky in any other city on Harmony. But here in Illusion Town, over the top was exactly what the movers and shakers who could afford Claude's substantial fees demanded. He had not been happy when the bride had insisted on giving the crystal contract to Singing Crystals.

"Maybe that pretentious blowhard hasn't heard the news yet," Clement said.

"Just a matter of time," Molly said. "Trust me, when the phone rings, it will be Claude calling to inform me that the contract has been canceled."

Clement shook his head. "We should have upgraded the lock on the back door."

Molly snorted. "I didn't upgrade because I couldn't afford it, remember? I was going to do that when I got the final payment on the Jones and

Bell wedding." Her phone rang. She flinched and stared at the screen. "It's Claude. I knew it."

"Want me to deal with him?" Clement asked. "I'll be happy to tell him to go to green hell."

"I appreciate the offer, but I'm the one who needs to handle this." She picked up the phone and took the call. "Singing Crystals. This is Molly Griffin. How can I help you, Mr. Claude?"

"You know why I'm calling." Mr. Claude sounded like he was speaking through clenched teeth. "The news about the murder in your shop is all over the media this morning."

"An intruder was killed in Singing Crystals, but rest assured, the crystals for the Jones and Bell wedding are in perfect condition."

"Death is death. Regardless of the cause, it produces energy that can easily be picked up by crystals that happen to be in the vicinity. Negative energy crystals at the wedding mean bad energy in the marriage."

"That's an old myth, Mr. Claude, as I'm sure you're well aware," Molly snapped. "But even if it were a real phenomenon, I have the talent to decontaminate any stone that might have been affected. Not that there's any need for decontamination in this instance, because the crystal flowers that I tuned for the Jones and Bell energy circle were nowhere near the scene of the incident. They were stored in a secure location."

"Unfortunately, my clients have taken your view of the situation. Ms. Bell seems to think that none of the other crystal artists she interviewed has your talent for infusing the wedding arrangements with the sort of energy she wants at the ceremony. In addition, she reminded me that she recently suffered a reputation-destroying incident herself and understands how that can affect a small business owner. She feels quite strongly that Singing Crystals should not be penalized because of circumstances beyond your control."

Braced for doom, Molly struggled to recalibrate. "That's very gracious of Ms. Bell."

"If it were up to me, I would cancel your contract immediately. Actually, if it had been up to me, I would not have hired Singing Crystals in the first place. But it is not up to me. The bride has the final say."

"I see." Molly waved at Clement and mouthed the words *He's not firing us.* "I'm delighted to hear that," she said into the phone, careful to keep her voice polite and professional. "You won't regret this, Mr. Claude."

"I have regretted the bride's decision to give Singing Crystals the contract from the start, Ms. Griffin. I have not changed my mind."

The phone clicked off in Molly's ear. She put the device down on the counter and took a deep breath. "I'm happy to report that Singing Crystals has been saved from a near-death experience."

Newton chortled and bounced a little, responding to the profound relief in her voice. She patted him on the head.

Clement grinned. "We've still got the contract?"

"Yep. Ms. Bell reminded Claude that she had been through a similar business disaster."

"That's true," Clement said. "And look what happened. They made a movie out of her experience down in the tunnels. *Guild Boss* is going to be released the day after the wedding."

"I know. Leona and I are planning to see it with the moms."

Clement started to say something but changed his mind. He nodded, his eyes bleak and sympathetic, and went back to sweeping up broken flowers.

"My sister is alive, Clement," Molly said quietly. She touched the yellow crystal she wore around her neck. "I'd know if she wasn't."

"Right," Clement said.

Molly started out from behind the counter, intending to give Clement a hand with cleaning up the shop. She stopped when her phone rang again. Returning to the counter, she checked the screen. Charlotte Griffin.

Molly stopped breathing for a beat. Her intuition flashed a high-rez warning in bright red lights. She warned herself not to read too much into a call from one of the moms. It could be bad news. It could be the worst possible news.

Or it could be a break in the case.

She grabbed the phone off the counter.

"Please tell me you tracked down Joshua Knight," she gasped.

"Looks like it." Charlotte's voice was infused with cautious optimism. "If our information is right, he's living off the grid in the desert a few miles outside of a little town called Outpost. There's no official address or coordinates, but the locals in Outpost are all well aware of the house and can provide directions."

"I'll find it," Molly vowed.

"I'm told you can't mistake the place. It's the only house on that stretch of the river." Charlotte paused. "And get this. It's made of fireglass."

Startled, Molly held the phone away from her ear and stared at it for a second. "Someone built an entire house out of fireglass? I didn't know it was used for construction work."

Eugenie responded on the other end of the connection. "Generally speaking, it's not. Evidently this particular house is the exception."

"According to our source, it has picked up a lot of energy over the years," Charlotte continued. "The locals who live in and around Outpost believe it sits over a hot zone. They call the mansion the Funhouse."

"Any idea why?" Molly asked.

"No, but I got the distinct impression the name was intended to be ironic. Something to do with the energy, I suppose."

Molly tightened her grip on the phone. "I can handle it."

"Eugenie and I are not worried about your ability to handle the house," Charlotte said. "The problem is Joshua Knight. According to the hospital records, he didn't simply discharge himself against medical advice. He escaped from a locked ward and stole a few things while he was at it. He was diagnosed as paranoid and prone to hallucinations and delusions. He may be dangerous."

"That's interesting," Molly said. "How did you get access to his medical records?"

"Don't ask."

"Right."

"I reviewed his matchmaking agency records, as well," Charlotte continued.

"He's registered?"

"Not anymore," Eugenie said. "The agency dumped him when they found out he had been locked up in a para-psychiatric hospital."

"No surprise." Molly glanced at the time on her phone. "Outpost is a long drive. I need to get on the road if I want to get there by nightfall."

"Definitely," Eugenie said. "I'm told you need to arrive during the daytime. Apparently you can't get close to the house after the sun goes down. Something about the fog."

"Who, exactly, is your source?"

"A Ms. Sandra Abernathy," Charlotte said. "She runs the Outpost Public Library. She was very helpful. Told me a man matching Knight's description has dropped in to the library to use the online computer a couple of times. He's also been seen at the general store. According to Ms. Abernathy, the locals refer to him as the Mad Doctor."

"That doesn't make sense," Molly said. "Knight is a navigator, not a doctor. Are you sure he's the right man?"

"Ms. Abernathy verified the photo I texted," Charlotte said. "She wasn't clear on why they named him the Mad Doctor. But she did say that even in a town filled with loners and eccentrics, he has made an impression. Molly, please be careful."

"Hey, Griffin women can take care of themselves."

"I know, but—"

"We talked about this, remember? We decided that of the three of us, I'm the best equipped to handle Joshua Knight. By the way, Ms. Bell refused to let Mr. Claude cancel the contract with Singing Crystals."

"Smart woman." Eugenie snorted. "I'll bet Claude was not happy. Serves him right. Pompous ass."

"Clement holds the same opinion of Mr. Claude," Molly said. "Got to go. Love you both."

"Love you, too, hon," Eugenie said.

"Love you," Charlotte added. "But be careful. One missing daughter is enough."

Molly ended the call and looked at Clement. "The moms located Joshua Knight. I've got to talk to him immediately. That means you're in charge here."

"What about the wedding?" Clement asked, alarmed. "It's in two days."

"I'll be back to set up the crystal arrangements." *I hope.* She headed for the stairs that led to her apartment above the shop. Newton bounded along beside her. "I'm going to pack. I'll be away overnight. Knight is living near a little town called Outpost."

"Long drive."

"I know. Apparently I have to arrive before sundown. There's a lot of fog."

"Good luck," Clement called. He did not hide the concern and the worry in his voice. "Be careful, boss."

"I'll be okay." She took the stairs two at a time. "This is the break the moms and I have been waiting for. Knight is the man who lost my sister. He's the only one who can tell me where to find her."

"According to the media, whatever happened in the Underworld fried his senses," Clement called. "That makes him unpredictable. Possibly dangerous."

"That doesn't mean that on some level he doesn't have the answers I need to find Leona. It's our only hope."

CHAPTER EIGHT

The fog was bad and getting worse by the minute. The amount of pavement revealed by the Float's headlights was diminishing rapidly when Molly finally turned into the graveled driveway of the mansion.

The woman at the Outpost General Store who had given her directions confirmed that the locals called it the Funhouse, but Molly's first impression was that the mansion could easily have been mistaken for a mausoleum. In the gathering mist the opaque gray fireglass walls seemed to absorb what little late-afternoon light was still available.

There was certainly nothing fiery or even mildly colorful about the pile of gray stone in front of her. The three-story structure loomed in the fog like an isolated fortress commanding a rocky bluff above the Illusion River. A chaotic mass of heavily overgrown vegetation formed a seemingly impenetrable barrier around the lower portion of the walls. Only the stone walkway that led to the colonnaded portico remained clear.

There were windows, but they were narrow and difficult to make out in the fading light.

She brought the little red Float to a stop, shut down the engine, and sat quietly for a moment, contemplating the mansion.

"I doubt that anyone ever threw a really fun party in the Funhouse, Newton," she said.

Newton had bounced up into the front of the Float while she was putting her suitcase and the satchel containing her dream-walking crystals into the trunk. Startled, she had tried to remove him. He had dodged her every attempt to snag him and made it clear he intended to accompany her. Unwilling to waste any more time on the eviction process, she had abandoned the effort, slipped behind the wheel, and pulled away from the curb.

Newton had been thrilled with the road trip. On the outskirts of Illusion Town she had given him one more chance to change his mind, but he had refused to get out of the car. "This is on you," she warned. Newton had chortled.

She stopped at a convenience store to stock up on Zing Chips and bottled water. Newton had spent the rest of the drive riding shotgun on the back of the passenger seat, munching chips and chortling exuberantly whenever they passed another vehicle.

It had been a very long drive. Molly had been grateful for the company.

"Stick close, pal," she said as she opened the door of the Float. "Knight is probably going to be a bit difficult. I may need backup."

Newton bounced a little, eager for the new adventure.

She unfastened her seat belt and got out. Reaching back into the front seat, she scooped up Newton and tucked him under one arm.

"Here goes." She went briskly along the stone walk that led to the portico and the front door. "I'm relying on you to tell me if this meeting looks like it's going to go to green hell, Newton. Your intuition is probably better than mine when it comes to men. My track record is not good."

She noted the dark SUV parked a few yards away in the drive and then went up the three broad steps to the imposing front door. She stopped to take a breath, centering her senses and her nerves. Leona's life depended on what happened next.

"No pressure," she whispered to Newton.

The door opened before she could bang the metal knocker. Joshua Knight loomed in the dimly lit hall. There was no mistaking him. His photo had been on the front page of every paper and in the news videos for days after the loss of the Hollister Expedition. She took a sharp breath and a quick step back.

Newton chortled a cheery greeting, unfazed. Knight glanced at him and then fixed Molly with a look that sent a trickle of ice down her spine.

"Whatever you're selling, I'm not buying," he said. "Get back in your little toy car and get out of here while you've still got a chance to escape before the fog closes in."

Maybe showing up unannounced on Joshua Knight's front steps had not been such a great idea. Then again, it wasn't as if she'd had a choice. There was no other way to contact him. He was truly off the grid.

In the wake of the Hollister Expedition disaster, the media had labeled him the Tarnished Knight, a highly regarded navigator who had worked for the legendary firm of Cork & Ferris Outfitters. The company had built an empire supplying outfitters and guides to corporations, research institutions, mining companies, and others who, for business or professional or personal reasons, wanted to go into the Underworld with the best equipment and personnel that money could buy.

Deep down she had expected to meet a real-life version of Jake Carlisle, Underworld Explorer. That was not the case. There was more than a five-o'clock shadow on Knight's hard face, and he was badly in need of a haircut. Instead of a lot of dashing khaki and leather, he wore a faded, oversized set of scrubs decorated with a few old coffee stains and the logo of the Amber Dawn Para-Psychiatric Hospital. A certain unmistakable fragrance clung to him. Knight had not bathed recently.

Yet another youthful dream crushed by reality, she thought. Still, if one overlooked the clothes and the unfortunate grooming practices, there was something compelling about Joshua Knight. Something intriguing. Under other circumstances, and if he was cleaned up, a woman such as herself—a committed free spirit when it came to dating—might find him interesting. Very interesting.

At least she was not picking up the sour smell that indicated a lot of heavy drinking. His eyes were sharp and clear. Fierce. She breathed a small sigh of relief. There was no indication that Knight was using drugs or heavy doses of alcohol to deal with the emotional fallout that must have descended in the aftermath of the disaster.

He was wearing amber. A nicely polished and tuned stone dangled from a narrow strip of leather around his neck.

Why did a man who had been psi-burned bother with tuned amber?

She braced herself for the battle of wills she knew was coming and rezzed up a cool, polished smile. "I get the impression you're trying to threaten me, Mr. Knight. If so, you're wasting your time."

He folded his arms across his broad chest. His intimidating gaze got a little more dangerous. "If I were threatening you, you'd know it. I'm trying to do you a favor. The fog around here is bad at night. It comes in off the river every day at this time, and it's infused with a lot of energy because this house sits on a hot zone. In about fifteen minutes you won't be able to see more than a foot or two in front of your face, and what you do see will scare the ghost shit out of you."

"Excuse me?"

"I'm warning you, if you stick around, you're going to end up spending the night in your car here in my driveway."

"Are you saying you wouldn't invite me to sleep inside your house?"

"Trust me, you don't want to spend the night in here." He stepped back and started to close the door. "Leave while you still can."

"I'm not going anywhere, Mr. Knight. I'll spend the night in your driveway if necessary, but I'll be here at your front door in the morning."

"You're a reporter, aren't you? I don't know how you tracked me down, but you wasted your time. I don't talk to the press, or anyone else if I can help it."

"I am not a reporter." She stepped forward and planted one foot firmly in the doorway. "My name is Molly Griffin, and I'm here because you need me and I need you."

"Shit." He closed his eyes. When he opened them, it was clear she was the very last person he wanted to see. "I'm assuming the Griffin name is not a coincidence?"

"I'm Leona Griffin's sister. Leona was on the—"

"Hollister Expedition. Yes, Ms. Griffin, I'm well aware of that. I'm sorry about what happened. Believe me, if I knew how to find your sister and the others, I would do exactly that."

"That's just it, Mr. Knight." She gave him what she hoped was a confident, reassuring smile. "I might be able to help you find the team."

The smile did not work. It had the opposite effect of what she had intended. Suspicion heated his eyes. "You're not really Leona Griffin's sister, are you?"

"Yes, I am. I have an art crystal shop in Illusion Town. Singing Crystals. Maybe you've heard of it?"

"No. I'm from Resonance, not Illusion Town."

"You can verify everything I'm telling you if you make a phone call or go online."

"I don't have phone or rez-net access, and as long as you're this far away from Outpost, neither do you. So don't bother offering me the use of your phone."

"I'm getting the feeling that *difficult* is your default setting, Mr. Knight."

"Your default is apparently *stubborn*," he said. "I've got better things to do than stand here and chat with you while the fog closes in."

"No, you don't, Mr. Knight. Here's what you need to know. In addition to being an excellent crystal artist, my talent makes me very good at crystal-focus work."

Mentally she crossed her fingers behind her back. The truth was a lot more complicated.

He scowled. "What's crystal-focus work?"

Newton chose that moment to wriggle out from under Molly's arm and vault down to the ground. Chortling enthusiastically, he bustled through the doorway.

"What the hell?" Joshua leaned down to grab him but missed.

With a farewell chortle, Newton disappeared into the big house.

Joshua rounded on Molly. "Call your dust bunny and leave. *Now.*"

"He doesn't always come when I call," she said smoothly. "If you'll kindly step aside, I'll fetch him. It will just take a minute."

The heat in Joshua's eyes went up another degree or two, and not in a good way. Reluctantly he moved back and opened the door wider. She went briskly past him.

"Why don't I believe you?" he said, sounding grimly resigned.

Probably because you're psychic, she thought. But she kept the opinion to herself, mostly because she had to take a beat to deal with the hot currents of energy that swirled in the shadowed hallway. She focused and succeeded in suppressing most of the effects on her senses.

She was still adjusting to the hot vibe in the hall when she stepped into the cold patch on the floor. She got a sharp jolt and hastily moved off the paranormal stain.

She cleared her throat. "Did someone die in here?"

"The man who built the Funhouse," Joshua said. He watched her closely. "They say he was trying to escape the mansion but it killed him before he could make it to the front door."

She took a breath and let it out with control. "I see. That is a rather grisly legend."

Joshua smiled an icy smile. "According to the locals, the original owner wasn't the only victim of the mansion. There have been other deaths in the decades since it was built. That's what the house does, you see. It murders people."

CHAPTER NINE

Molly took a deep breath. "Now you're trying to scare me."

"For your own good," Joshua said.

"Well, you're wasting your time. But I can see why the house has acquired a certain reputation. The energy in this space is . . . unusual, to say the least. It's coming from the mirrors, isn't it?"

The looking glasses covered both sides of the hallway, floor to ceiling. They came in all shapes and sizes, and they were all hot to varying degrees.

"The dust bunny, Ms. Griffin," Joshua growled.

She walked a few steps farther down the hall and paused to look back through the open doorway. The mist was so thick now she could barely make out the red Float in the driveway.

"You were absolutely right," she said. "It would not be at all safe to try to drive through that fog. Looks like I'll be stuck here tonight."

"You've still got a little time," Joshua said. He kept the door open.

The muffled sound of excited chortling echoed from somewhere deep inside the mansion.

"I'll be right back," Molly promised.

"I'm doomed, aren't I?" Joshua said.

The door closed with what could only be described as an ominous thud. Molly allowed herself a tiny flicker of optimism. She kept moving, trying to follow the increasingly distant chortles.

Joshua followed, closing in fast. She picked up the pace.

"Newton," she called. "Where are you, sweetie?"

Distant chortling answered her. It sounded like it was coming from an upper floor.

There were sconces on the walls, but the light did little to brighten the overall sense of gloom. Instead, the amber-yellow glow of the lamps sparked and flashed on the array of looking glasses.

A few of the mirrors appeared to be genuine Old World antiques that had been brought through the Curtain two hundred years ago by First Generation colonists. They were darkened with age. Others were obviously from the Colonial era, and the rest were relatively modern. Each simmered with energy—*tuned* energy.

She could not imagine anyone wanting to live in such a disturbing environment. What in the world had brought the Tarnished Knight to this place?

As she moved down the hall, she saw that some of the looking glasses on either side were arranged in a manner that reflected her image into infinity, but unlike in traditional funhouse mirrors, she was not viewing distortions of herself. The mirrors did not show her looking taller or shorter or monstrous. Instead, the scenes were strange and unique.

Each mirror showed her in a different landscape—a cavern of glowing ice, an eerie undersea grotto, the radiant green tunnels of the Underworld, the Rainforest, the ruins of one of the Dead Cities. The special effects should have been entertaining. But that was not the case. Instead, each of the landscapes generated a sense of deep unease. It was as if the looking glass was reaching out and trying to pull her into the vision; trying to trap her in another dimension. She had to exert some conscious effort to resist the hypnotic effects.

"I've got to tell you, these mirrors are a little creepy, Mr. Knight," she said over her shoulder.

"So you won't be spending the night, then?" Joshua said. "I'm devastated. You've got six minutes and counting to grab the dust bunny and leave."

She glanced back at him. He was right behind her now. She caught sight of his reflection in one of the larger mirrors. He appeared to be in a tunnel filled with endless night. She stopped, startled.

Joshua checked his watch. "Five minutes."

"That mirror," she said.

He went very still for a few seconds, and then he glanced briefly at the reflection. He looked away immediately. When he switched his attention back to her, she saw that the heat in his eyes had vanished. In its place was a bone-chilling cold.

"What about the mirror?" he asked, his voice too soft and too even.

She knew she was on dangerous ground. She had to move carefully.

"It shows you in a very dark tunnel," she said.

"You can see me in the tunnel?"

"I can now that you're the one standing in front of the mirror. But when I went past a moment ago, I saw my reflection set in a different landscape. The Underworld Rainforest."

"Tell me about the dark tunnel," he said quietly.

She walked back to where he stood, stopped beside him, and studied the reflection in the mirror. "Now I'm in the tunnel with you. Okay, this is weird."

"What, exactly, do you see?"

"We are standing side by side in an utterly dark tunnel that appears to recede into infinity behind us. What do you see?"

"A reflection of you. In the tunnel." He paused. "Alone."

She slanted him a sidelong look and thought about the para-psych doctors' diagnoses that Charlotte had discovered in the hospital records. *Paranoid. Delusional. Prone to hallucinations.* Maybe she had misinterpreted the sharp clarity she had seen in his eyes when he opened the door.

"You're telling me the truth?" she asked, feeling her way. "You don't see yourself?"

"It's been almost a week since I've been able to see my own reflection in the mirrors." He turned his head to look at her. "Changing your mind about spending the night with me in this house?"

She opted to ignore the taunt. Maybe he was not entirely sane, but there was another possible explanation for his inability to see his own reflection. She was willing to grasp at the flimsiest of straws.

"Do you recognize that tunnel?"

"Yes."

"So it's real?"

"Very, very real," he said.

"A moment ago, when I looked into the mirror, I saw the Rainforest."

"When I first arrived here, I also saw myself in the Rainforest when I looked into this mirror. But I've been diagnosed as psychically and mentally unstable. Oh, and by the way, my senses have been fried. What's your excuse?"

She watched him closely. "Ever dream about that dark tunnel?"

"Every time I manage to get some sleep."

"By any chance is that particular landscape associated with the Hollister Expedition disaster?"

"Yes."

Her spirits lifted. "That is very good news. I think we can both relax, at least a little. We've got some work ahead but we're on the right path."

"Haven't you been listening?" Joshua's eyes were stark. *"I can't see myself in the mirror."*

"I understand," she said, opting for the soothing tone she used with her clients at the youth shelter.

"Why can't I see myself? Tell me the truth. Is it because the doctors were right? Am I delusional?"

"Nope. At least I don't think so."

"Then how in green hell do you explain the fact that I can't see myself in this mirror or any of the other mirrors in this damned house?"

"I'm no para-physicist, but everyone knows the physics of mirrors is complicated. These mirrors are very hot, and I can tell you they were tuned by an expert who locked in the vibe. You've been living here in this house for, what? Two weeks?"

"Two weeks, three days," he said, making it sound like an eternity.

"According to the media, you suffered some serious para-trauma down in the Underworld, so your senses are probably still healing."

"My para-senses were burned out."

"Singed, obviously, but not destroyed," she said firmly.

"What makes you so sure of that?"

"The mirrors, of course." She waved a hand to indicate the multitude of looking glasses on the wall. "You can tolerate them. That means you're not a total burnout. If you had been deep-fried you either would have gone insane by now or you would have been driven out of the house. No one who didn't have a fairly stable core talent could handle this kind of energy for nearly three weeks."

"That's what I've been telling myself," he said, "but if I'm right, *why can't I see myself?*"

"Simple. The mirror is picking up a scene from one of your own dreamscapes. The reason you can't see yourself is because it's *your* dream. People don't see themselves when they are dreaming because they *experience* the dream. They don't watch it as if it were a video."

"Huh." He stared at her, looking stunned. When he recovered, he glanced at the mirror again. "Why can I see you in my dreamscape?"

"That," she said, "is a little more difficult to explain."

CHAPTER TEN

"Give me a minute to take a closer look." She reached out and cautiously brushed the mirror with her fingertips. A shiver of powerful energy stirred her senses. "It's some kind of crystal, not regular glass. I don't recognize it. Do you know where the mirrors came from?"

"No, they were all here when I moved in," Joshua said. He watched her with haunted eyes. "When I first got here I could see myself in the mirrors. The background images were weird funhouse landscapes. But now all I can see is that tunnel. If it's my dreamscape, what are you doing in it?"

"Okay, here's what I think happened. When you first moved into the house you were able to see the regular funhouse landscapes and your own reflection in the mirrors because you had not yet had a chance to lay down some of your own personal dream energy. But you've been sleeping here, and dreaming here, for almost three weeks now."

"So?"

"I told you, these are not normal mirrors, Mr. Knight. I think they were tuned to absorb paranormal energy. Recently they have been picking up your dreamlight vibe, which is evidently quite powerful."

"I used to be a strong talent," Joshua admitted. "But not any longer."

"You're still strong, but power without control is not only wasted, it's dangerous. It always comes down to tuning, and you need tuning."

"What the hell?"

"Later. Back to my explanation. As I said, the mirrors have been absorbing your dream energy for quite a while now, but you've been unaware of what is going on. Now when you look into one of these mirrors, you end up in an unfortunate doom loop."

"Well, shit."

"Sorry, poor choice of words," she said quickly. "The mirror shows you a scene right out of one of your own dreams and you get sucked into it because, hey, it's your dream energy. Your mind recognizes it, and the next thing you know, you are smack-dab in the middle of your own dream."

"While I'm awake?"

"Exactly."

"And I don't see myself because I'm experiencing the dream, not watching it like a video. Okay, I think I get some of that. I understand why I can't see myself. But you still haven't explained why I can see you."

She winced. "I'm afraid I walked into your dream by accident. My apologies. Usually I have much better control, but I've been under a lot of stress lately, and this house is really quite hot and, well—"

"Maybe you'd like to back up and try that explanation again," he said, his eyes tightening.

"Right." She took a breath. "My talent makes it possible for me to step into someone else's dreamscape. I stumbled into your dream because there's a lot of powerful energy in this hallway and because we're both rezzed on account of our emotional states—"

"Our *emotional* states?"

She raised her chin. "I get the impression that I am not the only person in this house who is feeling somewhat desperate."

He grimaced. "I'll give you that."

She waved one hand to indicate their surroundings. "And there is something very, very strange about these mirrors."

He eyed a nearby looking glass and then swiftly looked away. "Can't argue that point, either."

"I think you're desperate and frustrated because you don't know what your next step should be. Anger is the way you are channeling those emotions. I understand, believe me."

"Now you're practicing armchair psychology?"

"Shut up and give me your hand."

"What?"

"Give me your hand."

She was a little surprised when, without another word, he held out his hand. She took it before either of them could change their minds. His fingers closed around hers with the force of a mag-steel manacle. She flinched. He did not appear to notice.

"What now?" he demanded.

She tried to wriggle her fingers a little. When he didn't get the message, she gave a polite cough. "You don't have to hold my hand quite so tightly. A light touch is all I need to let you share my focus."

He glanced down at their hands and scowled. "Sorry."

He loosened his grip but he did not let go.

"That's better," she said. She paused. "You're really quite tense, aren't you?"

"Tell me what is happening here."

He did not raise his voice, but there was no mistaking the command. She reminded herself that, until the disaster, he had been an experienced, highly regarded exploration team leader, a navigator whose decisions could make the difference between life and death in the Underworld. He was accustomed to giving orders and having them obeyed.

A wide variety of people hired outfitters and guides to take them down into the tunnels for an equally wide variety of reasons. Leona had mentioned that navigators frequently complained about the academics in particular because they could be difficult to wrangle.

Research and exploration teams from universities and colleges were often made up of an assortment of temperamental, competitive, and obsessed individuals. Petty grievances, squabbles, and outright turf wars were common. And then there were the volatile personal relationships. It was easy to understand that the failure of the leader to establish discipline and maintain it could result in disaster.

From time to time in the past few weeks, the moms had speculated that perhaps Knight had lost control of the Hollister Expedition. They had wondered if that had been the cause of the catastrophe. But now that she had met him, she doubted the theory. There was no denying that Knight was currently a personal and professional rez-lev train wreck, but there was a core of mag-steel in the man. It was difficult to imagine him losing control of a team.

She held up their clasped hands. "Physical contact makes it possible for me to share my focus with you," she explained. "I'll show you what I see in your dream."

"You can do that?" he asked.

"Yes. But I will be viewing your dreamscape from my perspective, not yours. I will probably see things that you don't even notice because you take them for granted. But I'll warn you, the process can be unnerving." *Mostly for me,* she added silently.

"Just do it," Joshua said.

"Right."

She took a steadying breath. Like everyone else, she could use tuned amber to focus her psychic senses, but she preferred to channel energy through the yellow crystal she wore around her neck. She concentrated and cautiously rezzed her talent, searching for the currents that would allow her to resonate with Joshua's dream energy.

She had been braced for the disorienting and unpleasant sensations that always accompanied a dream link, but nothing could have prepared her for the shock of thrilling intimacy that hit her when she made the connection with Knight's aura. She had to fight the instinct to slam her barriers back into place.

It wasn't just the strength of his energy field—she had known he was a powerful talent, or had been at one time—it was the dissonance in some of the wavelengths that made her shudder. This wasn't the weak or unstable vibe that indicated mental or physical illness. Something else was going on. But now was not the time to try to diagnose the wrongness.

Joshua's hand abruptly tightened around hers. She gave a small yelp. He was oblivious, fixated on the image in the mirror.

"I can see my reflection," he rasped. "We're both in the tunnel now. Side by side. Holding hands. But the angle is off. It's not a true reflection of my position here in the hall."

"Remember, you're viewing the scene through my eyes."

He touched the beard stubble on his face and grimaced. "I look like I just rolled in from a weeklong bender."

"You've had a lot on your mind," she said gently.

He turned away from the mirror and watched her with feral eyes. "You have a very interesting talent, Ms. Griffin. But what good is it going to do me?"

"I can walk through your dreamscape with you," she said. "You will see it as I see it. Together we can find that which is hidden in your dreams."

"You think the key to locating your sister is locked in my dreamscape."

It wasn't a question.

"The only other possibility is that you're lying when you say you don't know where the Hollister Expedition was lost."

"I'm not lying," he rasped.

"I didn't think so."

He looked past her at the closed door. "You've missed your window of opportunity to escape this house tonight. You won't be able to leave until morning."

"My suitcase is in the trunk of my car."

"I'll get it."

Chapter Eleven

He was probably making the biggest mistake of his life, Joshua thought as he went out into the fog. But it was not like he had a choice. In any event the mist was so thick now he could barely see the red Float. No one would be driving in or out of the area until morning.

The dust bunny chortled behind him. He stopped and looked back. He could just barely see Newton on the threshold, brandishing a small object.

"Newton," Molly said. She spoke from inside the hallway. "Where did you get that? Put it back. You can't go around stealing Mr. Knight's stuff. He doesn't like us very much as it is. Newton, wait, no, you can't go with Mr. Knight. Please don't annoy him any more than I already have. *Newton*."

Ignoring her, Newton hustled forward and stopped in front of Joshua. The object in the dust bunny's paw was a small hand mirror.

Molly appeared in the doorway. "Sorry about that. He's very attracted to bright, sparkly objects."

"Aren't we all?" Joshua said.

This was probably not a good time to inform her that she was the only bright, sparkly thing that had appeared in his world in the past month. *I should have never opened the door.* But for some stupid reason he could not bring himself to regret it. In addition to being bright and sparkly, she had brought something else into his life—a faint glimmer of hope.

Weird. He had not expected hope, however faint, to arrive wearing a lot of artsy black—black jeans, black T-shirt, black sneakers—and a vividly patterned scarf around her throat. The dark, blunt-cut hairstyle provided an arresting frame for the angles of her face and her brilliant amber-brown eyes.

If he had seen her on the street, he would have imagined that Molly Griffin was an artist or a gallery owner or maybe a fashion photographer.

"Is the mirror valuable?" Molly called from the doorway.

"Beats me," Joshua said. "I haven't had an appraisal done on any of the mirrors in this place. I doubt if I could convince a dealer to hang around long enough to make an accurate estimate. The house isn't what you'd call comfortable."

"I noticed."

He glanced at the small mirror. "I think that hand mirror came from the séance room."

"There's a séance room?"

"Third floor. Top of the stairs."

"I've never seen a real séance room."

"Can't speak for séance rooms in general, but I can tell you that the one up on the third floor is hot. The previous owner of the house was a medium. I was told that she died in that room. Take my advice and don't go inside."

"I wasn't thinking of doing any such thing," Molly said quickly. "Certainly not without your permission."

She was lying, he thought, almost amused. But she had not lied when she claimed to be able to see the tunnel in the mirror. There was no way she could have known about his personal nightmare before she arrived at the mansion. There was no mention of it in the medical records because he had never told the doctors at the hospital about the recurring dream.

"I'm just giving you a little free advice," he said.

"Thanks," she said very politely. "I appreciate it." She paused briefly. "You said the medium died in the house?"

"Yep. The house murdered her."

"I see. How very Gothic. By the way, in addition to my suitcase, there's a carton of Zing Chips and a satchel in the trunk. You might as well bring those in, too."

"I'll get right on that."

He found the car when his knee collided with a bumper.

"Shit," he muttered, pausing to massage the sore spot.

Newton chortled in what sounded like a concerned sort of way, but who knew? He was a dust bunny.

"Everything okay out there?" Molly called.

He glanced back but he could no longer see her. "I found the damned car."

"Oh, good."

"I give up," he muttered.

"What?"

"Nothing."

He planted one hand on the side of the Float and used his sense of touch to work his way around to the back. He popped the trunk and hauled the rolling suitcase out of the back of the vehicle. Setting it on the ground, he hoisted the carton of Zing Chips and wedged it under his arm.

He gripped the handle of the satchel in one hand and pulled up the retractable handle of the suitcase with the other.

Newton bounced up onto the top of the rolling suitcase and chortled again.

"Right," Joshua said. "Why walk when you can ride? Don't get too comfortable, pal. You and Ms. Griffin won't be staying long. She may think she can handle the house, but trust me, by morning she'll have changed her mind. I'll bet you a bag of Zing Chips that the two of you will be on your way as soon as the fog clears tomorrow."

Newton did not appear concerned by that news. Using the faint glow of light in the doorway as a beacon, Joshua hauled the suitcase, chips, satchel, and dust bunny along the walkway, across the stone floor of the portico, and into the front hall.

Molly stepped out of the way. Joshua went past her and stopped. Evidently concluding that the short ride was over, Newton hopped off the suitcase and disappeared back into the depths of the house.

"He seems to be having a good time," Molly said, closing the front door.

"Oh, yeah. Here at the Funhouse Hotel we specialize in good times. Golf course, pool, hot tub, and rez-ball courts are available for your enjoyment. The gourmet restaurant is open twenty-four hours a day. Just contact the concierge if you need anything."

Molly gave him a dazzling smile. "I'm so glad you are able to handle this situation with a sense of humor."

He set the carton of Zing Chips on the floor. "I should have sent you packing when I had the chance," he said.

"Don't blame yourself. There was no getting rid of me. I'm not leaving until I find out what happened to my sister. Like I said, we need each other, Mr. Knight."

He considered her for a long moment, weighing the determination that heated her eyes. She was complicating his already complicated life, but respect where respect was due. He knew a fighter when he saw one.

"Follow me. I'll show you to your room," he said.

"Thank you."

"Wait until you see where you'll be spending the night before you thank me."

He shoved the retractable handle of the suitcase down into the closed position, picked up the bag and the satchel, and started toward the stairs. Molly hurried after him.

For some inexplicable reason he found himself remembering the exciting shot of intimacy he had experienced when she had taken his hand and invited him to join her in his dreamscape. The sensation had been intensely sensual, and it had blindsided him.

He had not thought about sex at all in the past month. Now was not the time to resume thinking about it. Besides, Molly Griffin was not his type. As it happened, he had a clear idea of what his type was, because shortly before the Hollister Expedition disaster, he had filled out an extensive questionnaire and endured an excruciatingly long interview with a counselor at a Covenant Marriage matchmaking agency in Resonance City. He had been given a spreadsheet detailing his type.

Okay, so Molly checked a few of the boxes. Yes, she seemed to be intelligent, and yes, she did not appear to be the clingy, needy sort, and yes, the fact that she had tracked him down and refused to be sent away indicated that she had a strong sense of family loyalty. You had to admire loyalty.

When it came to physical looks, he had never had a particular vision of what attracted him to a woman. He had always considered sexual attraction a you-know-it-when-you-see-it kind of thing. He was, however, very sure he had never been drawn to the artsy type. Until now.

The matchmaker at the agency had warned him that, in the end, it was the indefinable element of *energy* that determined the depth and seriousness of the attraction between two people. The matchmaker had also warned him that hot, immediate, and compelling energy was not always a good thing. It was powerful, however, and it could lead someone to make a serious mistake.

Lately, it seemed, he had become very good at making serious mistakes.

CHAPTER TWELVE

Molly Followed Joshua up the stairs to the second floor. She knew he did not expect anything good to come of allowing her to stay the night. It was all there in his body language—the rigid set of his broad shoulders and the way he paced up the stairs and down the hall. She was inside the Funhouse only because Knight was desperate. Well, so was she. They were both out of options.

Newton bounced up the staircase alongside her, evidently buzzed on dust bunny adrenaline. As far as she could tell, he had no problems with the mirror energy. No problems with Joshua Knight, either. She took that as a hopeful sign.

"I know you're not thrilled with this situation, Mr. Knight," she said. "Just to be clear, I'm not happy about it, either, but try to remember that I'm here to help you."

Joshua glanced back over his shoulder. Cold amusement glinted in his

PEOPLE IN GLASS HOUSES

eyes. "If you're telling me that you're doing this for my own good, save your breath. We both know you've got an agenda."

"Oddly enough, I was under the impression that, experienced Underworld navigator that you are, you would prove to be a mature, rational adult capable of rising above petty grievances."

"Surprise."

"Fine," she muttered. "Be that way."

Newton reached the landing on the second floor, chortled with excitement, and immediately disappeared down a dark, mirror-lined hall. Joshua followed and stopped in front of a door.

"It's a big house but most of the rooms on the second and third floors are unfurnished," he said. "There are only two that have beds. I'm using the one at the end of the hall. That means you get this one."

"I'm sure it will do nicely," she said.

"Let's hope so for your sake, because if it doesn't 'do nicely,' you'll be sleeping on a sofa or the floor."

"Your skills as a gracious host are a tad rusty, aren't they?"

"Try nonexistent."

He gave her another sharp smile and opened the door. She was startled to see that the lamps inside the room were on, steeping the space in a subdued light. The realization that Joshua had not had to rez a wall switch triggered her curiosity.

"Are you using this room for some purpose other than for entertaining houseguests?" she asked.

"Nope."

"Why are the lights on?"

"The house operates on its own schedule."

"I see." She didn't, but she decided not to press the issue.

Joshua moved aside to let her enter the room. She took a few steps over the threshold and paused to survey the dimly lit space. Most of the furnishings were in the dark, heavy style of the post–Era of Discord period. The descendants of the First Generation had accepted that they were on their own in the new world. They had triumphed over the mad chaos of Vincent Lee Vance's attempted insurrection, formed a strong federation, adopted a constitution, and established powerful social norms that reinforced the bonds of family and community. They had come back from the brink and they were determined not only to survive but to rebuild and flourish. It had been a serious time, and the art and architecture had reflected that vibe.

One could understand the social influences that had resulted in the style of decor that characterized the era, Molly thought. But there was no getting around the fact that to the modern eye, the dark colors, the heavy drapes, and the substantial-looking furniture were depressing.

The glaring exception to the decorating style in the room was the bed. It loomed in the center of the room. There were no sheets or blankets. The mattress appeared normal, but the base, headboard, and footboard were made of mag-steel, not wood. Four mag-steel posts supported the mag-steel canopy. Glass panels enclosed the bed on all four sides. A sliding glass door on one side provided access.

Her first thought was that the awful bed looked like a glass-and-steel coffin.

She went cold, aware of two absolute certainties. The first was that she would never sleep in the ghastly bed. The second was that she would not let Joshua Knight know that he had finally succeeded in unnerving her.

She rezzed up her best client smile and squared her shoulders.

"How unusual," she said.

Joshua regarded the bed with an unreadable expression. "Also practical. Mag-rez steel and glass are capable of blocking heavy energy."

"Steel has that property, but everyone knows glass can be very unpredictable when it comes to paranormal radiation."

"Probably a compromise." Joshua followed her into the room. "Maybe whoever commissioned the bed didn't want to sleep in a solid steel coffin."

Molly winced. "It does look like an avant-garde artist's notion of a high-tech sarcophagus, doesn't it?"

She looked around and was relieved to see a dark blue velvet love seat on the far side of the room. It would be a squeeze, but she could fit into it if she curled on her side.

Joshua set the suitcase and satchel on the bench at the foot of the glass-and-steel bed and angled his chin toward a door on the far side of the room. "The bath is through there."

The door to that room stood partially open. The lights were on inside. She wondered how long it had been since it had been cleaned.

"Don't worry," Joshua said, evidently reading her mind—or, perhaps, her wary expression. "The house doesn't pick up stuff, do the laundry, or change the beds, but it takes care of all the basic cleaning."

"Really? That's amazing. How?"

"The man who designed and built the mansion was an inventor."

"If he invented a self-cleaning house, he could have made a fortune."

"Maybe that was the plan, but the house murdered him before he could patent the technology. The librarian in Outpost told me the mansion has been humming along for decades and no one knows how or why it works."

Newton appeared in the doorway, chortled, and dashed across the room. He disappeared under the bed and then popped out and scurried to the velvet stool in front of the dressing table. From there he vaulted up to the top of the table to check out the mirror. He evidently lost interest when no bizarre landscapes appeared in the glass. He bounded back down to the floor and vanished into the bath.

"He's certainly having a good time here in your house," Molly said. "I think that, for him, it really is a funhouse."

"Evidently." Joshua went toward the door. "If I were you, I wouldn't bother to unpack. You'll be leaving first thing in the morning."

She opted to ignore that unsubtle threat. She would like nothing better than to get the answers she needed and leave in the morning, but her intuition warned her it wasn't going to be that easy.

"I see that the only mirror in here is the one on the dressing table," she said, trying to conceal her relief. She could handle the mirror energy when she was awake, but trying to sleep in a room full of it would be an entirely different matter. "It doesn't appear to be hot."

"It isn't," Joshua said. He paused in the doorway. "But there is one very high-rez mirror in here." He nodded toward a set of heavy black drapes that covered a portion of one wall.

"I'd offer to move it," Joshua continued, "but that's not possible. It's built into the wall. There are others like it scattered around the house. As far as I can tell, the covered mirrors are the most powerful."

She swallowed hard. "I see. Are there any actual windows in here?"

"Of course." Joshua gave her a grim smile. "There's one behind the maroon curtains."

"Oh, good. I like to have a little fresh air at night."

"Suit yourself, but I don't think you'll want to open that window, not at night."

"Why not?"

"The outside fog is not as bad as the inside stuff, but it's not exactly conducive to sleep."

"Inside fog?"

"Never mind. You'll see." Joshua indicated a closet. "There are sheets, blankets, and pillows in there. They were here when I moved in, so I have no idea how old they are, but as far as I can tell, they are clean. The towels are in there, too. Help yourself."

"Okay, thanks."

"Don't thank me." Joshua moved out into the hall. "You're going to regret talking your way into this house."

Molly raised her chin. "You have a rather negative outlook on life, don't you, Mr. Knight?"

He flashed another cold smile. "Not on life, just on people." He wrapped one hand around the doorknob. "I'll go see what I've got on hand for dinner. By the way, there are a couple of house rules."

A cold shiver raised the hair on the back of her neck.

"House rules?" she asked.

"The first one is, don't uncover any of the draped mirrors."

She folded her arms. "I can handle mirror energy."

"Right. Don't say you weren't warned."

"What's the second house rule?"

"Just the usual one for situations like this," Joshua said. "Don't go down into the basement."

"You're not joking, are you?"

"No," he said, "I'm not joking."

He went out into the hall and closed the door.

CHAPTER THIRTEEN

She waited a moment to be sure he'd had time to leave. Then she unfolded her arms and crossed the room to the draped mirror.

Sensing more entertainment, Newton appeared from the bathroom and hurried to join her. He stood on his hind paws and watched attentively as she reached for the tasseled pull cord.

"I need to know what I'm dealing with," she said as she hauled on the stout cord.

The dark drapes were made of silk and were surprisingly heavy. She had to throw most of her body weight into the task of drawing them aside. When they were halfway open, she paused to evaluate her progress. All she could see was the dark face of a mirror that extended from the floor to the ceiling.

Curious, she touched her fingertips to the surface and cautiously rezzed her senses.

It was as if she had pulled a trigger on a flamer. But instead of releasing a jet of fire, the mirror shot a bolt of paranormal lightning across the room, charging the atmosphere and illuminating the space in an explosion of energy that flashed across the spectrum.

She shrieked. Her entire nervous system went into overdrive, fueled by adrenaline and the disorientation caused by her wildly resonating senses. Her reflection in the mirror showed her hair lifting and whipping around her startled face. Her nerves screamed. Thoroughly rattled, she lost her balance. She staggered backward and came up hard against the glass enclosure of the coffin-bed.

Newton, meanwhile, was beyond excited. His fur was standing on end and all four of his eyes were open. He bounced up and down and chortled like a kid on a thrill ride.

Molly pushed herself away from the glass-and-steel bed and lunged toward the mirror. Seizing the tasseled cord, she hauled on it with both hands. The curtain slowly closed.

The lightning gradually disappeared. The energy level in the room started to calm down.

She released the pull cord and planted one hand against the wall to steady herself. Her pulse was still pounding and she was breathing hard.

The door opened. Joshua looked at her from the hallway.

"Told you so," he said.

Molly raised her free hand, folded three fingers down and extended the middle digit.

Joshua watched, curious. "Does that gesture have some particular significance?"

"One of my moms told me it was an Old World tradition. It conveys profound respect and admiration."

Joshua nodded. "Thought so."

He closed the door.

Molly sighed and looked at Newton. "It's going to be a long night, pal."

Newton chortled.

Chapter Fourteen

"What's the story behind this house?" Molly asked.

She was sitting at a black glass table in the dining nook off the kitchen, watching Joshua prepare a dinner of cheese-and-pickle sandwiches and canned soup. She had a large glass of wine in hand. It was a mediocre red from a box, but she was not about to complain. After the unfortunate incident in the bedroom, she was grateful for the therapeutic dose of alcohol. She needed it. Furthermore, she deserved it. She'd had difficult clients before, but they paled in comparison to Joshua Knight.

Still, to his credit, he had managed a quick shower. He had not taken time to shave, but he had changed into a clean set of Amber Dawn Para-Psychiatric Hospital scrubs. She noticed that he had poured a fortifying glass of wine for himself. Evidently they both needed a drink.

Newton was stationed on top of the refrigerator, taking a keen interest in dinner preparations. He appeared unfazed by Knight's less-than-hospitable attitude.

"The only solid information I have on the house came from the local library, and that's not much," Joshua said. He did not look up from the pot of canned soup he was stirring. "Like I said, the man who built this place was an inventor. He was generally considered to be an all-around eccentric. After the house murdered him—"

"You mean after he died inside the house," Molly corrected. "Stop trying to scare me with haunted house stories."

"Whatever. Afterward the heirs put the house on the market. Apparently it was a tough sell. It stood empty for a few years, but during that time a few people—transients looking for shelter and a couple of thrill seekers—went inside and tried to stay for a while. Some did not come out alive. The ones who survived were sure the mansion was haunted. Eventually the medium bought it. The house killed her a couple years ago. Unable to sell it, the heirs gave the mansion to the town of Outpost, which did not want it."

"Are you renting?"

"Nope." Joshua gave her a humorless smile. "I own the mansion."

She blinked. "You *bought* it?"

"No. After a few days during which I did not die or vacate the premises in a hurry, the town council voted to gift the Funhouse to me, free and clear. One afternoon the mayor and the sheriff showed up with the deed and that was that."

She shook her head. "That is . . . amazing."

"My life has taken some odd turns lately."

"Evidently," Molly said.

She watched him open a cupboard and take out a couple of soup bowls. The kitchen was as dated as the rest of the house, but none of the appliances bore familiar brand names. The refrigerator, oven, dishwasher, and cooktop all appeared to have been constructed of parts that had been found in a junkyard. The inventor who had built the Funhouse had obviously been a committed DIY kind of guy.

There was a narrow window in the nook that probably looked out over the driveway during the daytime. But tonight all that was visible was a solid wall of dark fog.

"The haunted mansion story really took off after the medium was found dead in the séance room," Joshua continued, ladling soup into bowls. "They say the door of that room was locked from the inside. The story is that she tried to barricade herself in there but the house got her anyway."

Molly narrowed her eyes. "You're wasting your time trying to scare me. You said the house sat empty for years on end in between owners. I wonder why it wasn't vandalized or emptied out by people stealing stuff. That's what happens to most abandoned buildings."

"As far as I can tell, the house seems to be able to take care of its own security as well as the housekeeping."

"If it has a built-in security system, how did you manage to get past it?"

"I'm pretty good with locks."

"The average vandal and the average burglar are pretty good with locks, too."

"I'm sure a few would-be thieves have tried to steal some things over the years. But once inside, they probably changed their minds. Would you really want to steal one of those mirrors? Everything in this house is hot, and not in a fun way."

Newton chortled. Joshua glanced at him. "Unless you're a dust bunny, apparently."

"Do you really believe that the energy in the mirrors in this house scared both of the previous owners and a few intruders to death?" Molly asked.

"It's a little difficult to believe they all died of natural causes."

"But you've been able to survive in this atmosphere for nearly three weeks."

"Maybe it's because I'm a total burnout and immune to the paranormal vibe."

She raised her brows. "Or maybe it's because you are not nearly as fried as you think you are."

"That's an interesting thought," Joshua said. He filled a third soup bowl and set it on top of the refrigerator for Newton. "What, exactly, do you think you can do for me, Molly Griffin?"

"The scene of you in the dark tunnel came from your dreams. It's based on a memory, isn't it?"

Joshua put a cheese-and-pickle sandwich on a plate and gave it to Newton. "What makes you say that?"

"A lot of dream imagery is symbolic. Vague. Disjointed. But that tunnel scene was quite specific. Detailed. I got the impression that it's a memory that is trying to surface in your dreams."

Joshua put the remaining soup bowls and a plate of sandwiches on a tray. "It's real. A totally dark tunnel in the Underworld. Somehow I found my way through it without amber after I lost the Hollister Expedition."

"Where did it lead you?" she asked.

He put the tray on the table and sat down across from her. "To this house."

"Here?"

"Yes."

Molly realized she was clenching the stem of her wineglass. Maybe Knight *was* delusional.

"What was the last thing you recall before you woke up in the dark tunnel?" she asked.

"I was with the Hollister Expedition. Our goal was an uncharted sector in the Glass House ruins."

"Leona has been talking about Glass House nonstop since the discovery was announced two months ago. She was thrilled to get a place on the Hollister Expedition."

"What little I've seen of the ruins is stunning." Joshua paused to drink some wine. "Crystal everywhere. But we were still in a standard green quartz sector when things went bad. I was walking point. There were six of us in all. The three academics, two security people, and myself."

"Tell me about the security detail. Had you worked with them before?"

Joshua dipped the corner of one of the sandwiches into his soup and took a bite. "You ask good questions."

"I'm asking you the questions the moms and I have been asking Hollister University's Department of Para-Archaeology and your employer, Cork and Ferris, ever since the expedition vanished."

"Get any answers?"

"Not the ones we wanted," Molly said. "The university refused to respond because of a fear of litigation. Cork and Ferris stonewalled us at every turn. They insisted that the two security people had a lot of experience and excellent reputations. The corporate line is that the disaster was caused by navigator error. We were reminded on several occasions that such things happen in the Underworld. It is an inherently dangerous environment."

Joshua dunked his sandwich again and took another bite. "Three months ago, Cork and Ferris decided to go with a private security firm rather than contract with the Guild. The new company assigned two people, Harkins and Barrow, to the Hollister Expedition. Both were former Guild men. They'd had a lot of experience in the Underworld. Now you want to know if I think they might have had anything to do with the disaster, don't you?"

She reached for one of the sandwiches. "Do you suspect them?"

"These days I suspect everyone, including the academics on the Hollister Expedition."

Shocked, she almost choked on the stale bread. She managed to swallow and quickly drank some wine to clear her throat. When she could breathe, she glared at Joshua.

"Are you saying you think my sister might have had something to do with the disappearance of the team?"

"I don't trust anyone who is in any way connected to the expedition."

"Well, you can damn well take my sister off your list. I guarantee you that she had nothing to do with the loss of the team. Get real. What possible motive would she have had?"

"Piracy comes to mind," Joshua said. "It's not unheard of for the bad guys to set up an off-the-books excavation site. Lots of money in Alien relics and artifacts."

"My sister is not a pirate. She's a dedicated para-archaeologist. Go on with your story."

"Like I said, I was walking point. I went around a corner and got the buzz that tells you there's ghost energy up ahead. That was no surprise. Happens all the time in the tunnels that haven't been cleared."

"Yes, I know," Molly said.

The dangerous balls of hot, unstable dissonance energy called ghosts drifted randomly through the ancient underground maze. No one knew what caused them—just another mystery left behind by the long-vanished Aliens. There was nothing supernatural about them. They were one of the primary hazards to exploration teams and the main reason the tradition-bound, male-dominated Ghost Hunter Guilds still existed in the modern era. It required a unique paranormal talent to de-rez the potentially lethal storms of acid-green fire, and that talent was strongly linked to testosterone.

She watched Joshua pick up another sandwich and dip it into his soup.

"Well?" she prompted when he showed no signs of finishing the tale.

"That's it, the last thing I remember," he said. "When I came to, I was lying on the sidewalk in front of the Outpost General Store. At the time I had no idea how I got there. But while I was locked up in Amber Dawn, I started having the dreams about the tunnel. Eventually I realized that if there were answers, I had to start looking for them here in the mansion."

"So you came back here and settled into the Funhouse. Any answers?"

"A few." His eyes were shadowed and intense. "I know now that the tunnel brought me here. This is where I surfaced from the Underworld. But that's pretty much all I've got in the way of verifiable memories."

She shivered. "Maybe you were overcome by that ghost you encountered. It could have put you into some sort of fugue state. The effects of Unstable Dissonance Energy Manifestations are unpredictable."

"Possible. But I'm good when it comes to avoiding ghosts. I've been a navigator ever since I got my license at eighteen. I'm not without experience, Ms. Griffin."

"I know. My sister said you had an unblemished reputation. You never lost a team. Never left anyone behind."

"Until the Hollister Expedition."

"Anyone can be overcome by a ghost," she said, "even someone with a strong talent."

"Sure, if you blunder into one accidentally. But there was no surprise involved in my case. I had plenty of warning. I was aware of the ghost energy."

Newton chortled and vaulted down to the counter and onto the floor. He fluttered across the kitchen and popped up onto the nook seat, and from there to the table. Molly offered him the remainder of her sandwich. He accepted it with his usual enthusiasm, but instead of eating it, he watched Joshua dip the corner of a sandwich into the soup.

Intrigued, he moved closer to Joshua's bowl and dunked the partially eaten sandwich in the soup.

"Newton," Molly said. "You're not supposed to do things like that. It's unsanitary."

"Don't worry about it," Joshua said. "There's more soup."

He pushed his bowl toward Newton and got up from the table to get a fresh helping of soup for himself.

Newton, evidently thrilled with his experiment, drowned the rest of his sandwich in soup and ate the drenched result.

"Sorry about that," Molly said, using a napkin to blot Newton's fur. "Newton and I are still getting to know each other. I'm learning that dust bunnies are very curious and very adventurous."

"Not a problem," Joshua said.

He brought a fresh bowl to the table, sat down, and dunked a cheese-and-pickle sandwich in the soup.

Aware that she was hungry and that she was going to need energy for the dream-walking work that lay ahead, Molly picked up another sandwich, peeled off the bread, and used a fork to eat the cheese and pickles.

Joshua watched. "What's wrong? Are you on a diet or something?"

"No. The bread is a bit stale, that's all."

"Well, sure, what did you expect? I bought it in Outpost last week. That's why you're supposed to dunk it into the soup."

"Thank you. That explains so much."

She dipped a corner of another sandwich in the soup and took a tentative bite. As far as she could tell, the technique did not improve the taste of the bread, but it did change the texture. She did not offer an opinion. It did not seem like a good time to insult her host's cooking.

"What happened after you woke up in front of the general store?" she asked in an attempt to get the conversation back on track.

"I realized I'd been psi-fried and that I had lost a chunk of my memory. I turned myself over to the doctors at the nearest para-psych hospital, Amber Dawn. When I realized they were not going to be able to help me recover my memories, I left."

"You mean you escaped." She looked pointedly at the logo on the front of his scrubs. "Evidently you grabbed a few clothes on the way out the back door."

He glanced down and then went back to eating. "I needed the orderly's keys and his uniform to get out of the building."

"The orderly didn't object?"

"The orderly was unconscious at the time because he had just accidentally ingested the medication that I was supposed to take."

She nodded. "I understand accidents happen all the time when it comes to medications."

"Yes, they do."

"I couldn't help but notice that is not the same set of scrubs you had on when I arrived."

"The orderly had two extra sets of scrubs in his locker."

Molly eyed the amber around his neck. "Where did the nav rock come from?"

"After I left Amber Dawn, I came back here to try to retrace my steps. I did a little shopping in Outpost when I arrived. That's it. That's my little tale of woe."

She studied him for a long moment, trying to read his eyes. "You have a theory about what happened to the Hollister team, don't you?"

He polished off the last of a soup-soaked sandwich, sat back, and picked up his wine. "I don't know how it was done, but I'm certain the team was kidnapped."

CHAPTER FIFTEEN

Molly stared at him, stunned. "Kidnapped?"

Instead of responding, Joshua drank some wine while he waited for her to process his theory.

"There hasn't been a ransom demand," she said after she had considered for a moment. "At least not that I know of. I realize the authorities would not have announced that kind of thing to the media, but surely they would have told the families."

"It's true that ransom negotiations are usually done in secret. But that's not the problem in this case. The people who grabbed the Hollister team are not after money, at least not in the form of a ransom."

"What other reason could there be for kidnapping three academics and their guards?"

"I think someone needed the skill sets of the people on that team and chose not to hire them through the usual channels."

Molly felt as if she had just been struck by another bolt of mirror energy. She took a moment to absorb the implications.

"Okay, I did not see that coming," she said. "But it makes sense. If the kidnappers are pirates working an illegal excavation site, they would need some serious talents and skills. My sister is a brilliant para-archaeologist. The other two members of the Hollister team are also well-respected academics."

"Pirates, claim-jumpers, and quasi-legit corporations have been engaged in illegal operations in the Underworld ever since the tunnels were discovered by the First Generation colonists. But they need expertise to locate, analyze, and evaluate the artifacts, just like the licensed businesses and academic institutions."

"I understand," Molly said. "But grabbing a high-profile team working for a major academic institution is an incredibly risky thing to do. The kidnappers had to know they would be bringing the full force of the Guilds and the FBPI down on their necks."

Joshua raised his brows. "But officially there was no kidnapping, remember? It was a search and rescue operation right from the start. The media focused on the incompetence and cowardice of the man in charge, the guy who, instead of having the decency to go down with the ship, lost his nerve and abandoned the team."

She tried to follow the logic but lost her way. "What does a ship have to do with this? Are you telling me that you saw a *boat* while you were down in the Underworld?"

"No," he said. "The idea that a captain goes down with his ship is an Old World tradition. You know, like the one-finger salute conveying profound respect and admiration that you gave me."

She tried and failed to suppress a hot flush. "Oh, yeah. Right."

"Your turn. Tell me exactly how you are going to help me regain my memory using that crystal-focus technique you mentioned."

"I think of it as dream-walking."

Joshua's eyes hardened. "Sounds like storefront psychic shit. Do you tell fortunes, too? Predict the future? Summon spirits?"

She reminded herself that she could not afford to be insulted. She had a mission. Nothing was allowed to get in the way.

"To be clear, Mr. Knight, I don't read palms or tell fortunes. I don't claim to speak to the dead. I admit that the kind of therapy I do is considered nontraditional by the modern medical establishment, but I am not a fraud."

"I went through a lot of different kinds of therapists at the hospital. They were not helpful."

She planted both hands on the table and learned forward. "I came here today because I need answers from you. I'm convinced my sister is still alive and I want to find her. I think you want answers, too. Neither of us has gotten very far on our own. What have we got to lose by working together?"

A crystalline silence gripped the table. Out of the corner of her eye Molly saw that Newton was watching Joshua very intently.

Joshua glanced at him. "Is he going to go for my throat?"

"You'll have to ask him," Molly said.

"I suppose the good news for me is that I don't see the teeth."

"Yet."

Joshua looked amused. "This is the first time I've been threatened by a dust bunny. But you're right about one thing. I have nothing to lose. I'll give your crystal-focus therapy a try tonight, as soon as we finish dinner. You get one shot."

She forced herself to breathe. "My technique sometimes requires a few sessions," she warned.

"Then we will both be up quite late, because tonight is all you've got."

She hesitated. The conversation was not going well. "A single session is usually exhausting for both the client and me. It takes time to recover. I don't think a series of back-to-back sessions would work well."

"In that case, let's hope the first one is successful, because you won't be hanging around tomorrow."

"Are you trying to scare me off again?"

"I won't have to. The house will send you packing in the morning."

"What do you mean?" she asked.

"This place is not much fun during the daylight hours, but after dark it's a nightmare that you can't escape."

CHAPTER SIXTEEN

In the mirror he was surrounded by the tunnel of endless night. He wasn't alone. Molly was with him, her hand locked in one of his. The image had been vague when it first appeared, but it was sharpening quickly. He could see details that had never been clear in his memories or his dreams—details like the powerful currents of energy that swirled in the depths of the darkness.

Details like a faint stream of light flowing through the night.

"We're in," Molly said. She tightened her grip on his hand. "I usually work with the much smaller, weaker crystals in my satchel, but under the circumstances we need all the power we can get. The mirrors inside this house are supercharged and tuned by a pro. Also, the large size will allow both of us to pick up details that might go unnoticed in one of my regular dream-walking crystals."

She had chosen the big mirror over the sofa for what, as far as he was concerned, was an experiment, one that was probably destined to fail. But she appeared calm and in control. He could feel the heat in her powerful aura. She knew what she was doing, he thought. Maybe this dream-walking thing really would work.

He had been braced for some theatrics, maybe a dramatic incantation or a chant. But she was going about the process very matter-of-factly. That was encouraging.

"How do we do this?" he asked.

"Think of the scene in the mirror as a police artist's sketch," Molly said. "Our goal is to fill in the details. We need a more complete picture. I'm going to ask you to walk me through your dreamscape and tell me what you're seeing. In turn, I'll tell you what I see. Next comes the complicated part."

"What, exactly, is the complicated part?"

"My talent allows me to use the energy locked in the crystal face of the mirror to sharpen the image and bring out details that you might not notice. But I have to take control of your dreamscape to do it."

"Define *take control.*"

She cleared her throat. "It's a lot like hypnosis except that you will be aware that you're in a trance and you'll remember everything. It's a lucid dream state."

"I'll be in a lucid dream state but you will be controlling the dream? I don't like where this is going."

"I was afraid you'd say that. Try to remember that we are working together. Our agendas are aligned. You're going to have to trust me. You simply don't have a choice. Neither do I."

"I'll probably regret this, but you're right. I'm out of options. Go for it."

"Try to think positive," she urged.

"I haven't had a positive thought since I lost the Hollister Expedition."

"We're going to find my sister and the others."

The already charged atmosphere got hotter—Molly's energy at work, he realized, not that of the mirrors. It was like standing next to a small, contained storm. He knew she was a strong talent, but he hadn't realized just how powerful she was.

Without warning the storm swept over him, dazzling his senses. He should have been terrified, running for his life. Instead, he had to fight an almost irresistible urge to abandon himself to the elemental thrill.

Belatedly he understood he was falling into the trancelike state she had warned him about. Instinct took control. He slammed his psychic barriers into place. The storm receded immediately.

"Sorry," Molly said. She sounded breathless. "I moved too fast. I should have been more subtle. But your energy field is very strong, so I went in at full-rez. Frankly, I'm amazed you were able to push me away."

He wiped the sweat off his forehead with the back of his arm. "Felt like I was hit by a hurricane."

"If it's any consolation, you threw me out immediately. It was like hitting a green quartz wall and bouncing off. Irresistible force meets immovable object, I suppose. You are obviously stronger than you think. The thing is, I need your cooperation to make my technique work. I'll be more careful next time."

"Give me a minute."

"Sure. No rush."

Except there was a reason to rush, he thought, and they both knew it.

"What did you mean about my aura being strong?" he asked. "I've been psi-burned. My senses were fried, remember?"

"I know that's what the media claimed."

"The doctors at the para-psych hospital made the diagnosis, not the media. I can tell you from experience that my navigation talents are gone."

"I think you were misdiagnosed because the doctors didn't detect the anomaly in one band of your aura. Not their fault. If I wasn't working with strong crystal at the moment, I might not be able to see it, either."

He tensed. The last thing he needed was one more problem with his paranormal senses. "What's the anomaly?"

"It looks like certain wavelengths are sort of . . . frozen."

He stared at their reflections in the mirror. "That doesn't sound good."

"It's actually good news. It means those wavelengths aren't burned out. They're in a state of suspended animation. I might be able to unfreeze those currents because they are in the dreamlight region." She tightened her grip again. "Will you let me give it a try?"

"What the hell. Nothing to lose."

Cautiously he lowered his defenses, opening the gate of his mental fortress. Molly's energy field whispered to his, seeking harmony. Resonance. It was a much different experience this time. She was not trying to overwhelm him. This was a seduction. Exciting. Intimate. Arousing.

Very arousing.

He definitely did not need this particular complication. But it was too late. He could have raised his defenses again, but he no longer wanted to resist. He liked having her close in the psychic sense as well as the physical.

Well, shit. She had done it, he realized. She had put him into a waking trance. The experience was intriguing. Not terrifying. Not scary at all.

"Don't worry," she said. "You can break the trance anytime you want. You're here voluntarily. I'm not holding you captive."

That amused him. "Are you sure about that?"

"Positive." In the mirror she looked offended.

"*Could* you hold me captive?" he asked. Curious. Not worried.

"That's a ridiculous question. Of course not."

But the answer came a little too quickly. He wondered what it would feel like to be locked into her aura. Would it work both ways? If she entranced him, would it follow that she was also caught in the trance?

"Stop it," Molly snapped.

She sounded annoyed. And somewhat unnerved. Shaken. He was not the only one who had just discovered that there was a primal sexuality infused into their intimate connection. Evidently it had caught her off guard.

"Stop what?" he asked, going for polite and innocent.

"Stop trying to make this a sexual experience."

"You can't blame me. You're the one in charge here."

"Focus, Mr. Knight. Pay attention to your dreamscape. Tell me about it."

"Right," he said. "Okay, I see us surrounded by heavy currents of powerful energy. Dark energy. There is one slim current of bright light. It wasn't there earlier when we looked into the hall mirror together."

"At the time I was not trying to hold the focus. This experience will be different."

Definitely different, he thought.

"Let's start with that narrow current of light," she said. "Any idea what it is or what it might indicate?"

A blurred memory surfaced.

. . . He was lost in the dark. Without his nav amber he could not orient his senses. He was vaguely aware that he was on his hands and knees on a hard surface. It felt like familiar green quartz but it did not glow. There was no light at all.

He put out a hand, searching for a wall, and fought to rez his shattered senses. He finally picked up a thin but distinct current of energy. It did not roil and churn like the waves of night that surrounded him. Instead, it was steady, a faint but distinct through-line.

"That's it," he said, disbelief warring with near-euphoric relief. "That's how I found my way through the tunnel to this house."

"I don't understand," Molly said. "Did you have some nav amber?"

"No. They took all my amber."

"Are you telling me you were able to follow that current even though you didn't have good amber?"

"All talent comes from an innate intuitive ability of some kind," he reminded her. "Mine is a sense of direction."

"But I didn't think it was possible for anyone to navigate the Underworld without tuned amber."

"Don't get me wrong, it's not easy. I don't do it on a regular basis, that's for damn sure. It's exhausting, for one thing. It requires a huge amount of sustained focus. On top of that, I have no idea how much I can trust my talent down in the tunnels because there's so much we don't know about paranormal physics and how the Aliens manipulated that kind of power. I always work with amber. But I didn't have it in that tunnel, so I was forced to use my core talent."

"You probably pushed it to the max," Molly said. "Stressed it. That's why it shut down. In effect, those particular wavelengths went into a temporary coma. They needed time to recover."

"Huh. Think so?"

"That's how it looks to me, but I'm not a doctor. You said you followed that current here. Can you backtrack it?"

"You mean now? In the dreamscape?"

"For starters, yes," Molly said. "Your memories are starting to fall into place. One will connect to another. We need you to remember as much as you can. Try following that current and see where it takes you."

It was a weird experience. He realized he was not trapped in the mirror dreamscape. He was capable of exerting agency in it. All he had to do was concentrate.

The dreamscape morphed into a silent video. He followed the slender current of bright energy. Molly accompanied him. They walked through the dark until the door appeared. It was a very ordinary door. Old. Wooden.

"That doesn't make sense," he said. "Why would there be a wooden door in my dream?"

"Dreamscape imagery is often symbolic," Molly said. "Sometimes the objects that appear require interpretation. Try opening the door."

He wrapped his hand around a crystal knob and opened the door.

Brilliant, senses-blinding energy blazed on the other side of the doorway.

Molly shrieked in surprise, just as she had that afternoon when she had uncovered the mirror in the bedroom. She clutched his hand.

"Close it," she yelped. "Close it. *Close it.*"

"Okay, take it easy," he said.

Reluctantly he willed the door to close. It shut, but not before he caught a glimpse of the pyramid of stacked crystals in the center of the white-hot room. He remembered those crystals . . .

In the next instant he was free of the trance. Satisfaction slammed through him.

"I hate when that happens," Molly said.

"When what happens?" he demanded.

"I hate when I get sucked too deeply into someone's dream-scape. It's weird. Really, really weird. It's been a long time since I lost control like that. There's just so much energy in this house . . . Never mind."

She sounded shocked. He was still gripping her hand, so he was aware of the shivers coursing through her. When he turned to look at her, he saw the dread in her eyes. She was sweating.

"Are you okay?" he asked.

She gave him a look that told him he had just asked a very dumb question. Unable to think of anything else to do, he pulled her close and wrapped his arms around her.

"I'm sorry," he whispered into her hair. "I didn't realize."

"Forget it," she said into the front of the green scrubs shirt. "Goes with the territory. My fault. I wasn't prepared. Got to admit, it's never been that intense before."

Newton vaulted up onto the coffee table and made concerned noises. Molly pulled away and leaned down to pat him reassuringly.

"It's all right," she said. "I just walked into a surprise, that's all."

She straightened, pulling herself together with a visible effort. "Looks like we made real progress."

"Yes," he said. He could feel the adrenaline hitting his bloodstream. Finally, his memories were returning. "I'm starting to recall more details. There's a pyramid in the chamber on the other side of the door."

"I saw it briefly. It looked like it was made out of a stack of very hot crystal rods."

"Quicksilver," he said. "Or, rather, some kind of material that looks like quicksilver. The room was full of energy, but not the dark kind in the tunnel. Some of it was . . . unstable. I've spent a lot of time in the Underworld, but I've never come across anything like it."

"Any idea what the pyramid is doing?"

"I think it's generating power, but who knows what the purpose is."

"Interesting," Molly said. "But those rods were not made of resonating amber."

"No. But just because we rely on amber for power doesn't mean that's what the Aliens used."

"Good point."

He turned back to the mirror. A flicker of *something* came and went at the edge of his vision. He struggled to see it clearly, but whatever it was stubbornly refused to come into focus.

"I need to get back into that dream," he said. He grabbed Molly's hand. "Do the trance thing again."

"I'm not sure that's a good idea," Molly said. "This is the first time I've worked with this crystal. It's unique, to say the least. I've already taken a few risks because your core talent feels strong. I think it would be a good idea for you to rest for a while."

"I'm so close to remembering *everything*," he said. "I just need a little more time in the dream. My intuition tells me that time is running out for the expedition team. Nothing to lose, remember?"

"Well—"

"Do it."

"All right."

She clutched his hand. He felt the currents of her aura heighten. The last of the shadows that had cloaked his talent lifted. He could focus again, *really* focus.

The flicker of energy at the edge of his vision sharpened. In the dreamscape he opened the door to the chamber that held the pyramid.

Energy blazed, dazzled, and stormed inside the room.

"I was in that chamber," he said.

"Are we good here?" Molly asked anxiously. "Because I really think we need to exit this dreamscape."

"Just one more minute," he said.

He walked through the doorway. Light exploded. An exultant sense of triumph swept through him.

"Yes," he said, dazzled by the experience. *"You did it. I remember every-thing now."*

He used his grip on Molly's hand to pull her into his arms. She was soft and sleek and warm and inviting. Her scent clouded his mind. Her eyes were very wide. Her lips were parted.

"The woman of my dreams," he whispered. "Where have you been all my life?"

"Mr. Knight, listen to me. I think you're trapped between the dream state and the waking state. You need to focus—"

He kissed her with all the fierce energy coursing through his veins. The taste of her thrilled his senses. He needed this, he needed Molly

Griffin, the woman of his dreams. He wanted nothing more than to pull Molly down onto the carpet and lose himself deep inside her.

Out of the corner of his eye he saw a flicker of lightning in the mirror over the sofa. He heard Molly gasp. Mad chortling sounded from somewhere nearby.

Before he could register what was happening, he plunged into a whirlpool of night.

CHAPTER SEVENTEEN

"The good news for us, Newton, is that he's not dead," Molly said.

Newton vaulted up onto the coffee table. Together they looked at the man sprawled on the carpet. Joshua had gone down in a heartbeat. There was no way to get him onto the sofa, let alone haul him up the stairs to his bedroom. He was going to have to sleep on the floor until he woke up.

Assuming he did wake up.

"This is exactly the type of accident that can happen when you let a client run the session," Molly said. "I should have had more control."

Newton chortled. Evidently not concerned with the situation, he lost interest in Joshua and switched his attention to a small crystal sculpture on the coffee table.

Molly crouched and took Joshua's pulse. It was strong.

"I think he'll be okay, Newton. He just needs a little time to recover from my slight miscalculation. This unfortunate turn of events is his fault. He insisted on moving too fast."

Newton chortled agreement.

"I'm sure he'll understand once I explain." But she knew she was trying to reassure herself. "The problem is that he's probably going to be really pissed off when he recovers. He might even try to throw us out of the house in the morning. What a mess. For a while there I thought I had made a breakthrough. Maybe I did. But we won't know for sure until he wakes up."

She pondered the problem of the sleeping man for another moment, and then she became aware of a chill in the atmosphere. The fine hairs on the back of her neck stirred. Everyone knew that paranormal energy was always stronger after dark. Like many people she enjoyed the pleasant little buzz of night. But this vibe was different. Unpleasant. Disturbing.

"I think I know why the locals say the house is haunted," she said aloud.

Newton ignored her. He was busy examining the empty crystal vase that sat on the coffee table. Curious, Molly touched the rim of the vase. Paranormal fire sparked.

"Ouch." She yanked her fingers off the vase.

Newton chortled and moved to an end table to check out the crystal base of a lamp. He soon lost interest in it and bounced across the room to a waist-high pedestal where a carved wooden chest was displayed. He leaped up onto the pedestal and tried to open the lid. When he failed, he chortled to Molly.

Intrigued, Molly walked to the pedestal. "Let's see what's inside."

She unlatched the lid and opened the box. The light from a nearby lamp sparked and flashed on a couple dozen colorful round crystals.

"Marbles," she said to Newton. "One of the previous owners must have been a collector."

Gingerly she rezzed her senses. The marbles began to heat. A frisson iced the back of her neck. Newton bounced up and down and made excited noises. He started to reach into the box to select a marble.

Molly slammed the lid shut. Newton protested.

"Sorry, pal," she said. "Something tells me that the combination of you and a Pandora's box full of hot marbles is not a good idea. Find something else to play with."

Newton muttered but he did not linger on the pedestal. He vaulted down to the floor and scurried to the large, elaborately decorated tassel that trimmed a drapery cord. Experimentally he gave it a push. The tassel swung. Thrilled, he seized the cord, pushed off with his rear paws, and rode the tassel as it sailed back and forth.

"That's better," Molly said. "Have fun."

She went back across the room to check on Joshua. He was sleeping soundly—very soundly. She leaned down and gave his shoulder a gentle shake. He did not respond.

She thought about the fog outside and crossed to one of the small windows. Hauling the heavy drapes aside, she peered out into the night. The darkness looked and felt absolute. It shrouded the house. She could not see the desert moon or the stars. Another chill rattled her senses.

"It's getting colder," she said to Newton. She looked around. "I don't see a thermostat. I'd better get a blanket for Knight. With luck there will be one in that awful bedroom I'm supposed to use."

She crossed to the stairs. Newton scurried across the room to join her. Together they climbed to the second floor. Molly paused on the landing and, looking up, contemplated the door on the third floor.

"Knight didn't actually forbid me to enter the séance room," she reminded Newton. "He just advised against it."

The same way he had advised against lifting the drapes on the wall mirrors, she thought.

"Okay, he *strongly* advised against it," she said. "Yes, there was an implied threat. But this will be different. Now I have a much better idea of what to expect from mirror heat. I'll be prepared for a jolt of hot energy."

Newton chortled.

"Clearly you agree with my logic," she said.

She started up the stairs to the third floor. Newton reached the landing before she did. When she arrived, she scooped him up and plopped him on her shoulder. Together they examined the partially open door of the séance chamber.

"You were in there earlier today," Molly said to Newton. "According to Knight, that's where you found the little mirror, so obviously, there's nothing really dangerous inside."

Newton made what she took to be encouraging sounds and waved the small mirror.

She pushed the door wider and moved cautiously into the séance chamber. Two wall sconces glowed softly, illuminating the room in a dim light.

She was surprised to see an old-fashioned amber lantern in the center of the table. Unlike the other lights in the mansion, it was unlit. It was the first device she had come across inside the house that was not hooked up to the mansion's main power supply.

"The medium probably used it as a prop for the séances," she said.

Mirrors covered the walls. Strange, fantastical landscapes appeared and disappeared in the looking glasses.

"It's okay, Newton. The energy in here is standard-issue crystal heat. Nothing I can't handle. When Knight warned me to stay out, he was just trying to scare me."

Newton chortled and hopped down to the table.

"I wish there was some way to turn up the lights," she said. "I'd like to take a closer look around this chamber to see what tricks and gadgets the medium used to make her clients think she could summon spirits."

She moved farther into the room and promptly stumbled into a pool of dark ice. She quickly stepped out of it and glanced down. With her senses rezzed, the stain of death was clearly evident. Luckily it did not feel recent.

"This must be where the medium died," she said.

Avoiding the stain, she worked her way around the chamber, peering into various mirrors. They were all infused with energy, and the eerie landscapes in them appeared and disappeared, depending on whether she focused on them, but none seemed dangerously hot.

One was draped. It was much smaller than the covered mirror in her bedroom. It could not hurt to lift a corner of the thick silk and take a peek.

She took a step forward . . .

. . . and stopped because the lights abruptly winked out. She glanced back toward the doorway. The hall was in deep night, too.

For a few seconds she was afraid to move for fear of stumbling into a chair or walking into a wall. She heard a reassuring chortle and saw two amber eyes pop open. They didn't work like flashlights but they did allow her to get oriented. Newton's gleaming eyes appeared to hover in midair. That indicated he was still on the séance table.

She remembered the old-fashioned amber lantern in the center of the table.

"Please stay right where you are, Newton," she said, feeling her way across the room. "Looks like there's been a power failure. I'm going to need the lantern."

Newton seemed to get the concept. He stayed put and made encouraging sounds. She worked her way toward him. When the toe of her sneaker struck a chair leg, she knew she was making progress.

She put out a hand, groping for the table. Her fingers touched wood. She stretched out her other hand, trying to make contact with the lantern.

Newton's eyes moved. She heard metal slide on wood. The next thing she knew, he had pushed the lantern into her hands.

"Thanks, pal."

Newton responded with a little chortle.

She found the switch and rezzed a little energy. To her overwhelming relief the lantern glowed faintly and then brightened.

"Hard to believe the First Generation settlers had to rely on such primitive sources of light after the Curtain closed," she said. "But it certainly creates atmosphere, doesn't it? I'll bet it made good theater for the medium's séances."

Newton chortled and hopped up onto her shoulder. Another eerie frisson stirred her intuition. Energy was rising in the chamber. Her palms prickled. She was very aware of the big, dark house enclosing her on all sides. The séance room felt claustrophobic.

"Maybe it wasn't such a great idea to explore this room," she said. Lantern in hand, she went toward the door. "Let's go get a blanket and head downstairs. If Knight wakes up in total darkness he might panic. Or not. Come to think of it, he doesn't seem like the sort to panic, does he?"

She was almost at the door when a flash of ghostly energy snapped across her senses.

No, not *ghostly* energy, she thought. She did not believe in supernatural manifestations of the dead. The only ghosts were the storms of green energy in the Underworld, and there was nothing supernatural about them. They were easily explained by the laws of paranormal physics.

But the cold vibe she was picking up was unfamiliar and deeply unsettling. Newton growled. She felt his hind paws tighten on her shoulder.

"You know," she said, "in another, less enlightened era—or if, say, someone happened to be highly suggestible—it would be easy to believe that the currents in this room are being generated by spirits."

Newton rumbled.

Annoyed that she was allowing the mirrors to rattle her nerves, she stopped and turned slowly on her heel, letting the glow of the lantern sweep the small space. The amber-yellow light glinted and flashed on the crystal faces of the looking glasses, but as far as she could tell, none of them was the source of the rising energy in the room.

She was about to continue out into the hall when the lantern light landed on the mirror draped in black. Another edgy frisson lanced her senses. Her sparking intuition abruptly shot to full-rez. It wasn't a fight-or-flight warning, she realized. It was the telltale signal letting her know there was something important about the looking glass.

She changed course and went to stand in front of the mirror. The icy currents were stronger now that she was so close. They leaked out around the edges of the black cloth.

She reached for a corner of the drape. "This is probably not a good idea."

Newton chortled. It wasn't a cheerful, enthusiastic chortle, but it wasn't a warning growl, either.

"Here goes."

She raised the corner of the drape. The chilling energy coming from the mirror got more intense.

"It's tuned energy," she said to Newton. "The normal human kind. No ghosts involved. It's different from the other tuned mirrors. I can tell you one thing for sure—whoever laid down the vibe in this mirror had a strong talent."

Newton muttered, but he was still fluffed. She took that as a good sign and gingerly pulled the drape entirely aside, revealing the dark crystal face of the mirror. She expected to see a reflection of herself holding the lantern, Newton on her shoulder. Instead, a spinning ball of light filled the center of the mirror.

She studied it, fascinated.

"I think it's a recording," she said to Newton, a little awed. "Someone left a message in this mirror."

It wasn't easy for even a high-rez psychic to embed a message into glass or crystal. It took practice and training, and the recipient had to have the ability to open the recording. When you got right down to it, the skill didn't have a lot of practical applications—not in the modern era, when leaving a message on someone's phone was faster and more reliable.

She reached out and cautiously put two fingertips on the crystal surface. The message was not locked. The spinning ball of energy brightened. A sharp jolt cracked across her senses. Instead of breaking off contact with the mirror, she heightened her talent, gaining control of the whirling image.

When she was satisfied that she could handle the energy, she gently opened the message. The whirling ball vanished, revealing a blurry video-like recording. A middle-aged woman appeared. She wore a high-necked dress studded with dark crystals. Her face was drawn into tight, haggard lines and her pale eyes were stark with fear. She delivered her message in a shaky, traumatized voice.

I am Madame Zandra. If you have opened this message, it means I am dead. I don't have much time. You must believe me when I tell you that this house holds terrible secrets. It is the portal to an Alien crypt in the Underworld. But the souls that are buried there are not truly dead.

I have come to understand that the Aliens put their dying into a state of suspended animation, no doubt intending to awaken them at some future time. But something went wrong for the Sleepers in the crypt below this house. I suspect that, centuries ago, when their people were forced to abandon Harmony, there was no time or perhaps no way to take the Sleepers with them. For whatever reason, those in the crypt were left behind.

The system that maintained the state of suspended animation has begun to fail. The Sleepers have partially awakened, but they are trapped in a terrible in-between state, neither truly dead nor truly alive. They have found this portal to the surface world, but they cannot go outside yet. For now the house is their prison. It has become mine as well. They know that I have been trying to find a way to lock the crypt. It is only a matter of time before they murder me.

I am leaving this message as a warning and a plea to whoever comes after me. You must find a way to lock the crypt. If the Sleepers escape this house, they will unleash the great power of their weapons upon we who have made Harmony our home. They will destroy the civilization we have created on this world.

The video dissolved. The spinning ball of energy reappeared.

CHAPTER EIGHTEEN

"Okay, that was different, Newton." Shaken, Molly took a deep breath and let the black drape fall back across the mirror. "Madame Zandra was obviously delusional. Maybe she had some serious psychological problems when she moved into the mansion, or perhaps the energy in this house drove her over the edge. We'll probably never know. I wonder if Knight knows about this message."

She stopped because Newton was growling softly—a warning growl, not a get-ready-to-fight growl. Her intuition spiked again. She became aware of a cold draft coming through the door of the séance room. She turned quickly and raised the lantern.

Wispy tendrils of glowing blue fog were drifting into the chamber. The mist was infused with a disturbing vibe, the kind of energy that raised the hair on the back of the neck and kicked up the heart rate. It was not difficult to imagine that what she was picking up was the chill of the crypt. She shivered.

"I think I know why the medium locked herself in this room," she said.

Newton muttered. She took that as an indication that he was not getting a pleasant buzz from the currents. He was definitely not bouncing around and chortling as if he had found a new form of entertainment. That did not bode well.

"Knight predicted that we would bail first thing in the morning. This is probably why he figured we wouldn't hang around. Hard to believe he's been able to tolerate the atmosphere in here for nearly three weeks. No wonder he's a wreck."

She focused her senses, pushing back on the graveyard vibe, and went out into the hall. When she reached the top of the stairs, she raised the lantern and looked down. Radiant blue fog swirled lightly in the living room. At first there was no sign of Joshua.

"Maybe he woke up and went to bed," she said, trying for a positive spin.

Newton growled. She got the impression the client was not safe in bed. Maybe there was no safe place in this house.

In the next moment the drifting fog in the living room thinned briefly, revealing the crumpled man on the carpet. He groaned and stirred restlessly, but he did not awaken.

"Oh, shit," Molly said. "He's still out, so he can't use his talent to push back on the fog. There's no telling what it's doing to his dreamscape."

Lantern in hand, she grabbed the handrail and hurried down the stairs to the second floor. Newton chortled encouragement. She could not tell if he thought they were playing a new game or if he was urging her to greater speed.

The welling fog was giving off so much eerie light now, she no longer needed the lantern. She started to set it down but changed her mind. The warm amber glow was a comforting barrier against the blue mist.

She made it into her bedroom and grabbed a blanket from the cupboard. She started to turn back toward the door but paused as a thought struck her. She took a second blanket.

She hurried out into the hall and descended the stairs.

By the time she reached the ground floor, faint and fleeting apparitions were starting to appear in the fog. Ghostly images and scenes took form briefly and then dissolved. She knew the visions were generated by her own dream energy, but that did not make them any less disturbing. In some ways it made them worse.

She located Joshua in the fog and dumped the bedding on the carpet beside him. She set down the lantern and looked at Newton.

"It's going to be a long night," she said. "We will need sustenance."

She fumbled her way across the fog-bound living room, aiming in what she hoped was the general direction of the arched entrance to the central hall. In the process she managed to accidentally blunder into a chair and send a crystal figurine crashing to the floor. The object landed on the carpet with a resounding thud.

"Lucky it missed my foot," she said to Newton. "Might have broken a toe."

Two steps later she stubbed her toe on the leg of a chair. She groaned. Newton made sympathetic noises.

She staggered out of the living room and into the hall. The fog was much thinner there. The kitchen was still clear. She picked up the tray that Joshua had used to carry dinner to the table and started piling stuff on it. She snagged a few bags of Zing Chips from the carton sitting on the counter, added some energy bars, and then opened the refrigerator. Newton was making very encouraging sounds now.

"The chips and energy bars will make us thirsty," Molly said. "We'll need to hydrate. We're also going to need caffeine."

The refrigerator was crammed with cans of Hot Quartz Cola. The labels boasted, THE EQUIVALENT OF TWO CUPS OF COFFEE IN EVERY CAN.

She grabbed a six-pack and started to close the refrigerator. She paused to consider the tray.

"This should keep us going until morning," she said. "Now to see if I can make it back across the living room without dropping the tray."

Newton vaulted up onto her shoulder and made it clear he was in favor of the project.

She moved out of the kitchen and across the hall. The fog was getting heavier. Newton huddled close and made comforting noises. She drew strength from his sturdy little aura and cautiously worked her way through the spectral fog.

She managed to avoid collisions with the furniture, but she almost stumbled over Joshua. He stirred when her shoe connected with his leg, but he did not open his eyes.

"He's dreaming, Newton. I was afraid of this."

She set the tray down within reach on the coffee table and shook out the blankets. Working quickly, she tucked one of the blankets around Joshua and then groped her way to the sofa, where she found a couple of pillows. Halfway back to her goal she felt a fresh draft across her ankles. Her first thought was that one of the windows was open, allowing the outside fog into the house.

"I'd better close it," she said.

Newton, still perched on her shoulder, muttered in disapproval. She felt her way through the mist and found herself in a short hall. There was a door at the end of the hall. Not just an ordinary door. It was made of mag-rez steel. It was the type of door used to seal bank vaults and hole-in-the-wall entrances to the tunnels. The draft was seeping up from what must be a basement. It was bringing the fog with it. The vapor leaked around the edges of the steel door.

Impulsively she reached out to grip the handle. Newton rumbled a warning, but it was too late. She yelped when a flash of psi heat shot up her arm.

"Shit," she said. "House rule number two. Don't go down into the basement."

She braced herself and gingerly touched the handle again. She got another shock, but it was manageable.

"You know, Newton, maybe it isn't a good idea to open this door tonight. I think I'll wait until morning and have a long talk with Joshua."

Newton chortled. He sounded relieved.

She worked her way back to Joshua and sank down onto the carpet beside him. Draping the second blanket around herself, she leaned against the sleeping man. It wasn't until she touched him that she realized he was warm. Too warm. It wasn't fever heat, she decided, relieved, but he was pulling hard on his psychic resources. Even asleep he was fighting the disturbing energy that swirled in the room.

She gripped his hand and cautiously rezzed her talent. In the next heartbeat the currents of their strong auras collided and swiftly began to resonate. A moment later Joshua grew calm. She knew he was drawing strength from her.

She struggled to ignore the intense sense of intimacy that was sending thrilling little frissons of sensual awareness through her. She had never experienced anything like it with her other clients. It was compelling. She could not think of any other word to describe the sensation.

"Nothing personal," she assured Newton. "It doesn't mean anything. It's just an example of paranormal biophysics in action. Everyone knows two auras are stronger than one. It will be easier for Joshua and me to suppress the hallucinations if we maintain physical contact."

Newton chortled.

"Are you laughing at me?" she said. "You are, aren't you?" She reached for a bag of Zing Chips with her free hand and tossed it to Newton. "Shut up and munch."

Newton deftly caught the bag and opened it with great care. He gave the process of selecting the perfect chip careful attention and finally made his choice. Molly snagged a can of Hot Quartz Cola, popped the top, and took a fortifying swallow.

She watched the visions come and go in the blue fog and thought about the medium's message. *You must find a way to lock the crypt. If the Sleepers escape this house, they will unleash the great power of their weapons upon we who have made Harmony our home. They will destroy the civilization we have created on this world.*

After a while she stopped thinking about the medium and turned to memories of the past . . .

CHAPTER NINETEEN

THE PAST . . .

Helen Inskip was too frightened to protest when Charlotte and Eugenie Griffin informed her that Molly and Leona would be leaving the school immediately. In the days that followed the kidnapping, the Inskip School was shut down by the authorities. The remaining students were transferred to another orphanage.

The press went wild with the story of the heroic rescue of a little orphan girl by the team from Griffin Investigations. The public loved that dust bunnies had been involved.

The kidnapper was identified as Nigel Willard, an eccentric chemist who had managed to get fired from every lab position he had ever held. He was dead when the Guild and the Federal Bureau of Psi Investigation agents arrived at the scene to take him into custody. Cause of death was officially undetermined, but the assumption was that he had succumbed to panic. The terror of finding himself on his own in the tunnels with no navigation amber had been too much for his unstable mind and had triggered a heart attack.

Little was known about Willard or his motives. The authorities concluded he was just another crackpot with some bizarre theories about the paranormal. Charlotte and Eugenie did not mention the notebook to the police or the Federal Bureau of Psi Investigation.

Helen Inskip died soon after the kidnapping. Cause of death was undetermined. Suicide was suspected but never confirmed.

Charlotte and Eugenie had a very serious discussion on the subject of their fitness for raising two little girls. Molly and Leona assured them that they were more than capable of parenthood. The adoption papers were signed within a week. Molly and Leona got a real last name—Griffin.

Charlotte and Eugenie made certain that the secrets in Willard's notebook stayed secret.

Molly and Leona did not pay any attention to the headlines. They were too busy discovering the world outside the walls of the Inskip School. Charlotte and Eugenie protected them from the media and refused all interviews. Eventually the story faded from the headlines.

Charlotte and Eugenie did not tell their daughters about the contents of the notebook until the girls turned thirteen and showed signs of coming into their talents.

"So, we were lab experiments?" Molly asked around a bite of birthday cake.

"According to the notebook, your mothers found themselves pregnant and on their own," Charlotte explained. "They were offered jobs as assistants in a research lab."

"During that time, they were exposed to some unknown paranormal radiation and given an injection of an unknown formula," Eugenie said. "They were told the radiation incident was a lab accident and that the injection would counteract any ill effects. They were assured that no harm had been done to them or the babies. But later they apparently discovered that they—or, rather, their babies—were unwitting research subjects."

"Why did they experiment on us?" Leona asked. "Were they trying to create monsters or something?"

"No," Eugenie said.

"Absolutely not," Charlotte added in her sternest voice.

But Molly thought both moms looked a little uncertain because they exchanged what she and Leona had labeled the mom-to-mom look.

Charlotte tapped the notebook. "From what we can tell, the goal of the experiment was to enhance the paranormal talents of the babies."

"What happened to our other mothers?" Molly asked.

"According to the notebook, they escaped and fled the lab," Eugenie said. "They went into hiding together. Evidently they managed to disappear for about a year and a half. During that time, you two were born. But something happened that made them afraid. Maybe they had reason to think someone was searching for them. They took the two of you to the Inskip School and left you on the doorstep along with a note assuring Inskip that she would receive a quarterly check so long as she took good care of the babies and made certain they were not adopted."

"It's clear your birth mothers planned to come back for you," Charlotte said. "But they were both murdered in what the police called a random act of street violence."

"We think that Helen Inskip would have eventually realized your mothers were never coming back and that there would be no more payments intended to keep you at the school," Eugenie said. "At that point she probably would have made you available for adoption. But it looks like Willard tracked you down at the orphanage. He made a deal with Helen Inskip. He offered to continue paying her to keep you in the school and continue raising you. He did not want to take the risk that the two of you might be adopted."

"Why did he kidnap me?" Molly asked.

"According to the notebook, he wanted to run some tests on you to see how your senses were developing," Eugenie said. "When he was finished, he would have returned you to the school and taken Leona for the same tests. He probably would have continued conducting tests on you until you were in your early teens and your abilities came in."

Leona drank some lemonade while she thought about that. "What kind of talents are we going to get?"

Charlotte exchanged glances with Eugenie. "That remains to be seen. Psychic talents appear in the early teens and continue to develop until they reach their full potential. That usually happens around eighteen or nineteen."

"That's a long time from now," Leona said, losing interest.

"Like forever," Molly said with a sigh.

"Yes, it is," Eugenie said, relieved to end the discussion. "We'll talk about it again in a few years. But in the meantime, you must promise us that you won't tell anyone else that someone used your birth mothers in an experiment meant to affect your para-psych profiles."

"Why not?" Leona asked.

"Yeah, why can't we tell anyone?" Molly asked. "It would be cool to have some really high-rez talents."

Charlotte cleared her throat. "Not necessarily, honey. People tend to get nervous around people who have very strong or unusual psychic senses."

"Especially if they believe those senses were artificially enhanced or altered in utero by unknown radiation and a formula," Eugenie added.

"What does *in utero* mean?" Molly asked.

"Obviously it means the kind of experiment that was conducted on us before we were born," Leona said.

Molly glared. Leona was turning out to be an overachiever with a bad habit of lecturing.

"The point is," Charlotte said, "every family has a secret. This is ours."

Leona looked at Molly, excitement widening her eyes. "We are the Griffin family secret."

Molly savored the drama. "This is so high-rez."

Eugenie and Charlotte exchanged speaking looks again but neither offered further comment.

"More cake?" Eugenie asked.

It wasn't until a few years later that Molly and Leona decided to read Nigel Willard's notebook together. When they did, they discovered just how much their secret would complicate their lives.

They marched into the offices of Griffin Investigations and informed the moms they were calling a family meeting. Eugenie and Charlotte locked the door and put the TEMPORARILY CLOSED sign in the window. Then the four of them gathered in Charlotte's office.

"The goal of Willard's experiment was to create multitalents, and he was successful," Molly announced. "Leona and I are doomed, aren't we?"

Statistically speaking, duals were rare in the population and tended to keep a low profile because powerful psychics made a lot of people uneasy. Triples were even scarcer, because most died by suicide at an early age or wound up in para-psych wards for the rest of their lives. The para-psychiatrists claimed that the human mind could not handle the overwhelming sensory overload that came with three paranormal talents.

"Are we going to end up in an asylum?" Leona demanded.

"Nope," Charlotte said. "Trust me, if you two were unstable, you would know it by now. So would Eugenie and I."

Leona, as usual, asked the bottom-line question.

"What are we supposed to tell our friends and our dates?" she said.

"There is no need to tell them anything at all," Eugenie said. "You are entitled to keep your secret."

"What about when we decide to get married?" Molly asked. "Everyone knows you have to fill out a full para-psych profile when you sign up with a matchmaking agency."

"There's no reason to worry about marriage now," Charlotte said smoothly. "You're both just starting college. It will be ages before you have to fill out a Covenant Marriage questionnaire."

"But what do we do when the time comes?" Molly asked.

Once again Eugenie and Charlotte exchanged the mom-to-mom look. Then Eugenie shrugged.

"You'll do what everyone else does when they fill out the CM questionnaires," she said. "You will omit the details of the family secret."

"You mean lie?" Leona asked.

"Omitting is not the same thing as lying," Charlotte said.

"Actually, it is pretty much the same thing," Eugenie said. "But don't worry, everyone does it when it comes to those questionnaires. The matchmaking agencies are not entitled to know your secrets."

But later that night, when Molly and Leona were alone in their room, they continued to contemplate the issue.

"I get that we shouldn't tell people that we're the result of some weird experiment that made us triple talents," Leona said. "But I don't think I'm going to want to marry someone I can't trust with the family secret."

"Neither do I," Molly said. "But what happens if we never find someone we can trust with the truth about our talents? Or, worse yet, what if we decide to trust the wrong person?"

"Maybe we will be free spirits our whole life," Leona said.

"Sooner or later, everyone gets married."

"Not everyone," Leona said. "There are a few exceptions."

"Very few," Molly said. "You know how it is. Every normal person gets married."

"We're not normal," Leona pointed out. "We're triple talents, and if people find out, we will be treated as unstable at best and as potential serial killers at worst."

Molly sighed. "At least you got a cool third talent. I'm stuck with a useless party trick that would scare the hell out of people if they knew about it."

"So don't tell anyone," Leona said.

Molly considered their uncertain futures for a moment. "Being free spirits might not be so bad when you think about it."

"Sounds good to me," Leona said.

CHAPTER TWENTY

PRESENT DAY . . .

Joshua woke to the fragrance of freshly brewed coffee and the chortle of a dust bunny. He opened his eyes and saw Newton hovering over him, the hand mirror clutched in one paw, a bag of Zing Chips in the other.

It took a moment to process the situation, but he eventually realized he was in the living room, sprawled on the carpet. One of the sofa pillows was under his head. There was a blanket draped over him.

Newton chortled again and graciously offered him a Zing Chip. He realized he was hungry, sat up, and took a couple of chips.

"Thanks, pal."

Memories snapped back into sharp focus. *Molly holding his hand. The incredibly intimate, incredibly thrilling sensation of her powerful aura resonating with his. A narrow current of energy offering a path through the endless night of the dark tunnel. The blast furnace of wild, unstable paranormal light behind the old wooden door. The quicksilver pyramid.*

He started to get to his feet but paused when he saw the empty cans of Hot Quartz Cola, discarded Zing Chip bags, and High-Rez Energy Bar wrappers on a tray.

"Just one question, Newton. Did I have a good time?"

"Truth be told, you slept through the entire party," Molly said from the doorway.

He turned to look at her. She had a mug of coffee in one hand. Her hair was damp from a shower. It dawned on him that the house had not come equipped with a hair dryer. He couldn't tell for sure if she had changed clothes, because she was once again in artsy, head-to-toe black, the brightly patterned scarf around her throat.

He glanced at the scene outside the nearest window and saw that the fog was starting to lift.

"You're not packing," he said, trying to process her calm attitude.

"Of course not. I'm not going anywhere. We're too close to finding the team." If she did not return to Illusion Town today, Clement would have to verify the energy circle for the wedding. She wanted to do that personally because the job was so important, but he was capable. That was why she had hired him, she reminded herself. He could handle things.

She watched Joshua with a wary eye. "How are you feeling?"

"Good." He did a quick internal check, pushed the blanket aside, and got to his feet. "Very good." He had slept for hours. Downstairs in the living room, which had no doubt been filled with hallucinatory fog. Evidently he had not been alone. He glanced at the tray cluttered with empty cans and snack food wrappers. "You were here? All night?"

"I couldn't figure out a way to get you upstairs, so Newton and I spent the night with you." She cleared her throat. "Speaking of which, I want to apologize for my slight miscalculation during the crystal-focus session."

"Miscalculation?"

"I did not anticipate that the dream-walking therapy would render you unconscious, but in my own defense, I would like to remind you that I was working with unfamiliar crystal energy. Also, you're the one who insisted on going straight into a second session before you had completely recovered from the first. I did try to warn you—"

"Stop. Please." He raised a hand, palm out, and then winced at the stiffness in his back and shoulders. The carpet had done little to soften the hard fireglass floor. "Whatever you did worked. I've got my memories back. That's all that matters."

Molly brightened. "I hoped you'd see it that way."

He eyed the mug in her hand. "Is that coffee?"

"Oh, right. Sorry." She hurried across the room and held out the mug. "Here you go."

He shoved the hair out of his eyes, reached for the coffee with both hands, and took a long swallow. He gave himself a moment to savor the heat and the caffeine.

"Thanks," he said. "I needed that." He shook his head in disbelief. "I can't believe you spent the night down here. How bad was the fog?"

"It got wild at times, but I had Newton and you. Your aura is strong, so between the three of us we got through it. You know the old rule. Two or more auras linked by physical contact are a lot more powerful than a single aura."

Physical contact. With Molly. The thought of her beside him— touching him—all night long made him sincerely regret that he had slept through the entire experience.

"Physical contact," he repeated.

"Right." She rezzed up a reassuring smile. "Nothing personal. Just an example of biophysics in action."

Nothing personal except that, in addition to helping him recover his memories, she had quite possibly saved his sanity by staying with him during the night. The *nothing personal* was depressing for some reason, but he shook it off and focused on the immediate future.

"You said you plan to stick around for a while?" he ventured.

"I'm not going anywhere." She narrowed her eyes. "You're stuck with Newton and me until we find Leona and the rest of the expedition team. By the way, something interesting happened last night," she continued.

He drank some more coffee. "That's one way to put it. Now that I've got my memories back, I need to come up with a rescue plan."

"That's not what I meant. I took a little tour of the séance room."

He groaned. "Of course you did. Because I advised you to stay out of there. I need to remember the basic principles of reverse psychology when I'm dealing with you. Well?"

"I've got questions about the mirror recording, but they can wait until breakfast."

He had been about to finish the coffee, but he paused the mug an inch from his mouth. "What recording?"

"The one the medium left in the séance room. Why? Are there others?"

Adrenaline spiked. Or maybe it was the caffeine hitting his system.

"I don't know anything about a recording," he said. "What does it say?"

"You really need to view the message yourself. The medium's theory was that the house is haunted by semi-dead Aliens. She called them Sleepers."

"The house got to her. Figures. She was probably hallucinating there at the end."

"Maybe, but I think there is something very important in the message."

"I'll check it out." He caught sight of himself in a nearby mirror. His first reaction was overwhelming relief because for the first time in days he could *see* himself in the mirror. The landscape was an underwater grotto, not an endless tunnel of night. He did, however, look like a man who slept in dark alleys and scrounged for leftovers in restaurant garbage bins. He downed the last of the coffee and held out the empty mug. "I need to shower and shave."

She took the mug. "Okay."

He headed for the staircase. "I'll just be a few minutes. You can start breakfast."

"Sure, boss."

He winced. "That did not come out right."

"I know, don't worry about it." She picked up the tray of empty cola cans and discarded wrappers. "Hey, you cooked dinner last night. I'll deal with breakfast."

"Great. I'm starving."

"Fresh berries and cream and poached eggs with hollandaise sauce coming right up."

He laughed—for the first time in weeks—and took the stairs two at a time, energized. Finally, a breakthrough, thanks to Molly. He had made the right decision yesterday afternoon when he had allowed her to stay.

Like he'd had a choice. The woman was a force of nature. And speaking of powerful natural forces, he was never going to forget that kiss. Hell, they had damn near set the living room on fire. At least, that was the way he remembered it. The question was, how did she remember it?

Chapter Twenty-One

ILLUSION TOWN . . .

The text message came in as Reed Latimer was unpacking a box of untuned crystal flowers that had been delivered that morning. He set a sunset-colored rose on the workbench and reached for his phone. His pulse spiked when he saw the code that identified the sender as the anonymous collector.

Have the arrangements for the consultation been made?

He groaned. Collectors were a notoriously demanding lot. Once they set their minds on acquiring an object—or, in this case, an evaluation—they became obsessive. He tried to think of a graceful way to dodge the question. Finally he settled on:

**Consultant was called out of town on a business
matter. Expected back soon. Will set up a meeting
after she returns.**

He sent the message and held his breath. The reply came back immediately.

> If you can't make the arrangements by the end of the
> week I will explore other options.

He sighed and responded.

> Understood. There won't be any more delays. I will get
> back to you with a firm date before the end of the week.

He dropped the phone into his pocket and glumly contemplated the sunset-colored crystal rose. He would do an excellent job with the tuning, but Molly could have made it sing for the client. Nobody could bring out the positive vibe in crystal and make it resonate with the senses in the unique way that she did. Her talent was extraordinary.

With Molly beside him, he could have taken his business to a whole new level. He would have proved to his family that he had inherited not only his grandfather's talent but the old man's business ability as well. He could have made everyone see that he was the heir best suited to become the president and CEO of the Resonant Crystals empire.

He had known he was taking a risk when he caved to family pressure and registered with the matchmaking agency in Frequency. Molly had made it clear that their relationship would end if, or when, he got serious about arranging a Covenant Marriage. In hindsight, he should have realized there was no way he could have kept his new status a secret. Her mothers were in the private investigation business, after all.

He had done his best to make Molly see that there was no reason they could not continue their relationship on both the business and personal level while he was in the process of finding a suitable spouse. It might take months for the agency to come up with a good match, especially if he stalled, which he planned to do. He was in no rush to get married. But Molly had lost her temper and stormed out of the shop, leaving the week's shipment of crystal flowers untuned.

Not long afterward she had opened Singing Crystals. The next thing he knew, she had landed the most important contract of the year—the art crystal arrangements for the Guild wedding.

It was so fucking unfair. After all he had done for her. He'd taken a chance on her and her talent, taught her the business, and she had repaid him by walking out on him.

Maybe he should have defied his family and married her. It wasn't the first time he'd had that thought. But even as it entered his head, he knew he was deceiving himself.

It wasn't just her status as an orphan that made him uneasy. He could have overlooked that in exchange for the prospect of bringing her amazing talent into the family business. When his relatives realized what she could do with crystals, they would have come around. Probably. In reality, they would have had no choice.

No one bothered to note Marriages of Convenience on the family tree—everyone understood they were nothing more than dressed-up affairs—but a Covenant Marriage was impossible to ignore and hard to terminate.

Divorce was not just expensive; it carried a ruinous social stigma for the families of both individuals. The times and attitudes were changing, but it was a slow process. It didn't matter who you wed, but sooner or later, you were expected to enter a Covenant Marriage. So, yes, if he had committed to a Covenant Marriage with Molly, his family would have been forced to accept an orphan into the clan.

But the truth was, even though he was attracted to her and found her talent as well as her claim to being a free spirit exciting, he had never wanted to marry her. Molly scared the ghost shit out of him on some primal level and he had no idea why.

No, he could never have taken the risk of marrying her.

But he was sure he could convince her to do some freelance consulting for him. It would be easy money for her and it didn't require a personal relationship. The job was just business. A win-win for both of them.

The problem was that Molly had disappeared. It made no sense. She had landed the most important crystal energy circle contract of the season and the wedding was tomorrow. She should have been consumed with a thousand and one last-minute details—checking and rechecking the layout of the venue, communicating with the event planner. There was a lot involved in a big wedding.

Where was Molly?

CHAPTER TWENTY-TWO

Twenty minutes later, showered, shaved, and wearing a clean set of scrubs, Joshua sat down in the dining nook and dug into a bowl of canned fruit and a plate of cheese and crackers. Molly was on the opposite side of the table. Up on the refrigerator, Newton was eagerly making his way through a similar repast, but he had some Zing Chips on the side.

It was all very homey, Joshua thought, except that the Funhouse could never in a million years be called a home. Still, it was unexpectedly comfortable sitting here with Molly. His world had changed overnight, thanks to her. He was no longer a prisoner of the mansion. He had a plan. A mission.

He surveyed the offerings on the table. "Nothing like fresh berries and cream and poached eggs with hollandaise sauce, I always say."

"Only the finest cuisine graces the table here at the Funhouse Hotel," Molly said. "Just so you know, you need to do some grocery shopping."

"With luck I won't be needing more groceries—not for this house, at any rate. Tell me about the message in the mirror."

"There's no doubt that Madame Zandra was delusional in the sense that she misinterpreted what she thought was happening here," Molly said. "She constructed a horror story involving half-dead Aliens to explain what she was seeing."

He thought about that while he ate some cheese. "I get that she tried to weave facts into a tale that fit her delusions. But if she was terrified of this house, why didn't she pack up and leave?"

"Who knows?" Molly drank some coffee and looked at him over the rim. "Why haven't you moved out?"

"I don't have a choice. The answers I need are here."

"Where, exactly?"

"The basement."

"Right," Molly said. "About the basement."

He shook his head. "Did you open that door, too?"

"No. Don't get me wrong. I thought about it, but when I realized that the weird fog was coming up from down there, I decided to wait and discuss the matter with you."

"That was a smart decision. Generally speaking, it's never a good idea to go down into a dark basement."

"But you've been down there," Molly said. "What do you know about that blue fog?"

"Not much. Just that it's heaviest at night and it has grown noticeably stronger in the time I've been here. Now that I've got my talent and my memories back, I intend to find out what is going on."

"Correction. *We* are going to find out."

"I appreciate what you've done for me, but you've gone far enough.

Whatever is down there is dangerous, Molly. I'll take it from here. When I find your sister, you will be the first to know."

Molly's eyes got an ominous glitter. "We will look for my sister together. You owe me that much."

So much for taking charge. He decided to try another approach. "How much time have you spent in the Underworld?"

"Not a lot," she admitted. "But I've gone down with Leona on a few occasions—often enough to know I can handle the energy, if that's what you're worried about."

Something in the restrained tone of her voice pinged his intuition. "Given your talent for crystals, it's interesting that you don't spend more time in the tunnels. I'm surprised you didn't go into the para-archaeology field like your sister."

"Para-archaeology work is interesting," Molly said. "But I'm an artist, not a researcher. My passion is making crystals sing with positive energy, not testing and analyzing artifacts."

She was telling the truth, he decided. But something was off.

"Are you by any chance claustrophobic?" he asked.

She hesitated. "Not any more so than most people."

"It's nothing to be embarrassed about," he said.

"I told you, I can handle the Underworld environment. I can even work gate energy."

"You're a gatekeeper?" he asked, startled.

"Gate energy is basically crystal energy. It always comes down to tuning. So, yes, I can work gates. At least I was able to handle the few I experimented with when I went below with Leona."

"Huh."

"Is that important?"

"Yes," he said. "I'll explain later. But if you can work gate energy, it's even more surprising that you didn't get involved in Underworld exploration or para-archaeology. A good gatekeeper is a valuable asset on any team."

Molly pressed her lips together and then apparently came to a decision. "When I was a little kid, I was kidnapped and held down in the tunnels for a while."

"What?"

"Leona and I were living in an orphanage at the time. One day when we were outside playing on the swings, a deranged man named Willard got through the gate and grabbed me. Leona called Griffin Investigations. Charlotte and Eugenie Griffin rescued me with the help of some dust bunnies. It was a big story in the media for about a week."

"You're serious," he said, more than a little stunned. "No wonder you weren't keen to have a career in the tunnels."

"My point is that I can handle the Underworld and I can work gate energy. That's all that matters."

"You and your sister were orphans?" he asked, trying to feel his way into her secrets.

"Yes. The Griffins adopted us after they rescued me. Look, my past is not important here."

She was right. He needed to keep his focus on his priorities.

"I understand where you're coming from," he said. "You're worried about your sister. I also realize that I am in your debt because of what you did for me last night. I know and respect the fact that your crystal skills are off the charts. But when it comes to the Underworld, I'm the expert, and to put it bluntly, I can't afford to be distracted by worrying about an inexperienced sidekick."

He saw the heat flash in her eyes and knew he had pushed too far.

"Let's get one thing straight, Knight," she said evenly. "I am not a sidekick. I'm an equal partner, and as you just pointed out, you owe me."

She was right. He was trying to find some logic to counteract her argument when he heard the muted crunch of gravel in the drive. Up on the refrigerator, Newton cocked his head, listening.

Distracted, Molly glanced out the window. "Are you expecting someone?"

"No." He got to his feet. "But then, I wasn't expecting anyone yesterday when you showed up. My social life is getting interesting."

Molly slipped out of the booth, alarmed. "I hope it isn't my assistant coming all this way to tell me the Guild wedding job has been canceled."

That stopped him. "What are you talking about?"

"My boutique, Singing Crystals, got the contract for the wedding of the Illusion Town Guild boss and his bride. It's the biggest event of the season. Things got a bit messy the night before last. There was some concern . . . Never mind. Do you recognize your visitor?"

Joshua went to a window, twitched a curtain aside, and watched a familiar figure climb out of a sleek, late-model Slider. "It's my boss, Auburn Cork."

"From Cork and Ferris Outfitters?" Molly joined him at the window. "Maybe he's got some good news about the Hollister Expedition search and rescue operation."

"They called it off, remember?"

"Yes, but maybe new information has come in. It's not like we'd know if that happened. Our phones aren't working out here in the desert."

Joshua let the curtain fall back into place and looked at her. "It occurs to me that you may have spent too much time getting irradiated by positive-energy crystals. Probably a hazard of the art crystal profession. All those weddings and anniversaries and Valentine's Days get to you."

She folded her arms. "Okay, what's your theory? Why did the head of Cork and Ferris drive out here to find you?"

"Best guess is that he's here to tell me he's going to fire me."

She dropped her arms, shocked. "Joshua—"

"Wait here. I don't think this will take long." He headed for the kitchen door. When he went past the refrigerator, Newton chortled and hopped down onto his shoulder.

"Sorry about that," Molly said. "Here, I'll take him."

"Forget it," he said. "Newton is fine. I might need backup."

At the front door he paused to check the peephole to confirm the identity of his visitor. Auburn Cork should have looked out of place dressed in an expensive hand-tailored suit, a discreetly striped tie, and polished shoes. This wasn't corporate headquarters in downtown Resonance City. This was the middle of nowhere.

But Cork was the owner and CEO of one of the Federation of City-States' most successful and most respected Underworld outfitters. He dressed for the role. He and Bruce Ferris had founded the firm ten years earlier. It had been a successful business partnership. Each had brought something important to the table. Ferris, an older man with a lifetime of experience in the tunnels, had a reputation that commanded respect in the outfitters' world. Cork was the financial expert who knew how to run a corporation. Together the two had built a major brand.

Two months ago, Bruce Ferris had died doing what he loved—exploring an uncharted sector of the Underworld. Auburn Cork was now in charge of the company.

In spite of what he was sure was coming, Joshua was glad he had taken the time to shower and shave earlier. A man wanted to look his best when he got fired. Or, in this case, almost his best. It was just too bad about the scrubs.

He opened the door.

"Good morning, Josh." Auburn eyed the scrubs and came up with a bleak smile. "You're a hard man to find."

"I wasn't looking to be found."

"I understand."

"How *did* you find me?"

"Long story. I'm sorry to intrude on your privacy, but I need to have a word with you. Under the circumstances I thought it only right to do it in person."

"I appreciate that." Joshua stepped back. "Come in."

"Thanks."

Auburn moved over the threshold. Newton rumbled.

"When did you get a dust bunny?" Auburn asked, amused.

Joshua closed the door. "I've got a guest. She and Newton arrived together."

"I saw the other car in the drive," Auburn said. He reached out to pat Newton on the head.

Newton growled.

Auburn hastily withdrew his hand. "I'm getting the impression that he doesn't like me."

"He's that way around strangers," Molly lied from the other end of the hallway. She hurried forward, scooped Newton off Joshua's shoulder, and tucked him under her arm. "He won't bite."

She was trying for a reassuring vibe, but Joshua almost smiled at the underlying anxiety in her voice. She knew full well that Newton certainly would bite if he was in the mood.

"Good to know," Auburn said. He studied Molly with a politely inquiring expression.

"Molly, this is Auburn Cork," Joshua said. "Auburn, Molly Griffin."

"We just finished breakfast," Molly said. "Can I offer you a cup of coffee, Mr. Cork?"

"Sounds great," Auburn said. "And please call me Auburn."

"How did you get here so early?" Joshua asked.

"I made it as far as Outpost late last night," Cork said. "Couldn't drive any farther. The fog is something else around here, isn't it? I spent the night at a motel and drove the rest of the way as soon as the road was clear."

"I'll show you into the living room." Molly turned to lead the way.

Auburn started to follow, but he hesitated, glancing uneasily into the mirrors on the walls. "Seems to be a lot of energy in this house."

"I'm told it sits on top of an uncharted hot zone," Joshua said. "Over the years the house has absorbed the vibe."

Auburn frowned. "The mirrors sure as hell don't help. Don't you find living here uncomfortable?"

"I haven't noticed the energy," Joshua said. "I was burned, remember? Psi-blind."

Auburn's jaw tightened. "Yeah, that's one of the reasons I'm here today."

"I know," Joshua said.

Molly stopped at the entrance to the living room. "Have a seat. I'll get the coffee."

Joshua followed Auburn into the living room and sat down on the sofa. Auburn took one of the large chairs on the other side of the coffee table. He glanced back toward the doorway, evidently making certain that Molly was out of earshot, and lowered his voice.

"Good to see you're not alone," he said. "There's been a lot of speculation about your state of mind. I admit I was afraid you might have succumbed to depression and taken a long walk in the tunnels without amber. Obviously you took steps to avoid that. Nothing like a little feminine companionship to lift a man's spirits. Good job."

Joshua said nothing.

"Known Molly long?"

"No," Joshua said. He did not offer any more information.

"I take it she doesn't mind the energy in the house."

"She can handle it," Joshua said.

"Evidently." Auburn cleared his throat. "Is that because she can't sense it, either?"

"I'm aware of the energy," Molly said from the doorway. She came forward carrying a tray with two mugs on it. "But I'm a crystal artist. My talent gives me some natural ability to suppress the energy in the mirrors."

Auburn nodded, satisfied with Molly's explanation. "That's fortunate for you. Will you be staying here with Josh for a while?"

"Nope." Molly set the tray on the table. "I have a crystal arrangements shop in Illusion Town. This is the wedding season. We do a lot of business at this time of year, so I can't afford to stay away for long."

Auburn picked up one of the mugs and chuckled. "I never thought of the art crystal business as dangerous until I saw the news about a dead body showing up in a boutique in Illusion Town. Apparently they're calling it a murder."

Molly stilled for an instant. She recovered immediately. "It was a shock to the entire art crystal community," she said smoothly.

Joshua didn't need his intuition to pick up on the new whisper of tension in the atmosphere. It was coming from Molly, not the mirrors. He remembered what she had said a few minutes ago. *My boutique, Singing Crystals, got the contract for the wedding of the Illusion Town Guild boss and his bride. It's the biggest event of the season. Things got a bit messy the night before last.*

"What's this about a murder in a crystal shop?" he asked.

Auburn shrugged. "The incident is a very big deal in Illusion Town because the crystal shop that was the scene of the crime is the one that has the crystal arranging contract for the wedding of the new Guild boss."

"What happened?" Joshua said. He kept his attention on Auburn, but out of the corner of his eye he could see that Molly was doing her best to appear politely unconcerned.

"All I know is what I saw in the Resonance City media," Auburn said, sipping his coffee. "The story got a lot of play in all the city-states because the new Guild boss in Illusion Town, Gabriel Jones, and his fiancée made headlines a few months ago. They got involved in an investigation that unfolded in the Underworld."

"I remember something about it," Joshua said.

"You'll be hearing more." Auburn snorted. "They've made a movie out of the story. It's due to be released soon."

"What about the murder?" Joshua said.

"Evidently the crystal shop was broken into the night before last,"

Auburn explained. "The thief was shot dead at the scene. The assumption is that he had a partner who turned on him."

"Were the wedding crystals stolen?" Joshua asked.

"No," Molly said. "They were safe."

"Then why did the break-in create headlines?" Joshua said.

Auburn looked amused. "Obviously you have never been involved in a Covenant Marriage. The crystal arrangements, especially the energy circle in which the bride and groom stand, are a very important part of the ceremony. There are a lot of traditions and superstitions connected to them. People like to say, *Negative energy crystals at the wedding mean bad energy in the marriage.*"

Molly coughed. "It's amazing that even in the modern era some people are still superstitious about that sort of thing. Every good crystal artist knows it's the two people getting married who bring the most important energy to the ceremony. All a professional crystal arranger can do is try to enhance the positive currents and dampen the negative vibes."

"Unfortunately," Auburn added, "there is an old-fashioned theory that crystals can be contaminated with the energy of a death that takes place in close proximity to them."

"Nonsense," Molly said. "I'm a professional. I assure you that is impossible."

Auburn fixed her with an intent look. "You said you're a crystal artist?"

"Yes," she answered.

"You seem to know a lot about the Illusion Town case."

She gave him her mag-rez steel smile. "The incident occurred in my boutique, Singing Crystals."

"I see," Auburn said. He winced. "I'm sorry to hear that."

"If you'll excuse me, I'll leave you two alone to discuss your business."

Joshua watched her go toward the door. She wasn't exactly fleeing the scene, but she was moving at a very brisk clip.

Before he could consider the implications, Auburn frowned.

"What is going on here, Josh?"

"It's personal," Joshua said.

"I see." Auburn's expression tightened. "Might as well move on, then. I have to ask you if there is any indication your senses are healing?"

"No."

Auburn sighed and put his mug back on the tray. "I'm sorry."

"So am I."

"The fallout from the Hollister Expedition disaster has taken a toll on Cork and Ferris," Auburn said. "There are rumors circulating in the industry."

"What kind of rumors?"

Auburn grimaced. "I think you know what I'm trying to say."

"No, I don't."

"There's talk that you've lost your nerve and your edge. That kind of chatter is leading to gossip about Cork and Ferris's overall reliability. I'm sure you realize that I have to think of the firm's reputation."

"Protect the brand."

"Right. I'm going to have to let you go."

Joshua nodded and picked up his coffee.

"I held off as long as I dared, hoping you would recover, but I don't think we should drag things out indefinitely," Auburn said. "I sincerely regret this, but rest assured you will get a severance check for two months' pay."

"I appreciate that."

Auburn set down his unfinished coffee and got to his feet. "That's it, then. I won't take up any more of your time."

Joshua stood. "Thanks for doing this face-to-face."

"I owed you that much. You've been a valuable member of my organization. Take care of yourself, Josh. Get in touch if your senses heal."

"I'll do that," Joshua said.

But they both knew he would not put either of them in that position.

Reputations in the exploration business were fragile things. No one wanted to work with a navigator who had lost his nerve and his edge, to say nothing of an entire expedition team.

He walked Auburn along the hall to the front door. Auburn paused on the threshold and looked back into the shadows of the mansion.

"Gotta tell you, I don't know how you can sleep in this house," he said.

"You'd be amazed at how peaceful the world becomes when you've been psi-burned. By the way, you never told me how you located me out here in the desert."

"Oh, right. I got concerned after you walked out of the hospital and disappeared. I felt a responsibility to find you, so I told our in-house security people to look for you. They were able to track you to Outpost."

"I was just curious."

Auburn started to turn away, but he paused. "Mind if I ask how Ms. Griffin located you?"

"Same way you did. Got some help from a private investigation firm."

Auburn looked thoughtful. "She's related to one of the members of the Hollister Expedition team, isn't she? The name can't be a coincidence."

"Molly's sister was on the team."

"It strikes me as odd that Molly Griffin went to the trouble and expense of hiring a PI to find you." Auburn's face tightened in apparent concern. "Is she harassing you because of what happened to the expedition? Has she threatened you in any way? Do you think she's dangerous?"

"Molly and I have an understanding," Joshua said. "Don't worry about me."

Auburn looked doubtful, but he clapped Joshua's shoulder once and, without another word, strode quickly across the fireglass portico. He got into the Slider and drove back down the road.

Joshua heard a cheery chortle and looked down to see Newton at his feet. The dust bunny was no longer growling. He appeared delighted to see their visitor depart.

"I got the feeling Cork was happy to leave, too," Joshua said. He leaned down, picked up Newton, and plopped him on one shoulder. "Now it's time to clarify a few details with your pal."

Molly was in the kitchen stacking dishes in the dishwasher. She looked decidedly pissed. "That dumbass fired you, didn't he?"

"I told you that's why he was here. Forget Cork. So you're the crystal artist whose shop was the scene of a murder night before last."

Molly sighed and closed the door of the dishwasher. "Yep."

"Why didn't you tell me?"

She rezzed the start button and turned to look at him. "There are a lot of reasons why I haven't mentioned it. Among other things, we haven't had much time for casual conversation. Also, there was no point bringing up the subject, because it has nothing to do with finding my sister and the others."

"I'm not buying either of those excuses. Keep talking."

"Fine." She widened her hands. "I was afraid you wouldn't let me through the front door if you knew about the murder in my shop. You were skittish enough as it was. I worried that you wouldn't even give me a chance to do some dream-walking work with you if you had any reason to think my crystals were tainted with bad energy."

"Skittish?" he repeated, focusing on the one word that made him ignore all the others. *"Skittish?"*

Molly folded her arms. "I didn't want to say nervous or anxious, but—"

"Stop right there," he said evenly. "For the record, I was not skittish."

"I know that now, but I didn't yesterday."

"I wanted you out of the house and as far away from here as possible before the fog closed in. *For your own good.* I figured you couldn't handle a night in this place."

Molly elevated her chin. "You were wrong about me, and I was wrong to assume that you might be skittish. That makes us even."

"No, it does not."

"Close enough. I vote we change the subject. Tell me why you lied to your boss. You let him think that your senses are still fried. Maybe you could have had your old job back if you had told him the truth."

"I don't think so."

Molly got a knowing look. "Yesterday you said you didn't trust anyone connected to the Hollister Expedition disaster. Does that include Auburn Cork?"

"Yes," he said quietly. "It does."

CHAPTER TWENTY-THREE

Joshua was serious. Molly took a breath and exhaled slowly. "I see. I hadn't considered that possibility. Do you have any evidence?"

"No. I'm pretty sure the kidnapping was an inside job. I just don't know how far inside."

Molly gave that some thought. "I can't see a man in Cork's position risking his firm's rock-solid reputation, let alone prison, for the sake of some illegal excavation work."

"Depends on what's being excavated."

He was right. She drew a tight breath. "Yes, it does."

"Tell me about the dead body in your shop."

"I don't know much more than what Cork told you. My apartment is over my business. I had a callout that night, so I was away when the thief broke in."

"A callout?"

"I do some volunteer work at a local youth shelter. I try to help street kids deal with their dream issues. I'm sure you remember what it was like when your psychic senses were starting to kick in. The dreams—"

"Were bad," he finished.

"And scary. When my client was finally sleeping calmly, I walked home. Newton was with me. That was about two a.m. We found the body when I unlocked the door of the shop."

"You walked home alone at two in the morning?"

It dawned on her that Joshua looked appalled.

She frowned. "I live in the Dark Zone in Illusion Town. It's a safe neighborhood. The youth shelter is only a couple of blocks away from my shop." She paused and then added, "The Griffin women can take care of themselves."

"How?"

"The moms gave Leona and me flamers when we moved into our own apartments."

"Because the neighborhood is so safe," he said.

She glared. "The moms are inclined to be a little overprotective."

He shook his head. "You had a flamer and a dust bunny for protection."

"Right." It was time to move the conversation along. "I opened the door of Singing Crystals, found the body, and called the police. That's it. That's all I know. The moms were worried for a while that I might be considered a suspect, but the cameras at the shelter and the one at the alley door entrance made it clear that I wasn't at home when the thief broke in. When the news got out, the event planner tried to cancel my contract, but the bride refused to let him."

"You said the wedding crystals were safe. Was anything taken?"

"No," Molly said. "As Cork told you, the police concluded the thief had a companion who turned on him."

Joshua pondered that briefly. "You're sure the thieves weren't after the wedding crystals?"

"They are the most valuable objects in my shop at the moment, but it makes no sense to steal them."

"Why not?"

"Because they are unique. I created them for the two individuals who are getting married, Gabriel Jones and Lucy Bell. I locked in the tuning. They are beautiful, of course, and the overall energy they radiate will feel good to those who get near them, but it will be a generic experience for anyone except the bride and groom. My signature tuning ensures those crystals will only truly resonate with those two people."

"The thieves might not have known that," he said.

"I suppose that's true. I just hope that after the wedding all everyone will remember is that my boutique did the crystal arrangements, including the energy circle, for the biggest event of the year in Illusion Town."

"Trust me, I understand what it's like to be stuck with a shredded reputation. I was registered with a matchmaking agency before my life went to green hell. They dropped me as soon as the news broke. Blamed it on my time in the para-psych hospital."

"I know." She braced herself. "You're okay working with me now that you know about the murder in my shop?"

"I've got no problem working with the dream therapist who healed my fried senses."

She gave him a wry smile. "Besides, you don't actually have much choice, do you?"

"Nope." He turned and headed for the door. "Let's go upstairs. I want to hear the medium's message."

CHAPTER TWENTY-FOUR

"You must find a way to lock the crypt. If the Sleepers escape this house, they will unleash the great power of their weapons upon we who have made Harmony our home. They will destroy the civilization we have created on this world."

The video in the mirror faded. The whirling ball took its place. Molly let the curtain fall across the crystal face of the looking glass and turned to Joshua.

"What do you think about her interpretation of the energy she sensed?"

"Madame Zandra obviously had some serious talent." Joshua turned away from the mirror. "Something is definitely raising the energy level in this house, but we're not dealing with half-dead, sleepwalking Aliens."

"I agree," Molly said. "I suppose it's a problem for the experts. We've got other issues. Do you think you've recovered enough to find your way back to the site of the Hollister Expedition disaster?"

Satisfaction heated Joshua's eyes. "Yes." He went toward the door. "Time to pack some gear."

She followed him out into the hall. "Do you have the things we need to go down into the Underworld?"

"Yes, thanks to the Outpost General Store." Joshua started down the stairs. "Early on I picked up what I knew I'd require if I was able to find my way back to the scene of the ambush."

"What about me? I've got my flamer but that's all."

"I'm a navigator," Joshua said. "I always go down with plenty of spares and backup. You can use some of it." He stopped on the second-floor landing. "Let's get your suitcase and that satchel you brought. We'll stow them in your car."

"Why? I told you I'm coming with you."

"We can't risk returning through the dark tunnel. We don't know what condition the Hollister people will be in, and even if they can handle the energy in that tunnel, surfacing here is the long way home. We'll use one of the mining camp entrances that is closer to Illusion Town. The camp will be able to supply the transportation we'll need to get everyone back to the city."

"Got it. So we're going to use the self-drive feature on our cars to send them back to Illusion Town."

"Right."

"Okay, makes sense, but just so you know, self-drive and the map programs don't work well in the Dark Zone, where I live. Too much energy. There's a big shopping mall on the border of the zone that we can put in for the destination address. The cars can park there until we arrange to pick them up."

Chapter Twenty-Five

Geared up with a lot of nav amber and a day pack stuffed with nutrition bars, bottled water, and her small flamer, Molly followed Joshua down the basement steps. Newton rode on Joshua's shoulder.

Wisps of blue fog glowed in the shadows. She could sense the paranormal heat, but it was nothing like the heavy mist that had swamped the first floor of the mansion during the night.

Newton chortled and waved his mirror, excited about the prospect of a new adventure.

Molly looked around. "I thought there would be more fog down here."

"Like I said, it isn't bad during the daytime," Joshua said. "At least, not yet."

"The Sleepers are probably afraid to come out during the daylight hours."

"There are no Aliens involved in this, Molly."

"I know. I was joking. Sorry."

"I've been living with night fog for a while now. I've lost my sense of humor when it comes to the Funhouse."

"Understandable."

Joshua led the way across the basement and stopped in front of an old mag-steel vault door. He had a length of drapery cord cut from a window curtain in one hand. He stopped at the door and looped one end of the cord around his waist. He gave her the other end. She secured it to her waist.

When they were finished linking themselves together, Joshua rezzed the lock, but he did not pull the door open.

"How did you figure out the code?" she asked.

"My navigation talent makes me very good at picking locks," he said. "All I have to do is identify the key currents and pay attention. It's an updated version of using a stethoscope to listen to the tumblers in the lock on an old-fashioned safe."

"Do the people who make locks know about that kind of ability?"

"Sure. Most professional locksmiths have it. So do a lot of burglars. But not many are as strong as I am."

"So you could have been a successful burglar?"

"Back when I had to make a career choice, I thought it would be more fun to go down into the Underworld," Joshua said. "In hindsight, that may have been a poor decision."

"I doubt it. I've only met one burglar, and he was dead."

"Fair point. All right. Amber check. It won't do you any good while we're in the dark tunnel, but you'll need it on the other side."

"Right." She ran some psi through her amber and got the clear response that told her the navigation stones were working. "All set."

"I'm good, too," Joshua said.

He hauled the massive door open. She thought she was ready for what awaited on the other side, but nothing could have prepared her for the wall of night that seethed in the opening. She knew she was not overreacting when she realized that Newton's second set of eyes had snapped open. There was no gleeful chortle. Like Joshua and herself, Newton was all business.

"That is . . . amazing," she said. "I've never seen anything like it."

"Take my hand and whatever you do, don't let go. We're going to need all the power we can get."

"Don't worry, I won't let go."

"With the physical connection you should be able to pick up some of what I'm sensing."

"Got it."

She reached for his hand. His strong fingers closed tightly around hers. The little thrill that accompanied the physical contact was familiar now, and reassuring. It felt right.

Joshua, with Newton crouched on his shoulder, moved over the threshold. She followed them into the currents of endless night.

CHAPTER TWENTY-SIX

The intense darkness was every bit as bad as it was in his nightmares. The stuff closed around the three of them, blinding, deafening, disorienting. Joshua could no longer see Molly, but he could feel her hand clenched in his and he was aware of the power of her aura. He could also feel Newton's hind paws clutching his shoulder. The dust bunny's second set of eyes glowed in the depths of the swirling currents of night.

"This is incredible," Molly whispered. "You're right, my amber isn't responding. How in the world can you navigate this stuff?"

"With an old cave-diving strategy."

"I don't do stuff like dive in flooded caves. Sounds like a nightmare."

"I thought you said you weren't claustrophobic."

"Got news for you, Knight. A lot of people would suddenly discover that they were claustrophobic if you took them into this tunnel."

He focused on the drowning-victim-clutching-a-life-raft grip she had on his hand. "Are you going to panic?"

"No."

"Are you sure?"

"Shut up and navigate."

"Right. Like I said, we're going to do what you do when you are in an underwater cave and your flashlight goes out. You stay very still until you find a steady current."

"There's a steady current in here?" she asked.

He heard the anxiety shivering just beneath the surface of her words.

"There is always a current," he said with more confidence than he felt.

"And you can sense it without amber?"

"Yes," he said. "Now please be quiet and let me focus."

She fell silent.

He rezzed his senses to the max, feeling his way into the storm of darkness.

And there it was, the thin but steady current that he had followed through the tunnel of night to the basement door of the mansion. Relief, followed by the rush of knowing that his talent truly was back to normal, sent another spike of adrenaline through him.

"Here we go," he said.

He started forward, moving carefully, one hand extended in front of his face. He did not remember colliding with any obstacles on his first trip through the tunnel, but that might have been sheer luck.

Molly stayed close. She was unnerved but in control. He sensed that her determination to complete the mission was mag-steel solid. Newton muttered from time to time but there was no question about his loyalty.

The three of them were in this together, Joshua thought. He had told himself he would never again take the risk of trusting anyone down in the Underworld, but here he was, walking through a dead zone with a not-exactly-claustrophobic crystal artist and a dust bunny addicted to Zing Chips. Life had a way of surprising you.

Time worked differently in total darkness. The trek seemed endless. He was starting to question his memories when he became aware that the flow of the current he was following was turning into the equivalent of an eddy in a river. He knew what that meant. He was picking up hole-in-the-wall energy.

He stopped. "We're here."

"Can I talk now?" Molly asked.

"What? Oh, right. Sorry. Yes, you can talk."

"Are you sure it's the right exit?"

"Good question. The answer is, probably."

"That's the best you can do? Probably?"

"It's been a bad month, Molly."

"I know. So, we're looking for an old wooden door?"

"No, we're looking for an old steel vault door. I remember it now. For some reason it showed up in my dreams as wooden."

He eased closer to the heart of the eddying currents, drawing Molly with him. His questing fingers found metal. "Got it. I should be able to work the lock."

It was a good lock, but it was human engineering and it was old. It dated from the same era as the Funhouse. It took him about twenty seconds to rez it. He left the door closed for a moment, remembering what lay on the other side.

"Ready?" he said.

"Maybe the chamber on the other side won't be as hot as it was in your dreamscape," Molly said. "Like the wooden door, the bright blast of energy we saw might have been symbolic."

"No, it's going to be real," he said.

He tugged on the big handle. Despite its age, the heavy door swung open on near-silent hinges. There was no rust in the Underworld.

The senses-dazzling light on the other side exploded in the opening.

The blast was all the more disorienting because they had spent the past several minutes in cave-like darkness.

"Should have brought sunglasses," Joshua said. But there was no way of knowing if shades would have worked. Some of the energy flaring inside the chamber was coming from the visible end of the spectrum, but a lot of it was from the paranormal end.

Newton's second set of eyes snapped shut. He rumbled.

Molly drew a sharp, shocked breath. The energy in the atmosphere lifted her hair. Newton muttered. His fur was standing on end.

"What *is* this place?"

"I don't know, but it feels hotter than I remember it. More unstable."

"Definitely unstable."

"How are you doing?"

"Stop worrying about me. I'm okay. As far as I can tell, it's crystal heat. Very powerful crystal heat, but still, the kind I can handle. I can't imagine what it must have been like for you, though. Talk about a shock to the senses. No wonder you got burned. How did you ever manage to locate the vault door into the dark tunnel?"

"I was going psi-blind, but I picked up a trickle of current that indicated an energy leak around the door. By the time I got the door open and made it through the dark tunnel to the Funhouse, though, I was not in good shape."

She squeezed his hand. "It's amazing you survived."

The full reality of what had happened during the night hit him with the same intensity as the white-hot energy they were confronting. She had put his world back together.

"I'd still be wandering around the Funhouse, trying not to get lost in the mirrors, if it weren't for you," he said.

"We're a team, remember? And we're still on a mission."

"Yes."

"You're in charge down here. What's next?"

He focused on the reason they were standing here in front of a para-normal furnace. "I remember stumbling into this chamber when I woke up after the ambush. I came through an open energy gate. It slammed shut behind me."

"Gates are very unpredictable. How did you get it open in the first place?"

He shook his head. "It was open when I found it. I knew I was being chased. Figured whoever was after me would not be able to follow me inside. Didn't expect the gate to close. When it did, I had to find another way out. I can't work gate energy."

"Fortunately you found the vault door."

"Yes, but now we need to locate the gate inside this chamber and open it. What we're looking for is on the other side."

CHAPTER TWENTY-SEVEN

She kept her grip on Joshua's hand as she moved into the chamber. The energy levels inside were far higher and more dazzling than anything she had ever experienced—but it was not unfamiliar energy. Crystal heat was crystal heat.

She drew on Joshua's and Newton's auras for the strength she needed to focus and suppress the violent impact of the blazing chamber. She knew Joshua was using Newton and her to do the same. There was no way to know how Newton was handling the paranormal radiation, but he appeared calm.

When she got things under control, she realized they were standing inside a circular, auditorium-sized space lined with . . .

"Mirrors," Joshua said. "I swear, when this is over, I'm never going to look in another mirror as long as I live."

"Well, we knew there had to be some connection between the mansion and this place," Molly said. "Apparently the link is mirrors."

"There's the pyramid that we saw in my dreamscape." Joshua indicated the neatly arranged stack of hexagonal rods in the center of the space.

The pyramid wasn't huge—Molly estimated that at its peak it was about ten or twelve feet tall—but it was infused with energy. A *lot* of energy.

Maintaining a tight grip on Joshua's hand, she began a circuit of the chamber. Newton vaulted onto her shoulder and hunkered down.

"The energy in these mirrors is tuned," she said. "But not by humans. This place has probably been running for the past few thousand years, ever since the Aliens vanished."

"It must be a machine of some kind," Joshua said.

Molly paused and carefully kicked up her senses. A faint, erratic current pulsed somewhere deep in the storm of energy. "Whatever it is, it's unstable. The bad vibe is coming from the pyramid."

"That adds up to a very good reason for not hanging around," Joshua said. "We need to get out of here. All I can see are mirrors. How will you identify the gate?"

"One of these mirrors will be different," she said.

I hope.

"Let's find it," Joshua said.

Halfway around the vast chamber, she sensed the difference she was searching for. Relief surged through her.

"Got it," she said. "Now to open it."

The gate was powered by a seemingly chaotic whirlwind of crystal energy, but there was no true chaos in the Underworld—just patterns that had to be deconstructed. The trick was to find the eye of the storm.

"I'm in," she said softly.

For the first time since they had embarked on the quest, Newton chortled.

The gate dissolved, revealing a vast, hexagonal chamber of green quartz. The stone glowed with the familiar acid-green energy that characterized most of the ruins the Aliens had left behind. Molly saw several corridors and hallways branching off from all six sides of the space.

"Nice work," Joshua said.

Molly was surprised by the little flush of warmth his words gave her. "Thanks."

With a pleased chortle, Newton vaulted down from her shoulder and set about exploring the chamber.

Joshua released Molly's hand, took his flamer out of the holster, and moved a few steps into the hexagon. She unzipped her day pack and gripped her small weapon.

"You can close the gate," Joshua said.

"Okay."

She released her focus. Energy shivered in the opening between the green quartz chamber and the mirrored room. The gate became translucent and then opaque and then, finally, a solid green quartz wall. There was no visible trace of its existence, but she could still sense the unique energy that identified it.

Joshua untied the drapery cord he had used to link them together. "You know, there aren't a lot of gatekeepers who can do what you just did. You could name your price on any corporate exploration venture."

"No thanks. Gate energy is an interesting challenge, but you can't make a gate sing. All you can do is open and close it. I'll stick with my artwork."

"I get it," Joshua said. He dropped the cord into his pack and turned his attention back to the green chamber. "I remember this space. The expedition team was moving down one of the tunnels that terminate here when we were ambushed. I remember seeing the open gate of the mirror chamber on the far side and wondering if the energy was going to be a problem. That was when I sensed the ghost energy. Not sure what happened after, but the next thing I knew, I was inside the mirror chamber and the gate had closed."

She looked around at the vast expanse of green quartz. "There must be a dozen exit points."

"The one we want is over there," Joshua said, sounding very sure of himself.

He started walking across the chamber, heading for the arched entrance of a corridor that, as far as Molly could tell, looked like all the others. She glanced around and realized she couldn't see Newton. For the first time since she had found him waiting for her on the night of the murder, it occurred to her that he might disappear from her life just as casually as he had appeared in it. She recognized the pattern. It was the same one she followed with the men she occasionally allowed to get close.

The same pattern she and Joshua would no doubt follow.

Well, shit. She did not need to be thinking depressing thoughts right now. There would be plenty of time to get depressed later.

"Newton," she called. "We're leaving."

He appeared from one of the many corridors, chortled, and fluttered forward to join her. She was so relieved to see him she scooped him up, kissed his furry head, and set him down on the floor again.

They both followed Joshua into the hallway he had selected.

"How can you tell which hallway is the right one?" she asked.

"I'm a pretty good navigator, Molly. Once I've been somewhere, I can always find my way back."

She smiled. "Amazing."

He stopped and studied the seemingly endless corridor and the dizzying array of open doorways that lined it. "This is where the team disappeared."

Molly got another little rush of hope. "Can you follow the trail?"

"Yes," he said. "They didn't go far." He stopped in front of an arched doorway. "They entered this chamber."

Molly moved to stand beside him and found herself looking into a long, narrow room. Two rows of green quartz pedestals rose from the floor, forming an aisle that extended the length of the space. The scene reminded her of an art gallery, but instead of displaying a sculpture, each pedestal was topped with a round, faceted crystal that measured about a foot in diameter. The stones were colorless and transparent. She sensed energy trapped inside each crystal.

Newton chortled and dashed across the floor. He came to a stop at the far end of the room, picked up a small object, and raced back to the doorway. He offered his find to Molly. A thrill of recognition hit her. She stared at the familiar yellow crystal that dangled from a delicate gold chain.

"Joshua, this belongs to Leona." She closed her fingers around the stone. "I'd know it anywhere."

"It looks like the one you wear."

"Yes. Both came from the chamber where I was held by the kidnapper. When I got older and came into my talent, I tuned each crystal with our personal signatures. Knowing Leona, I'll bet she dropped the necklace here. She hoped that whoever came looking for the team would find it. Don't you see? It's almost as good as a locator."

"We're going to need more than that," Joshua said. "The kidnappers took the team into this room, but the trail ends at that wall where Newton found the crystal."

"There must be another gate back there." Molly walked down the aisle formed by the pedestals, her senses open. The energy in the atmosphere covered the heat she was searching for until she was close to the wall. A familiar frisson alerted her. "Got it."

"Don't open it until I tell you, and be prepared to close it immediately if we don't like what's on the other side," Joshua ordered quietly.

"Understood."

"Use one of the pedestals as a shield," Joshua said. "Quartz will stop a flamer."

She did as instructed. Sensing that they were now on a combat footing, Newton set his little mirror on the stone floor, sleeked out, and crouched beside Molly's foot. He was ready for action. Joshua took up a position behind the opposite pedestal. He aimed the flamer at the blank quartz wall.

"Go," he instructed.

Molly pulled on her talent, searching for the currents that controlled the gate. The storm appeared quickly, a whirlwind of powerful energy in the center of the quartz wall. She sent a delicate pulse of energy into it, searching for the eye and the tuned anchor that had to be there. She found it and gently de-rezzed it.

A section of solid green quartz shimmered and swiftly grew transparent. The gate opened, revealing a radiant sapphire-blue crystal chamber. A wispy blue fog swirled in the space.

Objects loomed in the mist. At first glance they looked like abstract sculptures fashioned of blue crystal. They were about six feet tall and carved in graceful shapes that resembled the ethereal spires and towers of the ruins in the Dead Cities. Energy was infused into them but, as with the faceted crystals in the adjoining room, the power was locked inside. Contained. At least for now.

"Welcome to an uncharted sector of the Glass House Antiquity," Joshua said.

CHAPTER TWENTY-EIGHT

"A crystal sculpture garden," Molly whispered. "It's absolutely breathtaking."

"We're only just starting to explore Glass House, but from what little I've seen, it's all amazing," Joshua said. "The fog in that chamber is not heavy or unstable like the stuff that fills the Funhouse at night. I'm not seeing any visions. You?"

"No. Newton doesn't seem to be worried about it, either. He looks pretty casual now."

Joshua indicated a tunnel sled parked near the gate. "That's the sled the expedition used. We are definitely in the right place. Are you getting anything from your sister's crystal?"

Molly became aware of a trickle of energy in the stone. A frisson of certainty flashed through her. "Yes. Leona is somewhere nearby. She's alive, Joshua. I'm certain of it."

Newton chortled and fluffed up a bit. All four eyes were still open, but he was no longer in combat mode. Inspired, Molly crouched and showed him the crystal.

"Help us find Leona, Newton." She draped the necklace around his throat. It disappeared into his scruffy fur. "Please."

Newton bounced, ready to play the hide-and-seek game. He gave her his little mirror and scampered forward into the fog-drenched sculpture garden. Molly looked at Joshua.

"I think he understands," she said.

"Great idea," he said, moving out from the cover of the quartz pedestal. "Newton is the most qualified to walk point down here. Can you anchor the gate in the open position?"

"No. Pretty sure it will close if I don't hold the focus."

"I was afraid of that. You had better stay here."

"Why?"

"When I return with your sister and the others, we may be moving very fast, in which case there won't be time to wait for you to open the gate."

She wanted to argue, but Leona had told her countless times that in the Underworld, experience counted more than any other attribute. Joshua was the one with the skill set needed for a rescue operation.

"All right," she said. "Please be careful."

He inclined his head in acknowledgment of the inherently contradictory request. "Keep your flamer ready."

"I will," she promised.

Somewhere in the mist-shrouded sculpture garden Newton chortled again. This time the encouraging sound was muffled. Joshua plunged into the light blue fog to join him.

A moment later they were both gone.

An acute and eerie silence fell. Molly became intensely aware of the fact that she was deep in the Underworld and she was alone. The old nightmares from the day she was kidnapped stirred.

The fog in the crystal garden shifted. A new sculpture appeared. It had been there all along, she told herself. She hadn't noticed it because it had been veiled in the mist.

The tendrils drifted again, revealing another crystal object even as it concealed one.

The creepy mist created optical illusions, making the sculptures appear to be moving. *Just a trick of the light,* she thought.

She was not trapped, not the way she had been when she was six and a half years old. Except that she *was* trapped. She could not leave her post. She had a mission. She had to keep the gate open for Leona and Joshua and the others.

The fog twisted again, unveiling another sculpture. She flinched. The carved stones were *not* stalking her. She had to get control of her imagination.

She was doing okay, holding the focus. Then the pirates showed up.

CHAPTER TWENTY-NINE

"You are one hell of a tracker, Newton," Joshua whispered. He glanced down at the sleeked-out, four-eyed dust bunny at his feet. "Nice work."

Newton flicked his ears a couple of times, indicating that he knew he had been addressed, but he did not take his attention off the scene in front of them. He was hunting now. On a mission. *Like Molly and me,* Joshua thought.

He and Newton needed a strategy. They had found the Hollister Expedition team, but it was clear they would probably get only one chance at an extraction. Surprise was the sole thing they had in their favor.

The trail through the fog-bound crystal garden had ended in a jumble of large, faceted blue crystal boulders. He and Newton, concealed behind the boulders and draped in fog, peered through the small openings between the stones. In front of them was a large circular clearing. A ring of multicolored crystal pillars, each about fifteen feet tall, framed the space. There was no fog drifting inside the circle.

In the center of the circle was a pyramid-shaped building constructed of icy blue crystal blocks. The structure might have been intended as a place of worship, a vacation cottage, or anything in between. There was no way to know. When it came to guessing the purposes of various examples of Alien architecture, the debates among para-archaeologists were never-ending.

There was an entrance but it was draped in a curtain of shimmering, shifting, transparent energy. People moved around inside the structure. Three of them, by his count. He recognized Leona and the other two academics of the Hollister Expedition—Grant and Drayton.

He switched his attention to the two men lounging in camp chairs outside the entrance. They were dressed in khaki and leather, their hair tied back with strips of leather. Flamers were stuck in their gear belts. Typical ex-Guild men. He recognized one of them—Harkins—as a member of the security team assigned to the Hollister Expedition.

Bedrolls, a box of ready-to-eat field rations, and a case of bottled water were stacked haphazardly next to a tent. There were also several six-packs of Amber Haze beer. Empty cans, discarded instant-meal packages, and other assorted trash littered the area. Empty crates and packing materials stood waiting to be filled. There were also two portable out-houses, the sort used on construction sites.

It was a classic pirate operation.

Newton watched the scene with keen attention. He seemed to be aware that the action would start soon. *He's picking up my vibe,* Joshua thought. There was no way to know how much Newton comprehended, but he was a natural-born predator. He had a hunter's instincts. One could only hope that when the time came, he would be able to distinguish between the good guys and the bad guys.

Joshua checked the flamer again, making sure it was set on stun, and moved out from behind the boulders. Newton accompanied him, staying close. It was as if he was waiting for the signal. Maybe he was doing exactly that.

Joshua glanced down. Newton cocked his head, looking up at him. Joshua gestured with one hand and mouthed the words, *Go get the bad guys.*

Speed was everything. The guards were former Guild men. That meant the flamers were not their only weapons. They were both capable of manipulating certain paranormal forces in the tunnels to create powerful, potentially lethal energy ghosts. But rezzing a ghost took a little time. It was not an instant process.

Newton sprang forward, moving very quickly and very quietly. He reached the chair where Harkins sprawled, beer in hand, and pounced, landing on his target's leg. He raced up toward Harkins's throat.

"What the fuck?" Harkins yelled.

He scrambled out of the chair. The can of beer fell from his hand. He fumbled for his flamer while simultaneously clawing at his neck in a frantic attempt to dislodge Newton.

The second man jumped to his feet, trying to figure out what was happening. "Looks like a fucking dust bunny. First one we've seen in this sector."

Newton leaped off Harkins's neck and landed on the other pirate, who shouted and swiped wildly at his small assailant. Once again Newton nimbly bounced out of reach. By now Joshua was within firing range.

"That's enough, Newton," Joshua said. "I've got this."

At the sound of his voice, Harkins and his pal swung around, stunned.

Harkins reacted first. *"Knight."* He went for his flamer. "Where the fuck did you—"

Joshua rezzed the trigger of his weapon. The bolt of fire sent Harkins to the floor, unconscious. The other man had his flamer out of the holster now.

Joshua fired again. His target dropped hard on the unforgiving blue crystal floor.

Newton chortled, evidently thrilled with their success. He fluffed out and bounced a little.

"Good job, pal," Joshua said. "I'll go pirate hunting with you anytime."

He scooped up the flamers and turned to look at the pyramid. As he watched, the shimmery curtain of energy evaporated.

Leona and the other two members of the Hollister Expedition emerged, rushing forward.

Chortling, Newton bustled toward them and proudly offered the yellow crystal to Leona.

"Thank you," she said softly. "A dust bunny to the rescue of another Griffin. This is getting to be a habit." She pocketed the crystal. "I knew the family would find us."

Grant glanced at the pair on the ground. "Harkins and Miller. Bastards."

"There are two more guards," Drayton warned. "They could come back at any moment."

"Turns out Harkins is a gatekeeper," Grant explained. "Who knew? When they grabbed us, he's the one who opened the gate that controls access to this place. There were two other pirates waiting for us. The four of them brought us here."

Joshua handed one of the extra flamers to Leona. "I assume you know how to use this."

Leona gripped the weapon. "Oh, yeah. The Griffin women can take care of themselves."

"That does appear to be the case," Joshua said.

"I'll take the other flamer," Grant said.

Joshua gave it to him and then moved to the fallen men. "I'm going to confiscate their amber so they won't be able to go far. Then we're getting out of here. Stay alert and stay close. I do not want to waste time looking for stragglers."

"Don't worry," Leona said. "No one wants to get left behind. We're done with this place, at least until we can get back in to do some serious work."

"The site is amazing," Drayton said in reverent tones.

"Absolutely *incredible*," Grant enthused. "Can't wait to get some of these objects back to the surface and into a decent lab."

Joshua ignored the comments as he went about the business of stripping the nav amber off the two pirates. When he was finished, he looked at Newton.

"Let's go find Molly."

Newton chortled again and dashed toward the foggy crystal gardens. Joshua followed. The others hurried to keep up.

"What did you mean by telling the dust bunny to find my sister?" Leona asked. "Is she okay?"

"She's holding the gate open for us," Joshua said.

"I don't understand. She never comes down into the Underworld with anyone except me."

"And here you are," Joshua said.

"Well, yes, but she really does not feel comfortable . . . Never mind. Of course she would come looking for me. We're family."

He was missing something, Joshua thought. Again. Maybe that was simply the norm when dealing with the Griffin sisters.

But he could not stop himself from asking the next question. "Why doesn't Molly come down here with anyone except you?"

"She's a little claustrophobic," Leona said smoothly.

Too smoothly, Joshua decided, plunging into the crystal garden. He really was missing a piece of the puzzle that was Molly.

"Back at the start, the pirates told us you were dead, Knight," Grant said. "They made sure we knew the search had been called off. We figured that meant there wasn't a chance in green hell that anyone would find us. We knew they'd murder us when we finished analyzing the artifacts, so we tried to stall."

"Leona kept saying her family would never stop looking," Drayton volunteered. "But even if that was true, we didn't think it meant they would be successful."

"Griffin Investigations found me," Joshua said.

Leona looked satisfied. "And you found us."

"You can thank Molly for that," Joshua said.

CHAPTER THIRTY

She heard them first. The voices came out of the fogbound sculpture garden. Two men, she decided.

"What the fuck? The gate is open."

"The Hollister team. They escaped."

"Impossible. No way those three could have gotten past Harkins and Miller."

"So who the fuck opened the gate?"

"Must be another crew working this sector. Looks like we've got competition."

"That's what we're paid to handle."

Molly peeked around the pedestal that shielded her and watched two men, flamers in hand, emerge from the fog-laced garden. One had straggly blond hair that looked like it hadn't been washed in a while. The other was shaved bald. His head gleamed. Evidently he oiled it.

They came to a halt just short of the gate threshold and eyed the twin rows of pedestals in front of them.

Molly took a steadying breath. She had the flamer and she knew how to use it, but the odds—two against one—struck her as not very good. She also had her stupid third talent, the party trick no one wanted to see. Unfortunately, there was no knowing how it would affect the crystal in the space. She might easily doom them all and the gate would slam shut.

The gate. There was a great deal of energy locked in a gate. Crystal energy.

"Gentlemen, we seem to have a small problem," she called from behind the pedestal.

"Who's there?" Shaved Head shouted.

"What the fuck?" Dirty Hair said. "Sounded like a woman. She's hiding behind one of those pillars."

"Get her," Shaved Head ordered.

"I've got a flamer," Molly announced.

She rezzed the trigger and fired a random shot to prove her point.

"Throw out the fucking flamer, bitch," Shaved Head shouted. "Do it now or we'll come in there and get you."

She tossed the flamer around the edge of the pedestal. It clattered on the quartz floor.

"That's better," Shaved Head said, sounding somewhat surprised. "Come out with your hands on your head."

She edged cautiously around the pedestal, moving into view. She was out of the range of the flamers—barely.

"Come here," Dirty Hair ordered.

She took a few steps forward and stopped.

"Anyone else with you?" Shaved Head asked, peering at the rows of pedestals behind her.

"No," she said.

"You're lying," Dirty Hair said. "Where are the others?"

"There's only me," she said. "I got lost."

"Fuck you did," Shaved Head said.

"I dunno." Dirty Hair looked uncertain. "Maybe she's telling the truth. Look at her. She isn't dressed for the Underworld. Looks like the artsy type."

"Either way she's a problem," Shaved Head said. "The boss is going to want to talk to her."

"Fine by me," Molly said. "I've got some questions for your boss."

"Good luck with that," Shaved Head said. He nodded at Dirty Hair. "Get her. I'll cover you just in case there is someone else around."

Dirty Hair started forward. Both men were only inches away from the threshold now.

Close enough, Molly decided.

She cut her focus, releasing the gate. Energy flared in the opening, charging the atmosphere on either side of the threshold. The powerful currents struck the two men. Shaved Head's aura lit up. The shock twisted his face into a skeletal mask. An instant later he stiffened and collapsed across the threshold.

"Fuck, no," Dirty Hair yelled. Frantically, he tried to scramble backward, but he was too close. His aura flared for a heartbeat when the gate energy singed it, and then he, too, crumpled to the floor.

Molly hastily reversed the gate. When it was wide open again, she took a moment to catch her breath and steady her senses. Both men were sprawled across the threshold. Neither appeared conscious. She wondered if they were dead.

She did not know a great deal about the physics of gates, but, like everyone else, she had heard frightening reports of what could happen if they slammed shut without warning. People got seriously injured or killed. The mechanisms that opened the doors to the secrets of the

Underworld were, after all, Alien technology. Even professional gate-keepers admitted they did not know much about them.

First things first, she decided. She had to get the two men out of the doorway. Dead or alive, their bodies would probably interfere with the closing of the gate. Joshua had said that when he and the Hollister team returned, they might be running from the bad guys. If that turned out to be true, she would have to get the gate closed as quickly as possible.

Maybe if she grabbed them by the ankles . . .

She was a few steps away from Shaved Head when she heard a familiar chortle somewhere in the fog.

"Newton," she called.

He scampered out of the misty garden. She scooped him up and hugged him close. He was fully fluffed and the yellow crystal she had hung around his neck was gone. Both were good signs.

"Where is Joshua?" she asked.

"Right here," Joshua said, emerging from the fog.

He was not alone. Leona and the two men from the Hollister Expedition followed. Joy mingled with overwhelming relief shot through Molly.

"Leona," she said.

"I knew you and the moms would find us," Leona said. She sprinted forward. "What took you so long?"

Sparks flashed in the atmosphere. Everyone immediately switched their attention to the gate. Molly realized she had broken the focus. Hastily she concentrated, regaining control.

"Sorry about that," she said, hugging Leona. "There were a few complications."

Squashed between the two women, Newton wriggled free and vaulted down to the ground. Molly gave him the little mirror. He took it and then bustled over to investigate Dirty Hair and Shaved Head.

Joshua glanced at the two fallen men and then fixed Molly with an oddly fierce look.

"I can't leave you alone for even five minutes," he said. The heat in his eyes belied the light words. "Are you all right?"

"Yes," she said. "I'm okay."

"What happened to these two?" Joshua asked.

"Gate accident," Molly said.

His mouth kicked up in a knowing smile. "Son of a ghost. You closed it on them, didn't you? Sweet."

"Thanks."

Joshua looked at Drayton and Grant. "You're sure you only saw four pirates?"

"Yes," Drayton said. "Never did see the boss. Whoever he is, he's smart enough to stay clear."

"You're sure the boss is male?" Joshua asked.

"That's how the guards referred to him," Grant said.

Molly turned back to Leona. "The moms and I have been so worried."

"I know," Leona said.

"We were a little concerned ourselves," Grant muttered.

Drayton grunted. "It's been a fucking nightmare. We knew we didn't have much time left, so we came up with a plan. We managed to stockpile about ten days' worth of water and field rations inside the pyramid."

"Leona had figured out how to lock the entrance using one of the artifacts," Grant continued. "We went in one shift as usual, then locked the door behind us. The guards made a lot of threats but they couldn't get to us."

"The clock was ticking, though," Drayton added. "When the food and water ran out, we would have been forced to unlock the pyramid."

"The site is stunning," Leona said. "The most significant find since the Ghost City."

"There will be a lot of published papers coming out of this," Grant added. "Our names will be on every one of them."

"True." Drayton brightened at the prospect.

"Don't forget we agreed we would share the credit," Leona said, eyes narrowing. "We have a deal."

"That's right," Drayton said. "We need to get the site secured as soon as possible. We can't risk someone else staking a claim."

"Another thing," Leona warned. "When we get back to the surface, we need to form a united front to negotiate with the university authorities and the head of the department. You know as well as I do that they'll try to avoid giving us credit."

Joshua shook his head and went toward the fallen men. "Lord, save me from academics," he said to Molly as he went past.

She smiled. "They can be very focused. I know a lot of people like that. Present company included."

"Okay, you've got a point." He crouched beside Shaved Head. "These two are alive. Grant, Drayton, give me a hand. We have to move them. The gate might not close completely if they are in the way. I want to make sure they don't go anywhere until the Guild can send a team down to collect them along with the others."

"What others?" Molly asked.

"There were a couple of guards watching the pyramid where we were trapped," Leona explained. "Knight and the dust bunny took care of them."

"I see." Molly swallowed hard but told herself she would get the details later. "Well, hey, I'm all in favor of leaving the bad guys for Guild security, but I don't think just closing the gate and trapping them in the sculpture garden will do the job. These two mentioned that they have a gatekeeper on their crew."

"Not anymore," Joshua said. He did not look up from the task of hauling Shaved Head into the sculpture garden. "I used the flamer to stun him as well as the other guy. Stripped their amber just to be on the safe side. They won't be going anywhere for a while. Neither will these two."

"Not without nav amber," Grant said, sounding satisfied.

"Nothing scarier than being stuck down here without good amber," Drayton observed. "Talk about a death sentence."

Grant shuddered. "They say you go insane long before you die of starvation."

Joshua watched Leona and Molly exchange silent messages, but neither said a word. He let it go. There was no time to waste wondering what in green hell he was missing now.

"All right, everyone, listen up," he said. "We will be moving through uncharted territory. That means it hasn't been cleared of ghosts and traps and who knows what else might be down here. Check your amber. Maintain visual contact at all times. We have the sled, so no one has to walk, but the nearest exit point that can provide transport to Illusion Town is a Coppersmith Mining camp. It's going to take about an hour or so to reach it. Any questions?"

"I have one," Leona said. "What's with the hospital scrubs?"

"Fashion statement," Joshua said.

CHAPTER THIRTY-ONE

"The artifacts in that sector are absolutely stunning," Leona said. "Unlike anything we've seen. Hollister University is filing a claim as we speak. Grant and Drayton and I are negotiating an agreement with the university that will guarantee that the three of us direct all major research projects. We're waiting for the legal department to draw up the contracts."

"That's lovely, sweetie," Charlotte said. She folded her hands on her desk. "But shouldn't you be more traumatized or something? You've been through an ordeal."

Molly grinned and sipped some of the strong coffee that Eugenie had brewed. "Takes a lot to traumatize a Griffin," she said.

She and Leona and the moms were gathered in the offices of Griffin Investigations. The return to the surface had gone smoothly. They had reached the Coppersmith Mining site an hour after departing the crystal garden. As Joshua had predicted, the mining people had arranged transportation to Illusion Town via a high-speed mag-lev transporter.

Molly and Leona, Grant, and Drayton had returned on the transporter. Joshua had stayed behind to wait for Guild security to arrive. He was the only one who could lead them back to the pirate site. Coppersmith had provided a gatekeeper to accompany them. Newton, sensing more excitement, had stayed behind with Joshua.

The Illusion Town Guild had responded quickly after the phone call from the mining camp. A contingent of security personnel led by Gabriel Jones had been dispatched immediately. The Guild vehicles and the transporter carrying Molly and the others had passed each other on the road.

The press had gotten wind of events, thanks to the Guild's public relations department. The result was that a throng of reporters, representatives of Hollister University, and family members had been on hand to greet the rescued academics. Molly and Leona had avoided the press and slipped away with Eugenie and Charlotte. The moms had taken them back to the Dark Zone to shower and change clothes.

The news that Guild security and Joshua had returned to Illusion Town with the pirates in tow had come an hour ago. It was now three o'clock in the afternoon.

"I will admit I'd rather be relaxing around a pool drinking one of those cocktails that has an umbrella stuck in it," Leona said. "But first things first. Right now, Grant and Drayton and I have to protect our careers. I'll succumb to panic attacks later."

Molly saluted her with the coffee mug. "To a woman who knows how to set priorities."

Charlotte and Eugenie hoisted their mugs.

"To a Griffin," Eugenie said.

"To a Griffin." Charlotte smiled. "We are a tough bunch, but I think it's going to be a while before I recover from all the excitement. I'm not as young as I used to be. We've been so anxious, Leona."

"More like flat-out terrified," Eugenie said. "We were sure you were alive, but the authorities had abandoned the search and rescue operation. No one knew where to start looking. Joshua Knight was our only hope, but all indications were that he was psi-burned, paranoid, and delusional. The report was that he had lost his memories of the disaster. For the first week we couldn't get at him because they had him in a locked ward at a para-psych hospital."

"He disappeared from the asylum and the public forgot about him," Charlotte said. "The Hollister Expedition disaster was no longer in the headlines. But we kept looking for him because there was no other option. When we found him, we knew that Molly had the best chance of getting through to him because of her talent for dream-walking."

Leona's enthusiasm faded abruptly. "I'm a thoughtless person. I'm so sorry. I've been so rezzed since we got back to the surface that I haven't stopped to consider what the three of you went through during most of the past month. It must have been a nightmare. I know how I'd feel if one of you went missing."

Molly cleared her throat. "I did go missing once, remember? And you called the magic phone number that got me rescued."

Leona smiled. "Oh, yeah, right. I guess the good news is that the number for Griffin Investigations still works."

"Want answers?" Eugenie recited. *"We'll get them for you. Call now. No waiting."*

"Yep," Molly said. "But moving right along, we haven't had a chance to tell you about the body I found in my shop the other night."

"What?" Leona stared, dumbfounded.

Molly gave her a quick rundown of the discovery of the dead intruder.

"That is just horrible," Leona said, shaken. "It's a wonder you didn't lose the Guild wedding contract. Everyone knows that a lot of people take those old superstitions about contaminated crystals seriously."

"I was a tad worried for a while," Molly admitted. "But the bride saved me. She refused to pull the contract."

"Which reminds me," Charlotte said. "We have some news on that front. The police were able to identify the dead intruder. He was Blake Turnbridge, professional gambler."

"He had a side hustle as a cat burglar for hire," Eugenie added. "Turns out he's the thief the press nicknamed Mr. Invisible."

"They think he was shot and killed by whoever he was working with that evening," Eugenie added. "They haven't been able to find the partner."

"You *have* been busy," Leona said.

"And we're still busy," Eugenie said. "We're trying to find the client."

"What client?" Leona asked.

"The person who hired Mr. Invisible to steal the wedding crystals," Charlotte said. "We think it might be a collector."

"But a collector would never have been able to put them on display," Molly said. "The crystals would have been recognized immediately."

"Collectors don't always care about displaying their acquisitions," Eugenie said. "Sometimes all that matters to them is possessing the objects of their obsession."

"True." Leona drank some coffee and lowered the mug. She gave Molly a knowing look. "I couldn't help but notice that you and Joshua Knight made a good team down in the tunnels. You seemed quite . . . close."

Neither Eugenie nor Charlotte said a word, but Molly knew they were paying attention. She decided to play it casually.

"He's a grateful client," she said. "I was able to undo the damage that had been done to his senses and help him recover his memories."

"I got the feeling the two of you had something more than a therapist-client relationship going on," Leona said.

Molly rezzed up a bright smile. "Nope."

Charlotte gave her a stern mom look. "How much does he know about you?"

"Very little," Molly said. "It's not like we've had a lot of time for conversation."

Intense curiosity flared in Eugenie's eyes—mom curiosity. "Does he know about the kidnapping?"

Should have seen that question coming, Molly thought. She never talked about the kidnapping. It was hardly a family secret—the story had been in the press for a week—but she rarely felt comfortable sharing it. She had learned the hard way that people got a little weird when they heard that she had been abducted and held captive for a time. One date, a journalist, had wanted to write a true-crime book about the incident. A psychologist she had met in a bookstore café had become obsessed with discovering how the trauma had affected her dreams.

"Yes, he knows," Molly said. "He was curious about why I hadn't spent much time in the Underworld, given my talent for crystals. When I told him I'd been kidnapped, he understood."

"Hmm," Charlotte said, looking thoughtful. "So you didn't tell him the real reason you avoid the Underworld."

"There was no reason to tell him," Molly said. "Trust me, Joshua is not interested in a relationship, at least not right now. He has other priorities at the moment."

"Such as?" Eugenie asked, brows sharpening.

"He needs to find a job, among other things," Molly said. "He wants to get his life back."

"He has a job with Cork and Ferris," Leona said. "Everyone knows Knight is one of the best navigators in the business."

"The job with Cork and Ferris no longer exists," Molly said. "I was there when Auburn Cork fired him."

Leona snorted softly. "I'll bet it won't be long before Cork begs Knight to go back to work. The press is loving the story of the brave, bold navigator who refused to give up the search for the kidnapped expedition."

"Oh, yeah," Eugenie said. She held up her phone to display the screen and read the breaking news headline aloud. *"Expedition Team Freed. Pirates Arrested. Navigator Hailed as Hero."'*

Charlotte frowned. "It doesn't even mention Molly."

"Fine by me," Molly said. "I was just the gatekeeper." She took a closer look at the photo of Joshua standing next to Gabriel Jones while Jones gave a statement to the press. "Oh, look. Newton is in the picture. He's on Joshua's shoulder. Doesn't he look adorable?"

Leona leaned forward to examine the photo. "Newton has his little mirror and he's holding a bag of Zing Chips."

"He loves Zing Chips," Molly explained. "Joshua must have bought him a bag to celebrate."

Charlotte examined the photo. "What's up with the hospital scrubs that Knight is wearing?"

"The story is a bit complicated," Molly said. "When Joshua walked out of the Amber Dawn hospital—"

"You mean, when he drugged an orderly and escaped a locked ward," Charlotte clarified in a cool tone.

"Whatever," Molly said. "As I was saying, he couldn't find the clothes he had been wearing when he was admitted to the hospital. He grabbed three sets of scrubs on the way out the door. His apartment is a thousand miles away in Resonance City. He hasn't had time to go home and pick up his stuff."

"Or, apparently, time to shop," Eugenie said.

"Priorities," Molly reminded her.

"I understand that Knight has had other things on his to-do list lately," Leona said. "But I gotta tell you, I really do think he's more interested in a personal relationship with you than you realize."

Molly raised her eyes to the ceiling and then shook her head. "You came to that conclusion based on your observations of the two of us during the time it took to get you and the team out of the Underworld and back to Illusion Town?"

"Yep."

"Hmm." Charlotte glanced at her computer screen. "Joshua Knight is not currently registered with a matchmaking agency. However, he signed up with a firm in Resonance shortly before taking the Hollister job. They removed him from their list of clients when they learned that he was in a locked ward at Amber Dawn."

"He mentioned that," Molly said stiffly.

Leona cleared her throat. "The bottom line here is that Knight is not currently in violation of rule number one. What about rule number two?"

Molly grimaced. "It wasn't like that."

"Hah." Leona got a smug, knowing look. "You spent the night with him. You were still inside his house the next morning. Admit it. You broke rule number two for him. *Thou shalt be gone by morning.* That's our policy, remember? We decided long ago that spending the night and sticking around for breakfast was not a good idea for free spirits."

"Now you're just being mean," Molly said.

"I'm sorry." Leona's expression softened. "It's just that the energy around you and Knight felt so right. Maybe you should give the relationship a chance."

"At the moment it's an acquaintanceship, not a relationship," Molly said. But she could not hide the wistfulness in her voice.

"Oh, honey," Eugenie said gently.

Charlotte frowned. "What's that supposed to mean?"

"Damned if I know," Eugenie said. "I was trying to sound wise and maternal."

"Forget it," Charlotte said. "I'm the wise, maternal one. You're the pragmatic, no-nonsense mom, remember?"

"Oh, yeah, right," Eugenie said.

Mercifully, Molly's watch pinged. She checked the alert, leaped to her feet, and headed for the door. "I've got to run. The final energy circle setup and check for the Guild wedding is scheduled for four thirty this afternoon. Clement will be in a full-blown panic. I've got to get to the Amber Palace ballroom right now."

"I'm due to meet Grant and Drayton," Leona said. She came up out of the chair. "We agreed to go over our stories before we give our statements to the police. We also have to decide how we're going to handle the university people. Wait for me, Molly."

"Family dinner tonight," Charlotte called after them. "Ollie's House of Pizza. Six thirty."

"See you there," Leona said over her shoulder.

"Six thirty," Molly said. "Got it. I may be a little late. Start without me."

She and Leona reached the stairs at the same time and nearly collided with Joshua, who had just arrived on the landing. His face was etched with exhaustion but his eyes burned. Newton, riding on his shoulder, was chuffed. He chortled a greeting and vaulted onto Molly's shoulder.

"Thanks again for the rescue," Leona sang out as she swept past Joshua.

"Anytime," Joshua said. "Not like I've got a lot on my social calendar these days."

"Yes, you do," Molly said, dodging around him. "Dinner at Ollie's House of Pizza tonight. Six thirty."

"Thanks for inviting me."

"Ollie's is here in the Dark Zone. Ask some of the locals for directions. It's easy to get lost in this neighborhood."

"I'm pretty good at navigating," he said.

"Oh, right. I forgot. Got to run. Crystal check for the big wedding."

She flew down the stairs after Leona. When she reached the ground floor, she glanced back one last time and saw Joshua opening the door of Griffin Investigations. It occurred to her that it might not be a good idea to leave Joshua alone with the moms, but she did not have any choice. She had a business to save. Joshua was on his own.

Chapter Thirty-Two

Joshua moved into the small reception area of Griffin Investigations and closed the door. There was no one at the front desk. He was examining the minimalist decor when a woman opened the door of an inner office and walked out to greet him. She wore a sharply tailored business suit and heels. Her hair was done up in a sleek twist. She smiled.

"Joshua Knight," she said. "I recognize you from the photos. You are all over the news this afternoon. Well, you and the dust bunny. You even managed to push the Guild wedding off the front page for a few hours. I'm Charlotte Griffin, by the way."

"A pleasure, ma'am," Joshua said.

A second woman stepped out of an office. She was not as tall as her colleague, but she looked like she could do more damage—if she took a mind to do some damage.

"I'm Eugenie Griffin," she announced. "Very happy to meet you, Mr.

Knight. Charlotte and I are incredibly grateful. We owe you. If there is ever anything we can do for you—"

"I'm the one who owes the favor," he said. "If you hadn't tracked me down and sent Molly to find me, I'd still be slowly going out of my mind trying to find Leona and the others."

"Your family must be very happy to know that you rescued the Hollister team and that you're safe and sane," Eugenie said.

"I've been a little busy," Joshua said. "Haven't had a chance to call my parents."

"Really?" Charlotte frowned. "Don't tell me you're going to let them hear the story on the evening news. You need to contact your family immediately. I'm sure they've been very worried about you."

More like embarrassed and humiliated to have me in the family, he thought. "I'll get in touch with my parents soon," he said.

"Molly told us how the two of you worked together to rescue the expedition team," Charlotte said.

He smiled. "So she didn't tell you that she strong-armed her way into my house using Newton as a Trojan dust bunny?"

"What's a Trojan dust bunny?" Eugenie asked.

"Never mind," he said. "Did she mention that I tried my best to get rid of her before the fog rolled in, but she managed to talk her way into spending the night? Did she tell you that she rendered me unconscious for several hours when she ran me through her so-called dream-walking therapy?"

"I'm sure it was an accident," Charlotte said quickly.

"That's what she claimed," he said. "Something about working with unfamiliar crystal energy."

"Molly did not go into details," Charlotte said, her voice very cool now. "Why don't you step into my office so that we can get to know each other better?"

"Why not?" he said. "What could possibly go wrong?"

He walked into the office and sat down. Charlotte took the seat behind the desk. Eugenie opened a cupboard and took out three glasses. She set the glasses on the desk, reached back into the cupboard, and brought out a bottle of Amber River whiskey.

"The good stuff," Joshua said. "I'm honored."

Eugenie splashed the whiskey into the glasses and handed them around.

"Thank you for rescuing Leona," she said, raising her glass.

"You're welcome," he said. He took a fortifying swallow. "Is this where you tell me to stay the hell away from Molly?"

Eugenie's brows rose. "Would you stay away from her if we said that?"

"That would be up to Molly," he said.

Eugenie nodded. "Figured as much. As a matter of fact, we have no intention of warning you off. Molly is an adult. She makes her own decisions when it comes to relationships."

He allowed himself to relax a little. "Good to know."

"But under the circumstances, we feel we do have a right to ask a few questions," Charlotte said.

He drank an additional dose of medicinal whiskey and looked at the two formidable women. "You want to know my intentions toward Molly."

"Yes," Charlotte said. "We do. Molly has a lot of spirit and plenty of grit, but she suffered some serious childhood trauma."

"Because she spent the first few years of her life in an orphanage and was kidnapped by a deranged man named Willard," Joshua said. He leaned back in his chair and cradled his glass. "She told me the story and how the two of you rescued her."

Charlotte clasped her hands on the desktop. "Molly and Leona started out as orphans, and although they both became Griffins, they have had to live with the mystery of their past. We have been unable to trace their ancestries. All we have determined is that their mothers were both killed when the girls were a little over a year old."

"We have not been able to identify their fathers or any close relatives," Eugenie added. She started to swallow some whiskey but paused. "Believe me when I tell you that we are very, very good at finding people."

"I know," he said. "You found me."

"In fairness, you were not actually trying to hide," Charlotte conceded. "You just went off the grid. Big difference."

"If you'd been trying to hide, you would have gone down into the Underworld," Eugenie added.

"I'll remember that pro tip," he said.

Both women fixed him with a warning look.

"You're not taking this conversation seriously, are you?" Charlotte said.

"I was at first." He turned the glass between his palms. "Back when it was about my intentions. But then the discussion went in an entirely different direction."

Eugenie narrowed her eyes. "What do you mean?"

"Now you're trying to tell me that you think Molly is too fragile, too delicate, to handle the risk of a serious relationship."

"That's not what we meant," Charlotte snapped.

"No? Okay, then maybe you're nervous because you're afraid Molly has gotten involved with a man who got psi-fried so badly he wound up in an asylum where he was diagnosed as paranoid and delusional. A man who escaped a para-psych ward, disappeared, and became a recluse. A man who got labeled the 'Mad Doctor' by the entire population of the town of Outpost."

Eugenie eyed him. "The hospital scrubs send mixed messages."

"That's not my point."

"What is your point, Mr. Knight?" Charlotte said.

He got to his feet and put the half-empty whiskey glass on the desk. "My point is that you don't know your daughter nearly as well as you think you do. She's a lot stronger than you give her credit for. I understand why you feel protective of her, but trust me, she can handle a relationship with me."

"Is that right?" Eugenie asked.

"I've seen her in action." He went to the door. "You should be asking me if I can handle a relationship with her. You hacked into my hospital records and got my para-psych evaluation. You know I'm damned fragile and very delicate."

"Fragile and delicate, my ass," Eugenie growled.

Joshua pretended not to hear that.

"Call your parents," Charlotte ordered.

"Yes, ma'am."

He let himself out of the office and went down the stairs. He needed to find Molly. He had a few questions of his own about their relationship. He'd been focused on rescuing the Hollister team for most of the past month, and there were still some loose ends to take care of, but now he could afford to concentrate on Molly.

Also, he needed to call his parents.

CHAPTER THIRTY-THREE

Molly, he discovered, had her own priorities, and at that moment he was not at the top of her list.

He tracked her down in the vast ballroom of the Amber Palace Hotel & Casino. The glittering space was lavishly decorated in yards of drapery, bunting, and banners—all of it in the traditional Guild colors, amber and green. The room was abuzz with activity.

Everywhere there were people in black uniforms emblazoned with a logo that read *Illusion Town Event Designers*. Several were engaged in setting up what appeared to be a thousand foldable chairs on either side of a long amber-and-green carpet.

Other workers were adjusting the lighting. The massive crystal chandeliers overhead dimmed slightly and then brightened and dimmed again as technicians played with the lights. Several loud clicks crackled from hidden speakers as musicians ran sound checks.

A small, fierce man in the black uniform stopped him halfway across the room. Joshua glanced at the name tag. P. CLAUDE.

Claude took in the scrubs and managed to look both pained and suspicious.

"No one called for an ambulance," he said. "You obviously have the wrong location."

"I'm looking for the crystal artist, Molly Griffin," Joshua said.

"Why?"

"I'm a friend."

"I'm afraid Ms. Griffin is busy at the moment," Claude said. "She has no time for chitchat. She is putting the finishing touches on the energy circle. As a matter of fact, we are *all* extremely busy. Please leave immediately or I will summon hotel security."

Joshua held up one hand, palm out in surrender. "I can take a hint."

"Good." Claude started to turn away and then reversed course. "Why do you look familiar?"

"Probably the scrubs," Joshua said.

He heard a cheery chortle, looked around, and saw Newton bustling toward him. The dust bunny was waving his mirror and trailing a long amber-and-green satin streamer. Claude's expression softened a little at the sight of him.

"Isn't he just the cutest thing?" he said.

Joshua flashed on a mental image of Newton sleeked out and showing a lot of teeth as he raced forward to attack a pirate.

"Adorable," Joshua said. He scooped up Newton and plopped him on his shoulder. The long streamer trailed to the floor.

Claude's eyes tightened. "Hang on, you're the navigator, aren't you? The one who lost the Hollister team."

"Sorry to interfere with your work," Joshua said. "I'll be leaving now."

"I saw the headlines this afternoon," Claude continued on a sudden burst of enthusiasm. "They called off the search a while back, but you didn't give up. You kept looking, and a few hours ago you found the expedition people and brought them back to the surface. The Guild arrested the kidnappers."

"That's somewhat of an oversimplification," Joshua said.

"No, it's not," Molly said, hurrying toward them. She sounded a little breathless. "It's an excellent summary of events."

Joshua smiled at the sight of her. She was flushed and excited. There was a lot of energy in her eyes and in the atmosphere. *Good energy*, he thought. She was in her element. You'd never know that earlier that day she had been holding open a dangerous Alien gate and taking down a couple of pirates.

"I thought I'd drop in and see how things were going," he said. "But you're busy, so I won't hang around."

"Actually, we are right on schedule," she said, coming to a halt. "Aiden is pleased, isn't he, Mr. Claude?"

"Evidently," Claude said, looking somewhat gratified.

"Are you talking about Aiden Shore?" Joshua asked. "Gabriel Jones's administrative assistant? I met him today."

Claude grunted. "As the Guild liaison, he has a great deal to say about how the image of the organization is projected. He has taken a very hands-on approach."

"I thought it was supposed to be a wedding, not a public relations event," Joshua said.

Claude grimaced. "Wrong."

"Aiden is convinced that it's very important for this wedding to make a big splash," Molly explained. "He's committed to upgrading the Guild brand. He says it will require a spectacular event to make an impression on Illusion Town because, well, spectacle is pretty much the norm around here. By the way, he's absolutely thrilled with the rescue of the Hollister Expedition and the arrest of the pirates. He said the timing could not have been better."

"Better for what?" Joshua asked. "The expedition team spent nearly a month in the Underworld. I doubt they think the timing was terrific."

"The thing is, the arrests are making the Guild look very good on the eve of the boss's wedding," Molly said. "Isn't that right, Mr. Claude?"

"This is a city that takes luck seriously," Claude said. "There's no question but that the rescue and the subsequent arrests are being viewed as an excellent omen for the entire town."

"I see," Joshua said.

"Come with me and I'll introduce you to my assistant, Clement," Molly said.

"I've been asked to leave," Joshua said.

Molly looked at Claude.

"A misunderstanding," Claude muttered. "I didn't know who he was at first. For some reason I wasn't expecting the hero of the hour to show up wearing hospital attire."

"Right," Molly said before Joshua could come up with a response to the comment. "If you'll excuse us, Mr. Claude?"

"Certainly." Claude swiveled on one heel and marched toward a group of workers who were constructing a decorative arch at the front of the carpet.

Molly waited until he was out of earshot and then leaned in close. "How did it go with the moms today? Any problems?"

"I believe we all arrived at a clear understanding of each other," Joshua said.

"Oh, good." Molly relaxed. "I was a little worried. The moms can be intimidating."

"Really? I hadn't noticed."

She winced. "They scared the green hell out of you, didn't they?"

"Well, sure. That's their job."

Molly sighed. "I suppose so. I warned you they tend to be a little overprotective."

"They have their reasons."

"I will admit that, viewed from a certain perspective, I've been something of a screwup. In school my teachers mostly said I failed to reach my full potential. When I squeaked into college, I kept switching majors and barely graduated. I went through a long string of jobs until I opened Singing Crystals. Compared to Leona, I'm a slacker."

"You were searching for your passion. It just took you a while to find it."

She laughed. "Thanks. I needed that."

CHAPTER THIRTY-FOUR

They gathered in a family-sized booth at Ollie's House of Pizza. Molly and Newton were the last to arrive because she had felt it necessary to check the layout of the energy circle one more time after the lighting-and-sound crew completed their setup. The moms, Leona, and Joshua had been waiting when she and Newton rushed through the doors.

Luckily the short journey from the front entrance of the restaurant to the booth had given her time to recover from the shock of seeing Joshua—still wearing scrubs—chatting and drinking beer with Charlotte, Eugenie, and Leona.

She had been braced for a last-minute text from him advising her that something had come up and he would not be able to make it. She would not have blamed him. The meeting with the moms that afternoon had to have been uncomfortable for him. It wasn't as if they'd had grounds for grilling him. He had not shown any romantic interest in her—unless you counted that one hot kiss after she had helped him recover his memories.

It had been a gratitude kiss. Given that he had never mentioned it, she had begun to wonder if he remembered it.

But tonight he was apparently at ease sharing a meal with her family. The bigger shock was that the moms seemed to have accepted his presence at the table. Maybe that was because he had made it clear that his relationship with their daughter was strictly platonic. Nothing personal. Just two people with agendas that had happened to align for a few days.

Which was, technically speaking, true. Unfortunately.

She realized she could do with a little clarification herself.

Newton was in full adorable mode, charming everyone. Molly had ordered him his own pizza. When it was delivered to the table, he had been positively giddy. He had crouched over his plate, a small, fluffy dragon surveying his hoard of gold.

"Everything set for the big wedding tomorrow?" Joshua asked around a bite of pizza.

"I hope so." Molly reached for another slice. "I've reached the stage where I can truthfully say I'll be glad when it's over. Any updates on the pirate operation?"

"A few." Joshua picked up his beer. "The police confirmed that the two security people hired for the Hollister Expedition were ex-Guild men using fake IDs. Both had been kicked out of their organizations because they were suspected of illegal activities in the Underworld. Same with the other two pirates at the site."

Charlotte shook her head. "The Guilds have been cleaning house lately. Rebranding. Trying to upgrade their image. It's good to see new management at the top, but it has resulted in a lot of shady characters getting dumped onto the streets. They tend to go into what they like to call private security work. That term covers a great deal of territory."

"Have they figured out who was running the pirate operation?" Molly asked.

"Not yet," Joshua said. "But the investigation is, as they say, ongoing."

"Unfortunately, Grant and Drayton and I were not able to offer much in the way of help," Leona said. "We spent nearly a month down there, but we only saw the four armed men who were in charge of guarding us. As far as we could tell, the person they referred to as the boss was the broker who had hired them. We don't know who was paying the broker."

"The Guild is working with the police to track down the head of the operation," Joshua said. "Sooner or later there will be an arrest."

"What makes you so sure?" Eugenie asked.

"There are too many loose ends," Joshua said. "This was a complex operation, and now it's unraveling fast. There will be a lot of leads. One of them will pay off."

"I think you're right," Charlotte said. "That pirate operation required money—a great deal of it. There will be a paper trail."

Eugenie smiled a cool smile. "Meanwhile the excitement about the return of the Hollister Expedition and the wedding tomorrow has pushed the burglary attempt and the murder of Mr. Invisible out of the head-lines."

Charlotte looked satisfied. "After the wedding tomorrow nobody will remember a run-of-the-mill break-in-gone-bad at an art crystal bou-tique. What they will recall is that Singing Crystals is the premier crystal arrangements boutique in the city."

"Let's hope so," Molly said. She finished her pizza and checked the time. "I'm going to go home and get some sleep. Big day tomorrow. I have to be up early."

"You and Joshua must be exhausted," Leona said. "Neither of you has had a chance to sleep since you pulled Grant and Drayton and me out of the tunnels. Joshua had to turn around immediately and guide the Guild men back down to make the arrests. You had to go to work setting up the crystal arrangements for the wedding tomorrow."

"You haven't had any sleep, either," Molly said. She slid out of the booth and stood. "Ready to leave, Newton?"

He chortled and hopped onto her shoulder.

Joshua followed them out of the booth. "I'll see you home."

She hesitated. "That's not necessary. My shop is only a few blocks away."

"It's not a problem," he said. "I'll walk you back to your place and grab a cab to a hotel."

"Good idea," Eugenie said. "The Dark Zone is usually safe at night for the locals who know their way around, but you can't be too careful these days. After everything you've been through lately, Molly, I think I speak for all of us when I say we would feel better if Joshua walks you home."

Molly considered refusing the escort service and immediately asked herself why and in what universe would she do that. She was not ready to say good night to Joshua, let alone goodbye. If he walked her back to the shop she would have a little more time with him. Time to get some clarification.

"Thanks," she said. "I really am exhausted."

"You're not the only one," Joshua said.

Chapter Thirty-Five

Outside in the balmy desert night, Molly took a deep breath and allowed herself to relax. The neighborhood was comfortably busy, the restaurants, bars, and small casinos doing a brisk trade. Adventurous tourists from the flashier zones sometimes found their way into the DZ, but for the most part the businesses in this zone catered to the locals.

As usual, the DZ was steeped in the glow of the buzzy green energy that radiated from the nearby Dead City wall. It was all very romantic, Molly thought. At least that's how it felt to her. She could not tell if Joshua had the same impression. Probably not. He'd been through a lot lately. He needed sleep. So did she. So why was she thinking about her relationship with the man walking beside her?

Because I care about him. A lot. Maybe too much.

"I called my parents today after I left you in the ballroom," Joshua said.

She glanced at him, unable to read him. "They must be thrilled to know that you're stable and that you rescued the team."

"They seemed ... happy."

"You sound surprised."

"For the past month I've been a source of embarrassment and humiliation to my family. I expected them to be relieved by the positive twist the press is giving the story. And they are. But I think they were also genuinely happy. Mom couldn't stop crying. Dad said she hadn't slept for most of the past month because she was so worried. Dad sounded happy, too. They both told me they loved me and that they had been terrified that they would lose me."

"Of course they were frightened. Perfectly natural reaction. You're family."

"Family can be complicated."

"No kidding. But in this case maybe you had the dynamics backward."

"What do you mean?"

"Maybe you were the one who was too embarrassed and humiliated to face your family."

There was a moment of silence before Joshua spoke again.

"Maybe," he said after a while.

When they passed an alley Newton suddenly chortled and bounded down to the sidewalk. He waved his mirror at Molly, opened his hunting eyes, and fluttered off into the green shadows. She caught a glimpse of two more sets of gleaming amber eyes. There was a great deal of chortling, and then Newton and his two pals disappeared into the darkness.

"He likes to party with his friends at night," Molly said.

"He deserves some R and R," Joshua said.

"So do you," Molly said. "Got plans?"

"Not for R and R. I don't have the money for a vacation, even if I had the time, which I don't."

"I understand."

"I need to get my life back on track. Job one is figuring out how to set myself up as a freelance navigator."

She was an idiot. Here she was contemplating the possibilities for the future of their relationship, and the poor man was facing unemployment and, possibly, bankruptcy.

"You're getting a lot of excellent press at the moment," she said, going for a positive spin. "You're the heroic navigator who never gave up. You are a legend, at least for now. You'll be able to build on that."

His mouth curved in a faint smile. "And you're the heroic crystal artist who held the gate open while being attacked by pirates. But no one seems to have noticed."

She laughed. "No one ever pays any attention to the gatekeeper. That's fine by me. The last thing I want is a career in the Underworld."

"Speaking of career options, I had a short but interesting conversation with Gabriel Jones after his people picked up the pirates," Joshua said.

"And?"

"He wanted to know if I would be interested in discussing a navigator contract."

"Joshua, that's wonderful news." Molly stopped, forcing Joshua to stop, too. She turned to face him. "Why didn't you tell me right away? A contract with the Illusion Town Guild would be a terrific launch for your new business."

"It might not go anywhere."

"I certainly hope you said you would be open to negotiations."

Joshua's eyes glinted with amusement. "Oh, yeah."

"What else did Jones say?"

"That his administrative assistant will get in touch to set up an appointment as soon as the wedding nightmare is over."

She froze. "Oh, shit. That's *horrible.*"

"Think so? I gotta tell you, I am pretty damned thrilled."

"Thrilled?"

"Sure. You said it yourself—a contract with the Guild would set me up for work with other outfits."

"Yes, of course," she said. "That's not what I'm talking about. I meant the wedding nightmare thing. Jones used those words? *Wedding nightmare?*"

"I believe that was how he described it, yes."

She resumed walking, stunned by the implications. "This is awful. Just terrible. If the new boss of the Illusion Town Guild gives a statement to the media calling the biggest wedding of the season—his *own* wedding—a nightmare, everyone will blame my energy crystals."

Joshua fell into step beside her. "You're overthinking this. Talk about catastrophizing."

"Trust me, it will be a catastrophe for Singing Crystals. My business is toast."

"Jones said that in a private conversation. Weddings, especially Covenant Marriage weddings, make people nervous. Everyone knows that."

"Do you think Jones has commitment issues? I certainly did not sense that when I did the readings for the wedding. I could have sworn that he and Ms. Bell were a fantastic match."

"I'm no matchmaker, but my intuition tells me that Jones is one hundred percent committed to the marriage," Joshua said. "It's all the pomp and circumstance around it that's getting to him."

"It is a big event."

"How would you feel if you and your soon-to-be spouse were the center of attention for the entire city of Illusion Town for the past month? Jones says the paparazzi are everywhere. He can't even leave through the front door of his office without having to plow through a forest of cameras. Tomorrow every move he and his bride make will be photographed and videoed and scrutinized. The media will be blasting out features describing everything from the clothes to the food to the story of how the bride and groom met."

"And my crystals," Molly whispered, numb with the horror of it all. "Trust me, the media will have a *lot* to say about the energy at the wedding."

"The press might have a lot to say about your crystals, but Jones is not worrying about them. He just wants the wedding over with so that he can settle down to married life and get back to work."

"You're sure?" she said.

"I'm sure."

They walked in silence until they turned the corner and came to a stop in front of Singing Crystals.

"I suppose that, from Mr. Jones's point of view, the wedding preparations have been rather stressful," she said, rezzing the lock on the front door. "So many decisions to make. Rehearsals. Fittings. Menus. Music. Invitations. The crystal arrangements. He turned over as much of the load as possible to Aiden Shore and Ms. Bell and Mr. Claude. Still, he had no choice but to get involved at various stages along the way."

"Exactly." Joshua braced one hand on the doorjamb. "All while trying to get the new Guild organization here in Illusion Town up and running, deal with the murky politics of a city run by a handful of powerful casino moguls–slash-mobsters, and, oh, right, take down some bad guys while he's at it."

"You're right." She moved into the shop. "Okay, I'll try not to panic."

"If you ask me, that's what Gabriel Jones is doing. Trying not to panic."

"I'll take your word for it. Which hotel are you staying at?"

"I haven't had time to get a room." He pushed himself away from the doorframe. "Got a recommendation?"

"There are a couple of small places here in the DZ."

"If you'll give me directions—"

"In addition to being exhausted, you are unemployed at the moment, which means you need to watch expenses. There's no reason to waste money on a hotel room when I've got a perfectly good sofa. You're welcome to use it tonight."

He went very still. His eyes heated. But when he spoke, his voice was chillingly neutral. "Thanks, I appreciate the offer, but it's not necessary. I'll be fine."

"Don't be ridiculous. It's not like we haven't spent a night together." She felt herself turning a hot shade of red as soon as the words left her lips. She was very grateful for the green shadows. "Okay, that didn't come out quite right."

"It was an accurate statement. But spending the night at your place would feel . . . different."

"Relax," she said, regaining her composure. "You're worried because you met the moms today. Do not be intimidated by them. After what you and I went through together, we are definitely friends, and friends are comfortable with offering friends a sofa for a night."

"Friends." He paused, evidently testing the word. "I guess that works."

She stepped back. "In that case, stop arguing and come upstairs with me."

He moved through the doorway. It wasn't until she was leading him up the stairs that she realized he was right.

Inviting him to spend the night here in her apartment felt different.

CHAPTER THIRTY-SIX

He thought he would crash as soon as he settled on the very small sofa. He was exhausted. But the knowledge that Molly was sleeping a few feet away made him restless. His intuition pinged again and again, whispering that their connection would be ending soon. Their mission was complete. They no longer had a reason to stay close.

An hour later Joshua gave up trying to find a comfortable position on the ridiculous little sofa. Moving cautiously so as to make as little noise as possible, he got to his feet and used the blanket, sheet, and pillow Molly had provided to make up a bed on the floor of the cozy living room. He had spent more than one night on the hard quartz floors of the tunnels. The fact that there was an area rug available tonight was a bonus.

He was settling into the makeshift bed when Molly spoke from the bedroom.

"Joshua? I thought I heard you moving around. Everything okay?"

He folded his hands behind his head and contemplated the green shadows on the ceiling. "Everything is fine. Didn't mean to wake you."

"I wasn't asleep."

"Worrying about your crystals?"

"I won't be able to relax until the wedding is over," she admitted. "The tuning I did on those crystals was complicated. I locked in the signatures of the bride and groom, but if I screwed up the job—"

"Stop worrying. Everything will be fine." He paused. His future was on the line. Action was called for. "Speaking of the wedding, are you going?"

"Not as an invited guest. I'll be there, but I'll be working behind the scenes along with the lighting and sound techs and the rest of the crew. Mr. Claude wants everyone on hand in case there are any last-minute problems."

"What about afterward?" he asked. "I hear it's going to be one big street party here in Illusion Town tomorrow night."

"Oh, yes. This wedding really is a big event, right up there with New Year's Eve and Founders' Day. But I haven't had much time to think about afterward. I've been obsessed with the crystals and my sister's disappearance and tracking you down."

"I get it. But do you think you'll be in a mood to celebrate when the ceremony is over?"

There was a short silence in the bedroom.

"Are you kidding?" Molly said after a moment. "Leona is back, safe and sound. The wedding of the year will be over. You've got a potential job offer from the Guild. Yep, I will definitely be in a mood to celebrate."

"Need a date?"

There was another beat of silence. He heard some soft rustling and knew that Molly had gotten out of bed. The bedroom door squeaked when she opened it a bit wider.

"Are you volunteering?" she asked.

"I'm not volunteering for anything. I'm asking you out on a date."

"Thank you. I'd like that."

"Good. Tomorrow I'll see about renting a tux."

"That's not necessary," she said. "Illusion Town is actually quite casual."

"Tomorrow night you and the rest of this city will be dressed to party. I'll need a tux."

"Even if you can find one, it will probably cost a fortune. You're on a budget."

"I am not yet flat broke, Molly. I can afford the damned tux."

"If you're sure—"

"I'm sure."

"There's a discount mall over in the Shadow Zone that caters to the drive-through Marriage of Convenience market," she said. "You might be able to rent an inexpensive tux there."

"I'll figure out how to get a tux on my own. Is it always this hard to get a date with you?"

"It's just that—"

"Good night, Molly."

"You're annoyed, aren't you?"

"Getting there," he warned.

"I guess I shouldn't piss off my date for the wedding."

"Good plan," he said. "Probably too late to find another one."

"Good night, Joshua."

He smiled at the laughter in her voice.

There was a squeak from the door but she did not close it. He heard the soft rustle of sheets and blankets and knew she had gone back to bed.

Leaving the door open.

Probably for Newton, not him.

He lay quietly for a while, absorbing the good vibe of the little apartment. He had lived in a variety of rental units over the years, but none of those places had felt like home. Molly's apartment was different. There was a lot of good energy in the space. Molly's energy.

He thought about the kiss in the living room of the mansion and then he wondered if Molly thought about it. He reminded himself that action had been taken. He had a date with Molly, their first real date. It was up to him to make sure there was a second date.

He made a note to track down a tux in the morning and then he finally went to sleep.

He stirred briefly when Newton returned via a partially open kitchen window. Newton paused to chortle a soft greeting and then he disappeared into the bedroom.

Joshua went back to sleep.

CHAPTER THIRTY-SEVEN

The following night, shortly after one thirty a.m., Molly kicked off the heels she had spent hours dancing in and slipped into flip-flops. She threw open the glass doors of the apartment balcony and swept outside, the skirts of her black knee-length gown swirling around her. Fireworks burst, flared, blazed, sparkled, and roared overhead, as they had all evening, adding multiple layers of light and energy to a town that ran on both.

The celebration was going strong in all of the zones and would continue until dawn. Music spilled out of the open doors and windows of casinos and nightclubs. People filled the sidewalk cafés and mingled in the streets drinking cocktails with names like Alien Illusion and Green Ghost.

Newton had vanished at some point, presumably off to party with his dust bunny pals.

Buzzed on triumph, champagne, and the energy of the night, Molly turned to wave her phone at Joshua.

"Nobody fell over dead in my energy circle and the press is calling the Guild wedding the new definition of spectacular," she announced.

Joshua emerged from the shadows of the living room carrying two balloon glasses of brandy. Amusement glittered in his eyes.

"It's always a plus if no one falls over dead in the energy circle during a wedding," he said.

She got another little frisson of pleasure at the sight of him. He had, indeed, managed to rent a tux, and he looked awfully good in it, although, strictly speaking, he was no longer in the complete outfit. She decided he looked even better now. When they had entered the apartment a few minutes ago, he had stripped off the formal jacket and tossed it over the back of a chair. Next, he had loosened the bow tie, allowing the strip of black silk to drape around his neck. Then he had rolled up the sleeves of the white dress shirt and unfastened the collar. It was all she could do not to throw herself into his arms and ravish him.

Does he feel the heat between us? Does he remember that kiss?

Focus, woman.

"Listen to this," she said.

She read the headline in the special very early edition of the *Curtain* to him.

Wedding of the Year Dazzles Town
Storybook Nuptials Glow with Good Energy

The much-anticipated wedding of Gabriel Jones and Lucy Bell surpassed all expectations. The bride was elegant in a satin gown created by Illusion Town fashion designer Amery Ames. The groom wore the traditional amber-and-green dress uniform of the Ghost Hunters Guild.

It was generally agreed upon by those present that the energy circle, handcrafted by Molly Griffin, proprietor of Singing Crystals, provided a vibrant and truly harmonic resonance that infused the atmosphere of not only the circle but the entire ballroom . . .

"Congratulations," Joshua said. He lounged against the railing and raised his glass in a small salute. "You are now the premier crystal artist in Illusion Town."

"For a month or two." She put the phone on the table and took a sip of brandy. "All glory is fleeting. In my business you're only as fashionable as your last wedding. I will always be grateful to the bride for taking a chance on me."

"She wasn't risking anything. Good energy is good energy. You know it when you sense it. Obviously she was well aware of the vibe of those crystals you tuned for the wedding. According to that article you just read, so was everyone else in the room."

Molly laughed. "You are very good for my morale."

He watched her with unwavering attention. "I could say that's what friends are for, but I won't."

She was intensely aware of the charged atmosphere on the balcony. Not all of the heat was coming from the psi-infused night and the fireworks. She and Joshua were generating most of it.

She was afraid to move for fear of shattering the crystalline moment. It was all she could do to ask the question that needed to be asked.

"Why aren't you going to tell me that's what friends are for?" she whispered.

"Because what I'm feeling right now is not friendship."

"What a coincidence. I'm not feeling friendly, either."

He drew his finger along the edge of her jaw. "I want to kiss you."

"Great idea." She swiped the glass from his hand and set it down on the table next to hers. Moving very close to him, she wrapped her arms around his neck. "It's about time."

He fitted his hands to her waist and smiled a slow, sensual smile that had a melting effect on her senses.

"About time for what?" he asked in a low, husky voice.

"About time you took a break from fretting about your priorities and focused on us."

He brought his mouth very close to hers. "For the record, I do not fret."

"Obsess?"

"Possibly," he allowed. "But I would like to point out that I am not the only one who has been focused on other priorities lately."

"We've both been a little busy."

"I can, however, promise you that it is definitely all about us tonight."

She leaned into him, enthralled by the heat in his eyes. "That works. I am one hundred percent focused on us, too. But before we do this, I need to ask you a question."

"What?"

"Do you remember the first time you kissed me?"

His eyes burned. "Yes, Molly Griffin, I remember. Hard to forget a kiss that knocked me flat on my ass."

She winced. "I was afraid that was how you would remember it. I tried to explain. You see, there was so much heat in those mirrors, and—"

"And I can't wait to kiss you again."

His mouth came down on hers before she could ask any more questions. The setting and the atmosphere were different, but the intimate sensual energy that had infused that first kiss in the mansion was there, stronger than ever. She was suddenly riding the thrilling wave of a physical response unlike anything she had ever experienced.

For the first time in her life, she found herself standing in a man's arms and not waiting—hoping—for her senses to ignite. She was *rezzed*— not going through the motions in an effort to summon real passion.

Joshua was doing nothing to hide his response. Everything about him was hard—everything except his mouth. It was hot, damp, and demanding.

When he finally broke the kiss, she was very glad he was holding her tight, because she wasn't sure she could have kept her balance otherwise.

"I wanted to do that the day I opened the door and saw you," he said.

"No, you wanted me to turn around and leave immediately."

"Let's get one thing clear. I didn't *want* you to leave. I thought it would be *best* for you if you left."

"Whatever. For your information, the first time I saw you, I imagined that it would be very interesting to kiss you."

"Probably the scrubs."

"Yes, very sexy," she said.

"Well, now you know what it's like to kiss me. We've run the experiment twice. Do you have a verdict?"

"Kissing you is more than interesting. It's very exciting. I want to do it again."

"As another experiment?" he asked.

"No, for real this time. No more trial runs."

He smiled again—a deep, dark smile of anticipation—scooped her up in his arms, and carried her into the shadows of the apartment. Somewhere along the way her flip-flops fell to the floor.

When they reached her bedroom door, she pushed it open for him. He got her into the small space, stood her on her bare feet, and kissed her again. His hands went to the zipper of the black dress. The soft, silky garment slipped to her ankles and spilled onto the carpet.

Her fingers trembled as she undid the fastenings of his formal shirt. And then she realized that, although he was rock hard, he was not rock steady. She wasn't the only one who was having a problem channeling the wildfire. They were both losing control. For some reason that took the thrill factor to a whole new level, one she hadn't even suspected existed.

He kissed her again and then his mouth moved to the curve of her neck and his hands skimmed down her sides. It was not long before the only thing she was wearing was the yellow crystal around her throat. It glowed faintly in the shadows.

"It's been a while for me," he warned. "If I don't get this right the first time, promise me you'll give me a second chance."

She smiled, gripped the ends of the bow tie, and tugged him closer. "You can have as many chances as you need."

"Good to know."

He broke free of the embrace and ripped the comforter aside. The world spun again when he lifted her and settled her on the bed. She pulled the sheet up to her breasts, propped herself on an elbow, and watched Joshua get rid of his shoes, trousers, and briefs.

And then he was in bed with her, his body furnace-hot, his eyes burning with the raw energy of passion. Okay, she thought, *lust* was probably a more accurate, if considerably less romantic, term for what she was sensing. He was a man who had been on a mission for nearly a month, and now that mission had been successfully accomplished. Like her, he was in a mood to celebrate. So, yes, *lust* was the right word, but damned if she was going to use it. This was her fantasy. She had a right to tweak the details. She would go with *passion*.

He teased her nipples with his mouth until she was clawing at his shoulders. He flattened his palm between her breasts and stroked downward. When he reached her belly, he paused and then went lower still. His hand slipped between her thighs.

"So wet," he breathed against her parted lips. "And so warm. So soft."

Everything deep inside her was tight and tense. She turned into him, reaching for his impressive erection. When she found it, she closed her fingers around him. His aching groan was all the reward she needed.

When he finally rolled onto his back and settled her astride his thighs, she thought she would fly apart. He reached down to press the pad of his thumb to the tight little bud of sensation, stroked her intimately, and thrust deeply into her.

She did fly apart then.

A short time later, with a hoarse roar of triumph and surrender, he followed her over the edge.

Afterward she lay quietly for a time, savoring the intimacy and the sense of connection. This was so much more than passion. What had just happened between them was nothing less than a life-changing experience. If it had been the same for him, she was ready to tell him the full truth about herself.

"Joshua?" she whispered.

"Mmm?"

His response was heavy with the weight of oncoming sleep.

"I've been thinking," she said.

"Same," he mumbled. He rolled toward her and draped an arm around her waist. He did not open his eyes. "We need to go back to that damned mansion."

She froze. "What?"

"Got to lock the door of the crypt."

He did not say anything else. She realized he was rapidly descending into sleep. He hadn't had a lot of it lately, she reminded herself. But, then, neither had she, and she was ready to explore the possibility of a shared future, ready to trust him with her secret.

They had just had life-changing sex and all he could talk about was returning to a murderous house in the desert.

She contemplated the shadows of the bedroom and considered the possibility that she needed to revise her notion of what constituted a life-changing experience.

CHAPTER THIRTY-EIGHT

Joshua opened his eyes to the warm light of the sun streaming through the window. He pushed the covers aside and started to swing his legs over the side of the bed. He paused when Molly's scent whispered to him from the tumbled bedding. He realized he was getting hard. Sadly, he was alone in the bed. So much for plan A.

He got to his feet.

The aroma of freshly brewed coffee and something tasty that had just come out of the oven drifted through the partially open bedroom door. Time to pivot to plan B—a shower, a shave, and breakfast with Molly.

Newton appeared in the doorway, a half-eaten muffin clutched in two of his six paws. There were crumbs in his fur. He chortled a greeting.

"Save one for me," Joshua said.

Newton chortled again and disappeared.

Joshua spotted his pack on the floor and started across the small bedroom. Halfway to his goal he noticed that the clothes he and Molly had discarded on the way to bed were no longer scattered on the floor. He shook his head, bemused by the realization that he had been sleeping so soundly he had not heard Molly moving about the room, picking up the evidence of rez-hot sex.

Very rez-hot sex.

After which he had proceeded to fall sound asleep.

He groaned. He had never pretended to be a romantic man, but even he knew that turning over and going to sleep immediately after sex was not the way to make a good impression on one's partner. It was certainly not what he had intended when he had fantasized about sex with Molly— and in spite of everything else going on in his life, he had spent an inordinate amount of time fantasizing about her lately.

Last night his fantasies had come true, and afterward he'd gone to sleep.

He opened the pack and took out the new button-down blue shirt and khaki trousers he had bought when he rented the tux. He made a note to return the formal wear within the three-day limit so that he didn't get charged full price for the clothes.

Next time with Molly would be different, he vowed as he headed toward the bathroom—assuming he got a next time. The possibility that last night had been a one-night stand as far as she was concerned was unnerving.

Some twenty minutes later, showered and shaved and feeling a lot more optimistic, although he had no reason to be, he ambled into the cozy little kitchen.

He paused to savor the sight of Molly whipping up a bowl of eggs destined to be scrambled. She was once again in artsy black—flowing black trousers this time and a black T-shirt. The yellow crystal sparked in the light. No scarf, he noted. Probably her casual-at-home look. He realized he just wanted to watch her for a while.

Newton broke the spell by chortling from the top of the refrigerator, where he was keeping a close eye on breakfast preparations.

Molly glanced over her shoulder. "Good morning. Help yourself to the coffee. The muffins are right out of the oven."

She was smiling, but her eyes told him that she was watching him from the shadows. The woman he had held in his arms during the night had retreated into her secret place.

"Thanks." He crossed to the counter, gripped the handle of the coffeepot, and braced himself. "About last night."

"Stop right there." She held up the fork. "There is no need to discuss last night. We are friends who bonded because we went through a dangerous experience. We survived said dangerous experience, so we had plenty of reasons to celebrate, and that's what we did. We spent a night on the town, dancing and drinking. It's no wonder we had sex and then went to sleep. Perfectly normal under the circumstances."

He thought about that, trying to figure out exactly why the logic did not hold up for him. It wasn't enough, he decided. He wanted—needed— something more. He poured a mug of coffee and concluded he was irritated.

"I don't know about you," he said, "but I don't usually sleep with friends."

"Really?" She gave him a cool smile. "Who do you sleep with? Enemies?"

"How in green hell did this conversation go off a cliff so damn fast?"

"Good question." Her smile was now a little too sparkly. "Ready for breakfast?"

"Yeah." He swallowed some coffee. "I'm ready for breakfast."

The muffled sound of the shop doorbell ringing startled Molly just as she was about to pour the eggs into the pan. She set the bowl on the counter and glanced at the clock.

"Singing Crystals doesn't open until ten today," she said. She brightened. "Maybe it's a journalist who wants to do an article on my wedding arrangements."

She wiped her hands on her apron and rezzed the little video screen on the wall. A man appeared. He had blond highlights in his salon-styled hair, and the jacket he wore over a black pullover and black trousers had just the right amount of casual slouch. There was a single crystal stud in his ear.

Joshua glanced down at the inexpensive blue shirt and khaki trousers he was wearing. The clothes were an upgrade from the scrubs but not what anyone would call fashion-forward attire. He really did need to do some shopping.

"Shit," Molly said. Her eyes narrowed in an ominous manner.

Joshua watched her closely, trying to read her. "You know him?"

"Yes," Molly said. "Reed Latimer. He owns Resonant Crystals. He's my competition."

"And?"

"And I call him Big Mistake. Reed is one of my more embarrassing relationship screwups." She rezzed the button that activated the intercom. "Nice of you to drop by to congratulate me, Reed. I appreciate the gesture, but it's a little early. My shop isn't open yet."

"I need to talk to you, Molly," Reed said. "You owe me that much."

"I don't owe you anything. You are a lying, cheating creep. Also, I'm a little busy this morning."

"I never lied to you," Reed said, sounding as if he were speaking through gritted teeth. "I explained that what happened was a misunderstanding. It's been nearly a year. You need to let go of the past and move on."

"I did let go of the past. I dumped you, remember? In case you missed it, that was me letting go of the past, or at least the part of it that involved you."

"Look, I can see you're still a little upset."

"No, I've got better things to do than waste time being upset with you. Now go away. I'm in the middle of fixing breakfast."

"Damn it, this is important, Molly. It's not personal, it's business. What's more, it affects both of us. You've got to hear me out."

She had started to end the call, but she hesitated. "What are you talking about?"

The suspicion in her voice was as clear as a bell.

"I promise you, this is a platinum-quartz opportunity for us," Latimer said, speaking fast. "If we play our cards right, we can get into the collector end of the business. Do you realize how lucrative that sector of the market is? Look, I can't talk about this out here on the sidewalk. Let me in and I'll explain."

Molly drummed her fingers on the wall beside the video screen. Joshua smiled a little because he knew what her decision was going to be before she made it. He understood. Business was business.

"Okay," she said to Latimer. "But make it quick. I expect to be very busy today."

"Prepare to get a whole lot busier," Latimer promised, satisfaction heating his words.

Molly rezzed the door lock button. "Come on up."

She ended the call and looked at Joshua. "Sorry about this."

"Not a problem," he said. "I understand."

The muffled sound of the door opening and closing echoed from the lower floor. Newton's ears perked up.

Joshua looked at the tray of warm muffins on the counter. "Mind if I have one? I'm a little hungry this morning."

"Go right ahead," Molly said. "The butter is in the refrigerator."

Determined footsteps sounded on the stairs.

Joshua selected a muffin. "I'll disappear while you and what's-his-name talk about the, uh, platinum-quartz opportunity."

Molly's reassuring smile was far too polished. "Thanks, but don't bother to make yourself scarce. There's no need. Besides, where would you go? It's a very small apartment. Sound carries. Stay right where you are."

Three sharp raps reverberated on the apartment door. Molly squared her shoulders, elevated her chin, and stalked across the kitchen, heading for the living room.

Joshua looked at Newton. "I already don't like this guy."

Newton muttered.

"And we haven't even met him," Joshua added.

Chapter Thirty-Nine

This wasn't the first time she had encountered Reed since she had stormed out of his shop and out of his life. The DZ was a small neighborhood in many ways, the sort of place where everyone knew everyone else or knew someone who did know everyone else. She and Reed competed for the same crystal arranging contracts and they ran into each other at the same restaurants.

She was prepared for the twisted mix of self-recrimination and irritation she had experienced on previous occasions when they had crossed paths. But when he actually walked through the door of her apartment, she was mildly astonished to discover that the only thing she felt was a sense of impatience. She wanted to hear about the platinum-quartz opportunity, make a decision, and then send him on his way so she could sit down to breakfast with Joshua. And talk about locking the stupid Alien crypt.

For some reason the fizzy euphoria that had thrilled her senses last night had gone flat. Time to resume real life.

"Good to see you again, honey," Reed said with the smile that had charmed her the day she went to work for him, but which now did nothing.

He reached for her in what was no doubt meant to be a friendly, semi-intimate hug. She turned away before he could touch her and led him toward the kitchen.

"Coffee?" she asked, aiming for an aura of cool self-assurance, making it clear that she was a busy woman who had better things to do than chat with an ex. A woman who did not intend to repeat her mistakes. A woman who had provided the brilliantly tuned energy circle for the wedding of the year in Illusion Town.

"Sounds great," Reed said, apparently oblivious to her bold, assertive style.

He did, however, stop short when he saw Joshua lounging against the counter, eating a muffin.

"Uh," Reed said. He looked at Molly, surprised and bewildered.

A rush of satisfaction hit Molly. She realized she was suddenly enjoying the moment. *Call me petty . . .*

She picked up the coffeepot. "I forgot to mention I have a guest. Reed, this is Joshua Knight. I'm sure you know who he is. He's the navigator who rescued the Hollister Expedition after the authorities had given up. He also made it possible for the Guild to arrest a band of Underworld pirates. Joshua, this is Reed Latimer. I may have mentioned that he owns a nice little crystal arrangements shop here in the DZ."

The patronizing description of his business drew an annoyed frown from Reed, but he managed to incline his head, barely, at Joshua, who returned the acknowledgment. Barely.

"Latimer," Joshua said.

"Knight."

Atop the refrigerator, Newton rumbled ominously. He did not go into combat mode, but he stopped eating his muffin.

It occurred to Molly that the energy level in the kitchen was escalating quickly, the result of too many males circling each other and preparing to lay down markers.

She stifled a sigh of regret. Time to de-escalate. So much for allowing herself to savor a teensy bit of female revenge. Life could be so unfair.

"Have a seat, Reed," she said, gesturing toward the table.

"I see you have a dust bunny," Reed said. "A new addition to the household? He wasn't around when you and I were dating. Cute little guy."

He started to reach up to pat Newton. Newton growled a warning. Reed yanked his hand back. Joshua didn't say anything, but there was a glint of derisive amusement in his eyes. Reed shot him a savage glance and then dropped into a chair.

"He's sometimes a little surly before breakfast," Molly said smoothly. She did not specify which male she was referring to. She carried the mug of coffee to the table.

Reed gripped the mug as though he wished it were Joshua's throat. Joshua gave no indication that he noticed.

Molly had a sudden urge to blow a whistle, call a time-out, and phone home for maternal advice on how to manage a confrontation between an ex and a current lover. Unfortunately, that was not an option. She was annoyed with both men. The kitchen was *her* territory. For that matter, the whole apartment and the boutique downstairs belonged to her. She was in charge here.

She went with her female intuition, which dictated a quick change of topic.

Slipping into the chair across the table from Reed, she gave him a politely expectant look. "All right, let's hear the details of this platinum-quartz business opportunity."

Reed fixed his attention on her, pointedly ignoring Joshua, who helped himself to more coffee.

"This is a private business matter," Reed said. "It should not be discussed in front of others."

"Joshua isn't a potential competitor," Molly said. "It's fine if he listens in." She made a show of checking the time. "I'd appreciate it if you could move things along, Reed. I've got plans for the day."

Reed's jaw jerked a couple of times, but he apparently came to the conclusion that he had no choice but to talk.

"I've got a new client," he said. "A high roller in the collecting market who recently acquired a raw crystal that is a genuine exotic. This individual wants it tuned."

"So?" she said. "You're a professional and you're good. Tune it."

"You don't understand," Reed said. "I viewed the crystal. It is very unusual. I could feel the energy in it but I don't know how to unlock it."

"You think I can handle it?"

"Yes," he said, very certain. "I'll pay you a consulting fee, of course."

"How much are we talking about?"

Reed winked. "Name your price. The client doesn't care."

"Are we talking about a signature tuning or generic?"

"Signature. Like I said, this is a collector."

"I'd want full credit for the work and fifty percent of the fee, not just a commission."

"Absolutely," Reed said quickly.

"I'll need to see the crystal and make sure I can work with it before I agree to take the contract."

"Of course."

Something about the conversation did not ring true. Intuition and her history with Reed were sufficient to tell her that he was leaving out some important details.

"What makes you so sure I can tune your client's exotic?" she asked.

Reed flashed his magic charm smile. "I'm certain of it."

The confidence in his voice rezzed more red flags.

"*Why* are you so certain, Reed?"

He chuckled. "The client arranged for me to view the crystal. I'm almost positive it's the same kind of stone as the one in your pendant."

Shock lanced across her senses. The mug in her hand trembled. Drops of coffee spattered over the rim and splashed on the table. Out of the corner of her eye she saw Joshua go very still. Newton's second set of eyes snapped open. She knew the two were reacting to her emotional response to Reed's statement.

She recovered swiftly and set the mug down. "That's very interesting," she said, grabbing a napkin to mop up the spilled coffee. "Did your client tell you the provenance of the crystal?"

Reed snorted. "You know collectors. They never talk about their sources."

Joshua spoke for the first time since acknowledging the introduction a few minutes earlier. "Did you inform your client of the identity of the expert you intended to bring in as a consultant?"

Reed shot him an irritated look. "No, not that it's any of your business."

"In other words, you didn't tell the collector about me," Molly said.

"Of course not." Reed was amused. "Why would I send a client to my competition?"

He had a point. Theirs was a business, after all.

"Well?" he pushed. "How soon can you take a look at the crystal?"

She thought about Joshua's words last night as he was sinking into sleep. *We need to go back to that damned mansion.* She tried to calculate the travel time involved in a round trip to the Funhouse.

"I should be free in a couple of days," she said. "Better make it three. I have to go out of town on a short business trip."

Joshua, still lounging against the counter, raised his brows. She knew she had caught him off guard. Apparently he didn't realize she had been paying attention last night.

Reed was appalled. "Three days? That won't work. This is a rush job."

"I'm sorry but it's the best I can do."

"You don't seem to understand. This is an incredible opportunity for both of us."

"Sorry," she said. "Business."

"Don't be stupid." Reed shot to his feet, the legs of the chair scraping on the floor. "Postpone your out-of-town appointment. I just need one day. We'll take the morning rez-lev train to Frequency City. You can examine the crystal. Once you're sure you can handle it, we'll sign the contract and arrange for you to do the sig tuning at a later date."

The tension in the kitchen was rising again. Up on the refrigerator Newton watched Reed with a very intent gaze. There was a similar energy in Joshua's eyes.

"I'm afraid your client will have to wait," Molly said, getting to her feet.

"A little success has gone straight to your head, hasn't it?" Reed said. "Keep in mind that in our business, reputation is everything. You survived one near-disaster after the intruder was killed in your shop. You can't afford to have word get out that you were not able to tune an exotic for a collector."

"Are you threatening me?" she asked quietly.

"Interesting question," Joshua said.

Newton growled and sleeked out fully. All four eyes and a lot of teeth were now showing.

This was not good, Molly thought. She needed to get Reed out of the apartment before the situation deteriorated any further. Fortunately, he appeared to belatedly register the vibe in the atmosphere.

"All right," he said, heading for the door. "I'll see if I can talk the client into waiting another three days. A word of advice, Molly. Opportunities like this don't come around often. If you're as smart as I always believed you to be, you won't screw this up with more delays."

She ignored that to follow him out of the apartment and down the stairs. At the front door of the shop, he stepped outside and turned to face her.

"If that other priority you mentioned involves spending the next three days fucking your new friend Knight, you might want to remember that he's got a reputation, too, and it's not good," Reed said. "He may have rescued the Hollister Expedition, but don't forget, he's the one who abandoned it in the first place."

"He didn't abandon the team," she said. "Everyone knows now that the expedition was ambushed by a crew of pirates."

"So what? It's no secret Knight was psi-fried in the process. He wound up in a para-psych hospital, remember? You can't depend on him, Molly. There's a reason they called him the Tarnished Knight. You don't know what's going on in his head."

"There was a time when I didn't know what was going on in your head, either. Instead, I trusted you when you said you were not registered with a matchmaking agency."

"It was the truth—at least it was when we first started seeing each other. But I was under a lot of family pressure to register. Family is family. You know that. You're the one who insists on labeling yourself a free spirit. You made it clear a CM was not an option for us. What else could I do?"

"I dunno. Maybe not forget to tell me when you did decide to register?"

"Try to remember that I'm offering you a life-changing opportunity," Reed said.

"Oddly enough, I had a life-changing experience lately, and it didn't turn out quite the way I had hoped."

"Molly—"

"Goodbye, Reed."

"Listen to me—"

"No, you listen to me. I'll be back in three days."

She gave him the one-finger salute and started to close the door.

Reed frowned at her hand. "What's that supposed to mean?"

"Old World tradition. A gesture intended to convey respect and admiration."

She shut the door in his face, rezzed the lock, turned, and marched back to the stairs. Joshua, Newton on his shoulder, was waiting on the landing.

"Free spirit?" Joshua asked.

"You overheard everything?"

"The two of you were not exactly whispering. For what it's worth, I don't think you can trust Latimer."

"No shit."

"Well, it's your business."

"Damned right."

"Do you think the chance to tune his client's exotic crystal amounts to a life-changing opportunity?" Joshua asked.

"Maybe." She climbed the stairs. "Don't worry. My eyes are wide open. I'm well aware that life-changing opportunities aren't always what they are cracked up to be."

"I'll remember that."

When she reached the landing, she gave him a bright smile. "Luckily, there are a few things that actually can change a person's life."

"Such as?"

"Breakfast. Let's eat."

"I've heard it's the most important meal of the day." Joshua followed her into the apartment and closed the door. "Got a question for you."

"What?" she asked, heading for the kitchen.

"Think Latimer might have hired a professional cat burglar to steal the crystals you tuned for the Guild wedding?"

CHAPTER FORTY

Stunned, Molly stopped cold in the middle of the kitchen. It took her a couple of heartbeats to process Joshua's question. Her first response was to deny the possibility.

"No," she said. "I'm no longer Reed's number one fan, but I really can't see him resorting to what amounts to . . . what? Industrial espionage?"

"Are you sure?"

"I . . . think so." She threw up her hands and went back to the stove. "But who knows? I was wrong about him before. I might be wrong now. I no longer trust my own judgment." She rezzed a burner and put a large chunk of butter into the frying pan. "But why would he sabotage me? There was no guarantee he would have gotten the energy circle contract for the Guild wedding if the bride had decided not to use my crystals."

"When it comes to motives, never overlook the power of revenge."

"True. But still." She poured the beaten eggs into the pan and picked up a wooden spatula. "I guess I'll never know for sure. Time to move on. When are we leaving?"

"Leaving?"

"For the Funhouse. The last thing you said before you went to sleep last night was that we have to go back and lock the crypt. Hey, got to stop the Sleepers, right? Can't let them take over the planet. They already had their chance. It didn't go well for them."

Joshua picked up the coffeepot and poured himself another cup. "Glad you can see the humor in this situation."

"I'm in a really good mood today. Haven't you noticed?"

"If this is you in a good mood, I'm not looking forward to seeing you in a bad mood. Are you always this prickly the morning after a sleepover date?"

"I have no idea." She took plates out of the cupboard. "You had a couple of house rules. I have two when it comes to dating. The first is that I only date people who are truly single."

"Judging by what you said to Latimer, registering with a matchmaking agency means someone is no longer truly single."

"Right. It tells me someone is ready to get serious about marriage . . . with someone else."

"Fair point." Joshua drank some coffee, looking thoughtful. "What's the second rule?"

"Rule number two is that I don't do sleepovers at my place or anywhere else. I'm like Amberella. I always go home alone."

"Because you're a free spirit?"

"Exactly."

Joshua propped himself against the counter and watched her with enigmatic eyes.

"That explains it," he said.

She ladled the creamy eggs onto the plates. "Explains what?"

"Why your ex was so surprised to find me here getting ready to eat breakfast."

"Yes, it does. Reed knows my rules." She set the plates on the table and put a saucer of eggs on the refrigerator for Newton, who pounced on it. "Let's eat."

Joshua sat down and picked up his fork. "It occurs to me that you and I have spent three nights together and had breakfast the next morning on all three occasions."

She took a chair. "What can I say? My life has gotten complicated."

"Does breaking your own rules change your status as a free spirit?"

She came close to losing it then. *Yes,* she almost said out loud. *Yes. You have changed everything.* But she managed to reassert control over her churning emotions before she embarrassed herself. "Let's get back to the problem at hand. What do you think will happen if we don't find a way to stop the buildup of energy in the Funhouse?"

"I have no idea. Maybe nothing. But that house has murdered a few people since it was built, and it is getting stronger."

"That's a little melodramatic, don't you think? We're not dealing with a real haunted house."

"As good as," Joshua said around a mouthful of eggs. "People check in and they don't always check out. At the very least it will go on killing the occasional transient and thrill seeker if we don't lower the heat. The worst-case scenario is unpredictable, because we're talking about unknown Alien technology. I'd have the damn place bulldozed, but that fireglass stone is hard and major demolition projects are expensive. It would cost a lot of money to tear down the Funhouse. Money I don't have at the moment."

Molly gave the situation some thought. "Technically speaking, it's not your problem. You didn't buy the mansion."

"Technically speaking, it *is* my problem. I'm the legal owner of record according to the Outpost town council. I could abandon the Funhouse but that would not solve the problem."

"Maybe we could burn it down."

"Fireglass doesn't burn," he said, "at least not at normal temperatures. You'd need volcanic heat to melt it."

"You're right, something needs to be done about that mansion, and you and I are probably the two most qualified people to do it. You're the only person I know who can navigate that dark tunnel, and I'm the best crystal artist in Illusion Town." She touched the pendant with an absent gesture. "I might be able to stabilize the tuning in the mirror chamber."

"If anyone can do it, you can."

"Looks like the team is back in action." She looked at Newton. "Get ready to ride, pal. We're going to lock the Underworld crypt and stop the Sleepers from invading the surface world."

Newton chortled and bounced a little.

Joshua grimaced. "To be clear, we're dealing with an Alien machine, not a crypt, and there are no extraterrestrial sleepwalking zombies involved."

"Sure," Molly said. She waved a fork at him. "Take all the fun out of it."

He had been about to swallow some coffee. He sputtered as a laugh came out of nowhere and got in the way.

And just like that, for no good reason that Molly could see, the energy in the kitchen brightened.

When Joshua recovered, he checked the time. "If we leave within the next half hour we'll be able to get to the mansion before the fog closes in."

"I'll pack some food."

"Good idea." Joshua got to his feet, picked up his empty plate, and went to the sink. "Maybe on the way back to the mansion you'll tell me why examining that crystal for Latimer is so important to you."

She winced. "You're not buying that it's a life-changing business opportunity?"

"Nope."

Molly thought about that for the length of time it took her to put the dishes into the dishwasher. She had known Joshua for only a few days, but after what they had been through, she was certain she could trust him.

Maybe she was deceiving herself. No, it was more dangerous than that, she realized. She *wanted* him to know her secrets—all her secrets. She had to find out if their relationship was worth fighting for. His reaction would tell her what she needed to know.

"It's a deal," she said. "When we're on the road I'll tell you my origin story."

CHAPTER FORTY-ONE

"Your birth mother and Leona's were used in an off-the-books experiment designed to create multi-talents?" Joshua tightened his grip on the wheel as he processed the story Molly had just told him. He had braced himself for a sad tale of an out-of-wedlock birth and a tragic death that had left the infant Molly an orphan. The real version of events slammed him sideways. "Got to admit, I did not see that coming. No wonder you've tried to avoid signing up with a Covenant Marriage agency. What about your sister?"

They had been on the road for an hour and were making excellent time. As soon as the ragged outskirts of Illusion Town had disappeared in the rearview mirror, he had set the throttle to maximum speed. The highway to Outpost and the mansion was a long, straight strip of pavement that sliced through vast expanses of open desert. There was not another vehicle in sight.

Newton was perched on the back of the passenger seat, riveted by the way the scenery was whipping past. He had positioned his mirror on the dashboard where he could keep an eye on it while he opened his first bag of Zing Chips.

"Leona hasn't registered, either," Molly said. "And for some reason that was not the first question I expected."

Joshua glanced at her. Her attention was fixed on the view through the windshield. Her shoulders were rigid. *Back in the shadows,* he thought, but at least now he knew why. She was waiting—braced—to see how he reacted to the full truth about her birth.

He understood. It was not easy to be an out-of-wedlock orphan in a culture founded on tight family connections. It was far worse to know that someone had conducted experiments on your mother while you were in utero—experiments designed to make you a multi-talent in a society that was uneasy with especially strong talents and wary around doubles. Being a triple usually meant an asylum or early death. Those who survived were assumed to be dangerously unstable.

"Well?" Molly prompted.

He had no idea what he was supposed to say. "Well, what?"

"I have just told you the big, dark secret of the Griffin clan," Molly said. "No one outside our family knows the truth about Leona and me."

That he could respond to. He was a pragmatic man.

"Keeping the secret was the smart thing to do," he said. "I would have done the same. Hell, I *have* done the same."

She shot him a quick look. "You mean you haven't told anyone about your ability to navigate the Underworld without amber?"

"No one outside my family," he said. "Except you."

"Because you had to explain what I saw when I walked through your dreams."

"Yep."

"Why haven't you told anyone?"

"You know why. I'm not a multi-talent, but I am off the charts. Very strong talents make people nervous, too."

"True."

"Plus, there are those who want to study talents like me," he added. He grimaced. "Or make me a cult leader."

"Also true. The moms told Leona and me that we should omit the stuff about the experiments on the matchmaking agency questionnaires. They say we have a right to our secrets."

"My mom gave me the same advice. She said there was plenty of time for a conversation about talents when a match looked serious."

"So you didn't put your complete para-psych profile down on the questionnaire?"

He smiled. "I don't have a complete para-psych profile. I've never been tested. My mom made sure of it."

"I'm starting to think my mothers and yours would get along well together."

"An interesting thought," he said.

"Leona and I have resisted registration because we don't want to omit the information and end up wasting time on a lot of dates that have no chance of going anywhere. We made the decision to live as free spirits."

"You're avoiding marriage because you don't want to marry someone who might not be able to handle your secret."

"Exactly."

"Look at it this way," he said. "At least you've got the option of registering with an agency. That's off the table for me now."

"Because that agency in Resonance dumped you after you wound up in the para-psych hospital?"

"Once that kind of data gets into the system there's no dodging it."

"No, I guess not." She was silent for a moment. "What are you going to do?"

"Become a free spirit like you, maybe. But who knows?" He shot her a quick, assessing glance. "I might get lucky and find another free spirit who wants to do things the old-fashioned way."

"You're willing to take the risk of a Covenant Marriage without going through a matchmaking agency?"

"There's nothing guaranteed about an agency match," he said. "Yes, statistically speaking, it improves the odds, but it's not magic. Things can and do go wrong with matches made through an agency. People are complicated and life is unpredictable."

She smiled faintly. "And sometimes they lie on their registration questionnaires."

"Sometimes they do. Any Zing Chips left?"

Molly opened a fresh bag and held it out to him. "Help yourself."

He reached into the bag and took a handful of chips. "You've told me your big family secret. Your mother was the victim of an experiment designed to produce multi-talents. I assume that's how you explain your ability to make crystals resonate with people's auras and your talent for the dream-walking thing. You think you're a double talent."

She went back to concentrating on the view through the windshield. "Well, actually—"

"It's not such a big deal, you know. Being a double is rare, but it's not *that* rare. I've worked with a few over the years. In fact, I'd bet my one and only asset, the Funhouse, that Gabriel Jones is a double."

"I'm a triple, Joshua."

He did some more processing. "You're sure?"

"Yep."

"But you're stable," he said, not making it a question.

She took her eyes off the endless highway long enough to give him a quick, assessing glance. "Yes. But I would say that, wouldn't I? I doubt if the average triple goes around claiming to be unstable."

"There is no such thing as the average triple, because the number of them in the population is so small, no one has ever been able to do any serious research. We know about the unstable triples because they can't hold it together. We don't know anything about stable triples because they've got the good sense to keep low profiles."

"I hadn't thought of it that way," she admitted after a moment.

"So what's your third ability?" he asked, curious.

"It's a totally dumbass talent. Useless and scary. A party trick that no one wants to see performed."

"Sounds interesting. Tell me."

She told him.

"You see?" she said when she was finished. "I'm a potential hazard. A disaster waiting to happen. Sort of like an energy ghost or a shadow trap."

He considered briefly. "That does explain why you didn't take up a career in the Underworld."

She frowned. "Is that all you have to say?"

"I do have another question. Are there any more chips?"

CHAPTER FORTY-TWO

The fog was thickening rapidly by the time Joshua opened the front door of the mansion and stood aside to let Molly and Newton move into the hallway. Newton chortled and zipped ahead to check out his favorite mirrors. Molly stopped three steps in, icy frissons sparking across her senses.

"It's definitely hotter in here now than it was when we left," she said.

"Yes, it is." Joshua lowered his pack to the floor and closed the door. "The sooner we deal with that pyramid, the better."

"I wish we knew for sure what would happen if we don't figure out how to stabilize the pyramid," Molly said. "Maybe we're wasting our time. We're going on our intuition and the advice of a dead medium."

"You and I have both been inside that mirror chamber. I think we can trust our intuition."

"I agree." Molly let her pack slide off her shoulder. "When do you want to tackle the project?"

"No time like the present."

"It's not like we can relax over a glass of wine and canned soup first, not in this hot atmosphere."

She was still trying to get a clear read on Joshua. She did not know what she had expected in the way of a reaction to the Griffin family secret, but it certainly wasn't casual, unfazed acceptance.

After pondering his lack of concern, she was coming to the conclusion that he didn't have a problem with her three talents because he had not only survived a harrowing experience in the tunnels, he had also survived nearly three weeks in a mansion that had a nasty habit of murdering its residents.

Maybe there was some truth to the Old World saying *What doesn't kill you makes you stronger.*

She reminded herself that she had walked through one of his nightmares. You learned things about people when you did that. No, she had not known exactly how Joshua would react to her origin story, but deep down she had been very sure that he could handle it.

Half an hour later the fog was so heavy it was impossible to see anything on the other side of the windows. Not that it mattered, Molly thought as she adjusted her day pack and prepared to follow Joshua down into the basement. The tunnel of night that awaited them was darker than any mist-bound evening on the surface world.

Newton was on her shoulder, little mirror in one paw. It was clear he took the dark tunnel as seriously as she and Joshua did.

Joshua stopped at the bottom of the basement steps. The glowing blue mist seethed around his legs.

"The psi fog down here is more intense than it was the last time we went into the tunnel," he said.

"Definitely." Molly tried—and failed—to suppress the shivers that were rattling her senses.

Joshua used a long length of rope to chain himself to Molly.

"Ready?" he asked.

"As I will ever be," Molly said.

Joshua rezzed the lock on the vault door. The tunnel of night loomed in the opening. Newton muttered and snapped open his second set of eyes.

Joshua paused at the entrance of the tunnel. "Amber check."

Molly did not remind him that she had checked and rechecked all of their amber only minutes ago. She gazed into the cave-like darkness that awaited them and knew he was right to be cautious. Even with a talent like his, they could not be too careful when it came to making sure their nav amber was well tuned. If something happened to him or his paranormal ability, it would be up to her to get them out of the Underworld. For that she would need well-tuned amber. And a lot of luck.

She rezzed her senses, pulsing a little energy through the various pieces of nav amber she wore.

"All good," she said.

"I'm good, too," Joshua said.

He took her hand and led her into the darkness. She shuddered when the disorienting currents of non-light robbed her of her vision. The experience was as unnerving as it had been the first time Joshua had guided her through it.

He tightened his grip. "I've got the through-line current."

"Excellent."

There wasn't much else to say. They were committed. She concentrated on the strength in Joshua's hand and took comfort from Newton's weight on her shoulder.

The trip back through the tunnel seemed to go on forever, just as it had the first time. Relief surged through her when she began picking up a strong trickle of energy.

"Are we there yet?" she joked, trying to defuse some of the tension.

"We're there," Joshua said. His tone was anything but humorous. He was the guy in charge, and he was doing his job. "Hang on while I get the door open."

"Trust me, I'm not going anywhere on my own."

"Glasses," Joshua ordered.

She reached up to the top of her head and lowered a pair of dark glasses over her eyes. The shades had been a last-minute idea. There was no way to know if they would provide any significant protection from some of the brilliant paranormal energy inside the mirror chamber, but it was worth a try.

She heard Joshua working the lock on the old vault door, and suddenly, blazing light spilled out of the opening. The energy sparked, flashed, and dazzled. Even with the sunglasses it was like looking into a glassmaker's furnace.

Newton rumbled a warning but showed no signs of taking off for cooler locales. He was on the team.

"Hotter in here, too," Joshua observed. "Still think you can deal with the pyramid?"

"Let me take a look," Molly said.

She went through the doorway, her hair lifting and stirring in response to the energy charging the atmosphere. Newton's fur stood on end. He closed his hunting eyes against the glare and muttered a little.

Joshua followed them into the chamber, leaving the heavy metal door ajar. She did not ask why. She was pretty sure she knew the answer. He was prepared to evacuate them in a hurry if necessary.

She crossed to the pyramid pile of shimmering quicksilver-like crystal rods in the center of the chamber.

Joshua joined her. She took his hand and cautiously kicked up her senses. She was now aware of the power and stability in Joshua's aura. Newton's energy field was smaller, but it was sturdy and rather fierce.

"Here we go," she whispered.

She rezzed her talent higher still and studied the currents of paranormal fire seething inside the pyramid. She was strong, but she knew she could not stabilize the wild storm raging in the rods with brute power. The task called for finesse.

"Like making crystals sing," she said.

She found the out-of-tune vibe and followed it back to the source, a rod near the center of the pyramid. Working gently, deftly, she exerted just enough energy to nudge the current back into a stable pattern.

And then she stopped breathing for a moment, waiting to see if the fix held.

Newton sensed it first. He chortled, bounced down to the ground, and bustled around the chamber, investigating the mirrors.

After another moment, Joshua smiled, satisfied. "You did it. I can feel the difference already."

He was right. The chamber was still ablaze with mirror light, and energy poured from the pyramid, but the currents felt stable now. Relief and satisfaction crashed through her.

"It always comes down to tuning," she said. "I think it will hold steady, but it's still generating a huge amount of power and we don't know the purpose. I have no idea how to shut it down or even if that would be a good idea."

"We'll let the experts worry about it. Maybe the more critical question is, what destabilized it?"

She studied the pyramid. "It's Alien technology. That means it's a few thousand years old. No machine works forever, not without an occasional tune-up."

"True." Joshua started to walk around the pyramid. He stopped when he realized he was still gripping Molly's hand. "What you just did, rebooting that pyramid, was damned impressive."

"Thanks," she said. "I had a lot of help from you and Newton."

"We make a good team," he said.

He released her fingers and untied the rope that bound them together so that he could continue moving around the pyramid.

Team. Yes, the three of them were a team, but she and Joshua had something else going on between the two of them—an intimate connection that had nothing to do with teamwork or a mission. He had to be aware of it, she thought. The sense of connection was too intense, too real, to be one-sided.

Maybe he was trying to ignore the link because he had no intention of getting deeply involved with a woman he had decided he could not marry. Maybe he was trying to be strong for both their sakes. Trying to keep their relationship light. Superficial. No long-term commitments.

Maybe she should take a hint and end things before she got her heart broken for the first time in recorded history. In hindsight, it was obvious that she had spent her adult life protecting herself by avoiding the risk of love. Like Leona, she had been committed to being a true free spirit. But the situation with Joshua was not just another Big Mistake. It was shaping up to be an apocalyptic disaster.

Taking a step back from the edge would be the smart thing to do.

The thought of doing the smart thing brought tears to her eyes. She blinked them away.

Joshua paused on the far side of the pile of glowing rods and looked at her over the top.

"You know, when you think about it, there's plenty of proof that the Aliens' technology wasn't invulnerable," he said. "Their cities on the surface are in ruins, and there are holes in the green quartz walls throughout the Underworld tunnels."

That did it. Here she was having an existential crisis, and he was discussing para-archaeology. A woman could only take so much.

"I don't know about you, but I've had enough teamwork for today," she said. "I vote we go home."

He frowned. "We can't go home tonight. We won't be able to leave the Funhouse until morning. The fog, remember?"

"You know what I mean. Let's get out of here."

"Are you okay?"

"No, I am not okay."

To her horror, the tears welled up again, and this time they fell.

Alarmed, Newton abandoned his exploration of the mirrors and dashed back to her. She scooped him up and sobbed into his fur. He murmured soothingly.

"Shit," Joshua said.

"For your information, that is not an appropriate response," she mumbled into Newton's fur.

Joshua crossed to where she stood and wrapped his arms around her, squashing Newton in the process. Newton wriggled free and scrambled up onto Molly's shoulder. He hovered there, muttering anxiously.

"I'm sorry," Joshua said, tightening his hold. "I don't know what the right response is."

She pressed her face against his chest and sobbed harder. For a time they stood there together and Joshua held her while she cried.

The storm passed but it was replaced by mortification. Molly pulled free of the embrace, turned away, and shrugged out of her pack. Joshua watched her retrieve a handkerchief. He said nothing while she dried her face and stuffed the damp cloth back into the pack.

"Sorry about that," she muttered, avoiding his eyes. "Stress."

"Right."

She straightened her shoulders. "I'm okay now. Let's get out of here."

He watched her with a concerned expression. "Going back through the tunnel of night will be stressful—are you sure you're up for it? We can wait if you need time."

She gave him a steely smile and saluted him with her middle finger.

"Why do I get the impression that particular Old World gesture does not actually convey respect and admiration?" Joshua said.

"Probably because you are psychic."

"Probably. You're right. Time to leave."

CHAPTER FORTY-THREE

"Thanks, Mr. Sullivan," Charlotte said, adrenaline spiking. "Griffin Investigations appreciates that you have done the firm a very big favor. Please know that we are ready and willing to repay it at any time. Just give us a call."

She hung up the phone and looked at Eugenie, who was at the window watching the light traffic on the street. "We have the name of the client who hired Mr. Invisible."

Eugenie swung around. "Sullivan came through?"

Her eyes were ice-cold but Charlotte knew that was deceptive. Neither of them was feeling cold. This was not a routine investigation. This was family business.

"He was happy to give us the name of the client who commissioned Mr. Invisible to steal the Guild wedding crystals," Charlotte said. "Sullivan and, apparently, the entire community of professional cat burglars here in town are well and truly pissed because of what happened to their star. They feel he was set up. Conspiracy theories are flying."

"Naturally," Eugenie said. "Mr. Invisible was a local legend. When legends go down, people want answers. They want to know what went wrong."

"Just as they did when Joshua Knight returned alone and psi-fried from the Hollister Expedition disaster." Charlotte got to her feet, slipped into her sleek blue Amery Ames jacket, and headed for the door. "Let's go talk to the individual who commissioned the theft of the Guild wedding crystals."

Eugenie grabbed her denim jacket and followed Charlotte to the door. "Anyone we know?"

"Yes, as a matter of fact."

"I don't know what you're talking about." Reed Latimer locked the front door of Resonant Crystals, turned the sign in the window to CLOSED, and swung around to face the two women who had invaded his shop. "I didn't commission the theft of the crystals. How dare you accuse me? You can't possibly have any proof."

He was sweating. Charlotte didn't need her talent to know he was lying. "According to our source, you were the client who booked the services of a professional burglar who went by the street name Mr. Invisible."

"Who told you that?" Reed yelped.

"We never divulge our sources," Eugenie said.

"Whoever they are, they're lying." Reed's voice turned surly as he recovered from his initial panic. "Why would I hire someone to steal the crystals?"

"You had two motives," Eugenie said. "One business related and one personal. First, you were furious because another art crystal business, namely Singing Crystals, got the contract for the Guild wedding."

"It's a new business," Reed fumed. "That shop has been open for less than a year. It doesn't have a long-standing, highly respected reputation like Resonant Crystals. Molly didn't deserve to get the highest profile contract of the wedding season."

"That was the bride's decision, not yours," Charlotte said. "Which brings us to the personal motive. You wanted revenge because Molly quit you and quit her job after she found out you had lied to her."

"That is not true," Reed said, straightening his spine. "I never lied to Molly."

"You knew she has two rules when it comes to relationships," Eugenie said. "The first rule is that she does not date people who are either married or registered with a Covenant Marriage matchmaker. No exceptions."

"Back at the start, she asked if I was registered. I told her the truth at the time. *I wasn't registered.*"

"We know," Charlotte said. "We checked. But a month later you took a business trip to Frequency City, which happens to be your hometown, and registered with an agency there. When you returned you neglected to mention that change of status to Molly. Then you started making so-called business trips to Frequency to meet the dates the agency arranged for you."

"But I didn't lie," Reed insisted. "It's not my fault Molly never again asked about my CM status."

"We admit we're stuck with some of the responsibility," Eugenie said. "We got busy with a couple of back-to-back investigations and neglected to check in on you for a few weeks. Imagine our surprise when we discovered that you had registered."

"It was none of your business," Reed said, his voice rising. "Or Molly's, either, for that matter. She wants to be a free spirit? Fine. That's her affair. But it works both ways. I'm free to have a private life."

"You broke her number one rule," Eugenie said.

"Why should she get to make the rules?" Reed shot back. "It's not my fault she never registered with an agency. Maybe we would have been a good match. I told her it was worth a try, but she refused."

"That was her decision," Charlotte said. "And it's beside the point. We're here today because we know you hired Mr. Invisible to steal the crystals that had been tuned for the Guild wedding."

"You can't prove it," Reed said.

"That's the thing," Charlotte said. "We don't have to prove anything, because we're not planning to take this to the police."

Reed blinked a couple of times and pulled himself together. "I'm glad you realize that would be a waste of time. Just to be clear, if you do go to the cops or try to smear the reputation of my business, I will sue you straight into bankruptcy."

"Save your threats," Charlotte said. "And your money. You'll need the cash to pay for your move to another city."

"You can't run me out of town. Why in fucking hell would I move? I've got major contracts here."

"Your problem is that a lot of people in certain quarters of the local criminal community are speculating that whoever hired Mr. Invisible through a broker is the person who murdered him," Eugenie said.

Reed stared, horror flaring in his eyes. "No. That's not true. It makes no sense. Say I did hire a professional thief. Why would I kill him while he was carrying out the job that I was paying him to do?"

Eugenie shrugged. "Maybe because you got nervous and were afraid that if he was caught, he would talk? Or maybe you thought he might decide to blackmail you afterward? There are all sorts of reasons why you might have changed your mind and decided to get rid of the only witness."

"Don't be ridiculous," Reed snapped. "Why would I shoot him at the scene of the crime?"

"That's obvious," Charlotte said. "You did not know Mr. Invisible's identity, but you knew where he would be that night. All you had to do was watch the rear door of the shop until he showed up. Then you followed him inside and shot him."

"You stupid bitch," Reed said. "I did not kill the thief. And there's no way you two can pin this on me. I was assured—"

He stopped, evidently realizing what he had just said.

"You were assured of confidentiality?" Charlotte said. "Your secret would have been safe if you hadn't shot Mr. Invisible. Unfortunately for you, the broker you used has a few rules, too."

Eugenie smiled a chilly smile. "Our advice is to leave town within twenty-four hours and not come back."

"You can't threaten me," Reed said.

"We're not doing any such thing," Eugenie said. "Think of it as a public service announcement. The broker has a private security department that is used primarily for collecting overdue payments from deadbeat clients. However, it also takes care of maintaining the reputation of the business. Reputation is everything in this town, isn't it?"

"Are you saying there's a contract out on me?" Reed asked, shaken.

"If there is, it wasn't commissioned by us," Charlotte said. "That's all we can tell you. We just dropped by to give you a friendly heads-up."

"Maybe not exactly friendly," Eugenie said. "But you get the point, I'm sure." She looked at Charlotte. "Are we done here?"

"I believe we are."

Eugenie unlocked the door and walked out onto the sidewalk. Charlotte joined her. They headed back toward the offices of Griffin Investigations.

"What do you think?" Eugenie asked.

"I think he'll leave town."

"So do I. But I was talking about the other thing. Do you think he killed Mr. Invisible?"

"No," Charlotte said, mentally rerunning the scene with Latimer. "He hasn't got the nerve it would take to follow a professional thief into a shop and murder him in cold blood."

"I agree," Eugenie said.

"We have just eliminated our prime suspect. That leaves a very big question. Who murdered Mr. Invisible?"

"One problem at a time."

"I never did like Latimer," Charlotte said.

"Neither did I."

"I like Knight."

"So do I. The problem is, Molly is clearly losing her heart to him. This isn't one more free spirit flirtation for her. She could get hurt."

"Because sooner or later Knight will feel the pressure to register with an agency?"

"Sooner or later everybody does," Eugenie said. "We're as much to blame as the rest of society. Look how hard we're pushing Molly and Leona to sign up with an agency."

"Professional matchmaking worked for us."

"Yes, but our daughters have a lot of complicated issues, thanks to their personal histories. They don't have the basic ancestry data they need to fill out the questionnaires properly. They don't even know the identities of their fathers. Their mothers were orphans who left almost nothing in the way of personal information. And then there's the problem of their para-psych profiles."

"Their profiles are pristine," Charlotte said. "Stone-cold normal. I made sure of it myself, remember? No one has ever questioned the records."

"You cleaned up the profiles that the private lab did when Leona and Molly turned thirteen, but the girls know the truth."

"It wasn't something we could hide from them," Charlotte said. "They needed to know what they would be dealing with when they came into their talents."

"Regardless, the end result is that they both refuse to register with a matchmaking agency." Eugenie got a thoughtful look. "Huh."

Charlotte glanced at her. "What?"

"It occurs to me that in the process of tracking down Joshua Knight we acquired a considerable amount of personal information about him. And, as Molly's parents, we know her better than she knows herself."

"So?"

Eugenie's eyes heated with excitement. "So there's no law that says the matchmaking questionnaires have to be filled out by the individuals who are seeking to be matched. The questionnaires aren't legal documents, after all. No one can arrest you if you lie or omit information."

"I'm sure each agency has a firm policy in place."

"Maybe a new agency that is trying to build a client list in a niche market that caters to high-rez and difficult-to-match talents would be interested in taking the old-fashioned approach."

Charlotte frowned. "There's an old-fashioned approach?"

"According to my research, back on the Old World, it was often traditional for the parents to consult with professional matchmakers to produce a list of suitable matches for their offspring."

"Do you know of a local agency that is operating in that niche market you described?"

Eugenie smiled. "I believe I do."

Charlotte considered that. "I consider myself a modern-thinking person, but occasionally there's something to be said for the old ways."

CHAPTER FORTY-FOUR

"Too bad we don't have a bottle of champagne," Joshua said as he emptied the pot of canned vegetable-noodle soup into three bowls. "Don't know about you, but I am in a mood to celebrate. This will be my last night in the Funhouse. There were times when I felt like I'd be trapped here for the rest of my life."

That was nothing less than the truth, he thought as he set one of the soup bowls on the refrigerator for Newton. He was finally free of the damned house. Free to focus on his future. That meant focusing on Molly, because he could not see a future without her—at least not one he wanted to contemplate.

"The energy in this place would make it impossible for anyone to live here indefinitely," Molly said. She sat back in the nook and drank some of the boxed wine he had poured for her. "The only reason you and I can handle it is because our core paranormal senses are strong, but we would never be able to sleep well, and eventually we would be forced out. It's no wonder the mansion has a reputation for murdering people. It probably drove its victims mad first."

"I'm sure it caused the medium to hallucinate and conclude that co-matose Aliens were escaping a crypt and preparing to return to the surface," Joshua said. "A couple more weeks here and I might have started seeing the Sleeper Aliens, too."

He put a bowl of soup and a small plate of cheese and crackers on the refrigerator. Newton surveyed the spread with enthusiasm and carefully chose a cracker to dip into the soup.

Joshua carried the tray holding the rest of the meal to the dining nook and sat down across from Molly. He studied her covertly as he handed out the soup bowls. As far as he could tell she had recovered from the emotional low point that had brought on the tears back in the mirror chamber. Stress had been the cause, she claimed—and maybe that was partially true—but he had a feeling there was more to the story.

"Don't," she said, munching a cheese-topped cracker.

"Don't what?" he asked.

She was amused. "Don't look at me like that."

"Like what?"

"Like you're afraid I'm going to fall apart again at any moment."

He could feel the heat rising in his face. "I think I have a right to be concerned. We're—"

"A team?" Her cool smile started to look dangerous. "Partners?"

"Yes, but that's not all. We have a relationship, damn it."

"Friends? With benefits? Oh, wait, you don't sleep with friends."

Now he was getting mad. So much for the celebratory mood. "We're lovers, in case you have forgotten. Yes, it was only the one time, and yes, I'm guilty of rushing things and I wasn't good with the postcoital pillow talk. I apologize. But in my own defense, I would like to point out that it had been a long day—a long month—and I was trying to figure out what to do about this damned mansion."

She nodded in a knowing way. "I get it. Priorities."

"Exactly." He swallowed a fortifying mouthful of wine and reached for a cracker. "Priorities."

"I really do understand, you know," she said, her voice softening. "I've had a few priorities myself lately. There's no need to apologize for the sex, by the way. It was good for me, too."

"Then why am I apologizing?"

"Mostly because afterward I wanted to talk about our relationship and you interrupted me to announce that we had to return to the Funhouse and lock the crypt. Then you went to sleep."

"So this is about me having a problem with my priorities?"

"It was, but not anymore because, as I just said, I understand where you were coming from."

"Is this what the tears were about today?" he asked, feeling as if he was groping his way through the dark tunnel without benefit of a through-line current.

"Not exactly."

"Are you going to tell me exactly why you cried?"

She went silent for a beat and then she evidently came to a decision. "All right, the truth is, I've been wondering if you took me dancing the night of the wedding and then went home with me and made love to me because you were feeling grateful."

He stared at her, stunned.

"Huh," he said, giving himself time to work out the screwy logic. "Huh."

She frowned. "Are you okay? You look a little weird."

"I think I just had a blinding flash of the obvious."

She shuddered. "Trust me, I know the feeling."

"Let me make sure I've got this straight. You're afraid that my feelings for you are being generated by gratitude because you helped heal my senses."

She flushed. "I'm not saying there isn't some mutual physical attraction involved."

"Nice to know the physical attraction, at least, is mutual."

"Joshua, I think we've said enough. It's been a very long day—preceded by several long days—and we're both exhausted. Again."

The pieces of the puzzle that was Molly were finally falling into place.

"Oh, no, you don't," he said. "You don't get to use exhaustion to dodge this conversation. We're going to clarify a couple of things. First, I did not rent the tux, dance with you for hours, and then have amazing sex with you because I was feeling grateful."

She blinked as if she was suddenly uncertain. "Did you rent the tux, dance with me, and go to bed with me because you were in a celebratory mood?" she ventured.

"No." He paused. "Although I admit I was in a pretty damn good mood."

"Why did you do all that stuff, then?" she demanded.

"Because I wanted to be with you," he said, exasperated. "Why did you wear that hot dress, dance with me all night, and then go to bed with me?"

She gave him a shaky smile, but her eyes were heating. "I wanted to be with you."

He drew a deep breath, released it, and picked up another cracker topped with cheese. "Okay, that settles it. We're not friends. We're lovers."

"Okay." Molly munched some cheese.

"That's it?" he said. "That's all you've got to say about our relationship?"

She swallowed the bite of cheese. "Should I say something else?"

"I guess not." That didn't feel right, but he didn't know where to go with it. "But just so you know, I can prove I didn't go to bed with you because I was feeling grateful."

She picked up her wine. "Really?"

"Yes. I've never used sex to say thank you to anyone. Frankly, it never occurred to me that it would work. Sounds like it would complicate things in a million different ways. When I want to say thank you, I just use the words. I figure that's why they were invented."

She had just taken a sip of wine. It did not go down well. She sputtered and choked on a gasp of laughter. She grabbed a napkin and covered her mouth until she got herself under control.

"Amazingly," she said, "that actually sounds logical. Thank you. I feel much better now."

He watched her for a moment, bemused. Fascinated.

"Will you give me another chance?" he asked.

"Another chance?"

"I know I'm not a romantic man, but I am a damn good navigator. Give me time and I will find the way."

She smiled, but he recognized the glitter in her eyes. Panic hit him.

"Shit," he said. "Are you going to cry again?"

"No. Absolutely not." She grabbed a napkin and swiped it across her eyes. "It's just that what you said was so romantic. Using your last dime to rent that tux and dancing all night with me was also very romantic."

He winced. "To be clear, it wasn't my *last* dime."

She ignored him. "You are much more romantic than you think. And, yes, I would like very much to give you—give *us*—another chance." She raised her eyes to the ceiling. "But not in that glass-and-steel coffin you tried to foist on me when I first got here."

"If we use my bed, we should probably change the sheets. I wasn't paying much attention to housekeeping before you arrived. It was a good day when I remembered to take a shower and shave."

As soon as the words were out of his mouth, he wanted to slap himself upside the head. *Way to sound romantic, Knight.*

Molly appeared unfazed. "Changing the sheets is a terrific idea."

Chapter Forty-Five

The bed in Joshua's room was another four-poster made of mag-rez steel, but there were no glass walls around it. Most of the mirrors had been removed. The single remaining one was heavily draped in black silk.

The house lights had gone out a short time ago, but Joshua gripped the handle of an amber lantern. The soft light illuminated the room.

"I think this will work," Molly announced from the doorway. "The energy level in here is fairly low compared to the rest of the house. Where are the sheets?"

"Cupboard," Joshua said. He set the lantern on the nightstand. "I'll get them."

There was something intimate about the task of making up the bed together. The touch of domesticity infused the situation with a small but pleasant vibe of normalcy. The relationship felt real. The future was still murky, but she was catching glimpses of it.

She looked at Joshua across the neatly turned down bed. He was watching her with eyes that burned. She caught her breath. Who was she kidding? Nothing would ever be normal with this man, and suddenly it was blazingly clear that was a very fine thing.

"Screw normal," she said.

He gave a low, sexy laugh that surfaced from somewhere deep inside him. He rounded the end of the bed, stopped directly in front of her, and caught her face between his hands.

"You must have read my mind," he said. "I was just thinking the same thing. Where's the fun in normal?"

She wrapped her arms around his neck. "Good question."

The kiss started out as a slow-burn affair, a compelling, seductive exploration that stirred the senses. Initially she let herself sink into the embrace, savoring the escalating excitement and the delicious intimacy. But the charge in the atmosphere built quickly. When Joshua moved his hands down to her waist, she went to work unfastening the front of his shirt.

He caught her hands in one of his. "Not so fast. Not this time."

"It's okay, really," she whispered.

"No, it's not okay. I've got something to prove, remember?"

"That you aren't going to fall asleep afterward. Yes, I know. But this isn't afterward. This is the before part."

"Trust me, I'm well aware of where we are in the process," he said a little too evenly.

"Are you getting irritated?" she asked, startled.

"It's a distinct possibility."

She frowned. "I wasn't trying to start an argument."

"Is that right? Could have fooled me. Probably the best way to avoid that outcome is to stop talking."

"The thing is, I have control issues."

"No shit. So do I. I'm a navigator, remember? I'm supposed to be the one in charge."

She smiled. "That sounds . . . interesting."

"Good."

He kissed her again, an irresistible, all-consuming, overwhelming kiss that demanded a response and made it impossible to talk. She stopped trying to rip off his shirt and abandoned herself to the glorious sensation of knowing that he wanted her as fiercely as she wanted him.

Their clothes seemed to melt away, and then they were falling together onto the silk sheets. She thrilled to the sight of his broad shoulders gleaming in the lantern light.

He took her to the brink—and left her hanging there until she could not take any more. She fought back, making her own sensual demands, pulling him over her so that she could wrap her legs around his waist. He groaned. Sweat slicked the skin of his back.

He reached down between their bodies and used his fingers to tip her over the edge. She abandoned herself to the climax. He thrust into her while the waves of release were still sweeping through her. She heard his hoarse, muffled shout, triumph infused with surrender, and wanted to laugh with the sheer pleasure of it all, but she could not catch her breath.

Afterward he pulled her close. She let herself fall into his warmth and strength. She opened her senses a little and savored the luxurious sense of rightness that whispered between them.

"That was amazing," he said into her hair.

"Yes, it was." Molly paused. "Think the energy in this house enhanced our experience?"

"What the hell?" He pushed her onto her back and sprawled on top of her, pinning her to the bed. His eyes glinted in the soft light. "What just happened between us was all you and me. There was no third party involved, especially not this monster house. Got that?"

She laughed. "I was teasing you."

"I am not laughing."

She speared her fingers through his hair. "I noticed. You're right. About the house not having anything to do with the great sex, I mean. You know, viewed from one angle, that's a shame."

"What are you talking about?"

"It occurs to me that if the energy in this place actually did have an enhancing effect on sex, you could make a fortune renting out the rooms. I doubt if anyone ever went broke promoting products that are designed to rez up a couple's sex life. If you convinced people that a night here in the Funhouse would take their lovemaking to a whole new level, the money would roll in."

"That," he said, "is the dumbest idea I've ever heard."

"Just a thought. I know you're worried about what to do with this place. I was trying to help."

"Don't bother." He looked down into her eyes. "Let's talk about something else."

"Such as?"

"How about our future?"

She stilled, and the sensual warmth that had enveloped the bed vanished. She was suddenly torn between a bone-deep longing to get a sharper vision of what a future with Joshua would look like, and the fear of discovering that she might not like what she saw.

As long as the view was clouded, she could allow herself to hope that there was a reason to take the risk of love and commitment. She did not want to enter another affair with one foot out the door—not with this man.

But the habit of protecting herself was strong.

"We probably shouldn't rush things," she said, her chest a little tight.

"We really haven't had what anyone would call a normal start to a relationship. Everything has been so hectic. There's a lot we don't know about each other."

His eyes got a little hotter. "You're the one who said, 'Screw normal.'"

She caught her breath. "Yes, I did say that, didn't I?"

"I realize there's a lot you don't know about me, and I understand that you want time to make sure we're right for each other—"

He broke off because she had clamped her hand over his mouth. His brows rose in silent inquiry, but he did not attempt to continue talking.

"The problem," she said, trying to steel herself for the risk she was about to take, "isn't that I don't know much about you. I know I can trust you. That's the important thing. The real problem is that you don't know as much as you deserve to know about me, and I can't tell you because I don't have the answers. I don't know anything about my ancestors. I don't know how the experiment that was done on my mother will impact me long-term or how it will affect any children I might have. Yes, you know my big secret. I'm a triple talent. But most people think that is the working definition of a psychic monster. Your family would be horrified if they knew the truth about me."

He did not respond, he just watched her with a steady gaze. She realized she was still covering his mouth with her palm.

"Sorry," she mumbled, flushing. She removed her hand.

"Here's what I know about you," he said. "I know you will drop everything and go down into green hell to rescue your sister. I know you will walk into the house of a man rumored to be half-mad and possibly dangerous and you will take the risk of trying to heal his shattered, psi-fried senses. I know you will spend a sleepless night protecting that man from nightmares and hallucinations. I know you can make crystals sing with good energy. I know you are the most exciting woman I have ever met. I know I wanted you the minute I opened the door and saw you. I know I want a future with you."

"Joshua," she whispered. She touched the side of his face with her fingertips. "I want a future with you, too."

He lowered his mouth to hers. She began to respond, joy igniting her senses. For now she could believe in the possibility of a future together. In the morning she would probably discover that she was deluding herself. But in the meantime, she had tonight.

Muffled chortling shattered the dreamy atmosphere. She froze.

"Uh-oh," she said.

She pushed Joshua aside, got to her feet, and grabbed a quilt.

"Sounds like Newton is back," Joshua said, levering himself up on his elbows.

"He's back, all right, and he's not alone."

CHAPTER FORTY-SIX

Molly's grim tone made him smile. Joshua folded his arms behind his head and watched her grab the lantern. She marched to the door, the bottom edge of the quilt trailing behind her, and disappeared into the hall.

"Newton," she said, her voice rising. "What are you doing?"

With a sigh, Joshua climbed out of bed, pulled on his briefs, and went to the door. Molly was at the top of the stairs, lantern in hand. She was leaning over the railing to look down into the living room. The chortling was much louder now.

He walked down the hall to join Molly, gripped the railing, and studied the chaotic scene on the ground floor. There wasn't much blue fog tonight, but there was enough to illuminate the living room in a weak blue radiance. Newton was, indeed, back, and he had brought what appeared to be twenty or thirty of his best friends with him. Maybe more.

It was difficult to get an accurate count, because the dust bunnies were bouncing on and off the furniture and dashing from mirror to mirror. It was clear they were enthralled with their own images set against the bizarre, ever-shifting landscapes in the crystal looking glasses. The chortling was in overdrive.

And in the center of it all was Newton, waving his small mirror.

"It's an invasion," Molly said, shocked.

"No, it's a party," Joshua said. "Look on the bright side."

"What bright side?"

He gestured at the living room. "There's a lot less fog in the house tonight. The energy level in here is still high, but it hasn't escalated since we returned from the mirror chamber."

Molly turned toward him, her eyes widening. "You're right. My tuning job must be working."

"Looks like it."

She smiled a satisfied smile. "It always comes down to tuning."

He grinned, put an arm around her shoulders, and hugged her close against his side. "And when it comes to tuning, you're the best there is."

"Thanks," she said. "But I'm not sure my work will do much to improve the value of your property. Got a hunch it will take a long time for the mirrors to cool down. Years, maybe. I doubt if this house will ever be comfortable."

"Now, see, this is where I'm going to think positive," he said. "The house is unique. Granted, it will require a very specific sort of buyer, an individual who appreciates its one-of-a-kind amenities."

"Like an eccentric horror film director or a medium who believes she can communicate with dead Aliens? I suppose it's possible someone will want to turn it into a haunted house theme park and charge admission, but I doubt it. It's too far away from Illusion Town."

"I'm sure the right buyer is out there," Joshua said. "My luck has turned, thanks to you."

He tightened his grip on her and started to kiss her. A loud crash stopped him. The noise was followed by delirious chortling. He glanced over the edge of the balcony railing.

"What was it?" Molly asked. "I'm afraid to look."

"Apparently there's a limit to how many dust bunnies can dance on a coffee table," he reported. "The vase just fell off. Don't worry, it didn't break."

A thud reverberated from the ground floor.

Molly shuddered. "Now what?"

Joshua studied the scene below. "A table lamp." He watched Newton demonstrate how to swing from a curtain tassel. "Got a feeling the drapes are coming down."

"At this rate you won't be able to list the house as fully furnished."

"So? The next buyer will bring in a decorator who will see the place as a blank canvas upon which to create a uniquely personal space for the client."

Molly started to laugh. He took her hand and led her back into the bedroom.

CHAPTER FORTY-SEVEN

Molly emerged from the bathroom dressed for the long day of travel that lay ahead in her uniform—black pants and a black tee. She glanced at the tumbled sheets on the big four-poster and gave herself a moment to remember the time spent in Joshua's arms. A rush of anticipation hit her like a tonic. Morning had arrived, and as it always did, it had brought clarity. The good news was that she could still believe that she and Joshua had a future together.

His pack was gone. It was probably sitting in the front hall, waiting to be loaded into the car. She zipped up her own pack and headed for the door.

The scene of the disaster did not become visible until she was at the top of the stairs. It brought her to a full stop.

"Newton," she shouted.

He chortled a cheery greeting and appeared from the direction of the kitchen. Hustling to the foot of the stairs, he rose on his hind paws, offering her a small bowl of dry cereal.

Ignoring the cereal, she swept out a hand to indicate the evidence of the apocalypse in the living room. Empty cans of Hot Quartz Cola were scattered across the floor. The discarded wrappers of what looked like an entire case of High-Rez Energy Bars littered the scene. Crumpled bags of Zing Chips were everywhere.

In addition to the overturned vase and the table lamp, crystal figurines had been swept off the end tables. Window curtains sagged on their rods, gold tassels lying forlornly on the floor. The drapes that had covered the large built-in mirrors had been pulled aside and, in some cases, torn down. Yards of black silk pooled on the floor.

The atmosphere felt hotter. Molly realized that paranormal light from the far end of the spectrum was sparking and flashing and burning in the dark crystal faces of two floor-to-ceiling wall mirrors that had once been safely covered.

She gave Newton a stern look and descended the stairs. "You and your hooligan friends trashed the place. What do you have to say for yourself?"

Newton chortled and bounced out of the living room with his bowl of dry cereal. He vanished into the hall.

"Be careful where you step," Joshua called from the kitchen. "There are marbles all over the floor."

"I can't believe this mess," she muttered.

When she arrived in the kitchen, Newton was back on top of the refrigerator, munching cereal. Joshua had a mug of coffee ready. He grinned when he handed it to her.

"Here, you need this," he said. "You look like you're in shock."

She sat down at the nook table and wrapped her hands around the mug. "I apologize on behalf of Newton and his pals."

"Don't worry about it," Joshua said. "Do you want dry cereal or the Chef's Special, cheese and crackers?"

"I'll go with the cheese and crackers."

"Good choice."

She drank some coffee and shook her head. "Evidently the party really took off after you and I went back to bed."

"Yep." Joshua was amused. "They even figured out how to open the refrigerator."

"That explains the empty cans of Hot Quartz Cola in the living room."

"They went through most of my stash. They must have been really buzzed on all that caffeine." Joshua opened the refrigerator. "Luckily they left a couple of cans for us."

"Anything else? We'll need some road food for the long drive home."

"I took inventory while you were upstairs. In addition to the cola, we've got a few personal-sized bags of Zing Chips, three energy bars, and some bottled water."

"What about the cheese and crackers?"

"We're eating the last of both this morning."

Molly glanced at one of the cupboards. "We should pack up whatever is left of the canned goods."

"Forget it. I've had enough canned soup to last me a lifetime."

Joshua carried two plates of cheese and crackers to the table and went back into the kitchen for his coffee. When he sat down, she saw that he was smiling.

"What?" she asked.

"When you said we'll need road food for the long drive home, it made me realize that I hadn't thought of Illusion Town as home until now. But it sounds . . . right."

She realized she was suddenly feeling a little giddy. "Does that mean you're thinking of establishing your navigation business there?"

"It looks like a good location for my kind of talent. There's a lot of exploratory work going on in the Underworld sectors below the city. If I get that contract with the local Guild, I'll be able to reestablish my reputation. Yes, I can see building a business there."

Satisfied, Molly ate some cheese and crackers. They were making progress. Firing up a for-real relationship, the kind that had a future.

"When do you want to leave?" she asked.

"In about twenty minutes, I think," Joshua said. He studied the scene outside the narrow window. "The fog is lifting rapidly."

"Sounds like a plan," she said.

"When we get home, I'm going to ask Griffin Investigations to see if they can dig up any information on Latimer's mysterious collector."

She finished her coffee and set the mug down. "Do you really think there's something off about that gig?"

"Yeah," he said. "I do. The coincidence thing. What are the odds that, out of all the crystal artists in Illusion Town, an anonymous collector contacts Reed Latimer, your ex, looking for a consultant who can assess a unique chunk of crystal that just happens to look like the one you wear around your neck?"

She took a deep breath and exhaled with control. "When you put it like that, it does sound a little too coincidental, doesn't it? You do realize I'm not thinking of taking the job because of the money? Leona and I want answers about our past. This is the first solid lead we've had in ages."

"I know," Joshua said. "We'll get answers, Molly. One way or another."

Within fifteen minutes the fog around the mansion had thinned to the point of being drivable.

"We're in luck." Joshua closed the cargo door of the SUV. "The mist is clearing faster than usual."

"More proof that the ambient energy level is going down outside the mansion as well as inside," Molly said from the doorway. She had Newton tucked under one arm. "Did you put those bags of Zing Chips and the energy bars and the colas in the back seat?"

"Along with the bottled water. Don't worry, we won't starve." Joshua walked toward her. "I'll take one last look around to make sure I'm not leaving anything important behind. I don't want to have to come back here if I can avoid it unless it's to sign the papers in a real estate deal."

She stepped aside to allow him through the doorway. Newton chortled and wriggled free of her grasp. He bounced up onto Joshua's shoulder.

"Maybe he wants another souvenir," Molly said. "He knows we're leaving."

"He's welcome to whatever he can carry. Pretty sure he and his buddies are the only ones who ever had a good time in this house."

Joshua headed down the hall. A moment later his footsteps sounded on the stairs, moving quickly. He was not taking a long, leisurely farewell stroll, Molly thought. He wanted to leave as soon as possible. Fine by her.

She glanced at the nearest hallway mirror and saw a reflection of herself alone in a glowing green Underworld chamber. Experimentally she lowered her defenses and allowed the mirror to tug at her senses.

There was plenty of power left in the mirror. The longer she gazed into it, the more ominous the image became, threatening to pull her into another dimension, trapping her . . .

"Shit," she whispered.

The house was no longer heating up, but it was still too hot for comfort. It had a long way to go before it cooled down to a level that a real estate agent would be able to describe as cozy.

With a shiver, she suppressed the unpleasant vibe and stepped outside onto the fireglass floor of the portico.

She heard the low hum of an expensive engine a few seconds before the sleek Slider appeared out of the last wisps of gray mist and glided to a stop in the driveway. The car door popped open. Auburn Cork climbed out.

"Ms. Griffin, a pleasure to see you again," he said, striding swiftly toward the portico. "Congratulations on that big wedding in Illusion Town. I understand that all went well in spite of the unfortunate events that took place beforehand."

"Thanks," she said. "The bride and groom were pleased, and that's what matters." A chill that had nothing to do with the energy in the mansion iced her senses. Everything about Cork's arrival felt wrong. "Are you here to offer Joshua his old job?"

I hope not, she added silently. She wanted to tell Cork that Joshua had other plans for the future, but she had no right to interfere. Still, maybe a small, discouraging hint wouldn't be amiss.

"He's been considering a new focus for his career—" she began.

"No, Ms. Griffin, I am not here to rehire Knight. I have other business to conduct with him. Where is he?"

"Inside. He'll be downstairs in a minute or two." She waved a hand at the SUV. "We're leaving momentarily. Long drive ahead. Don't want to dawdle. I'm sure you can understand."

"Looks like I got here just in time." Cork reached inside his jacket. When his hand reappeared, there was a mag-rez in it. "Let's go inside, Ms. Griffin. I don't like talking business out in the open."

She stared at the gun. A connecting line appeared between some previously vague dots. Then she met Cork's eyes.

"It was you," she said. "You're the one who set up the ambush in the Underworld. You kidnapped my sister and the others. Joshua said he didn't trust anyone involved in that assignment, including you."

"Inside," Cork ordered, his voice edging upward.

His eyes flared with rage and something else. Desperation, she decided. Maybe panic.

"Sure," she said.

She turned and slowly walked back into the house. Cork followed, closing the distance between them until he was a couple of steps behind her.

"Stop," Cork ordered when they were a few feet inside the front hall. Molly obeyed.

"Fuck," Cork muttered. "I'd forgotten how fucking hot it is in here."

Joshua appeared in the shadows at the far end of the hall, Newton, sleeked out and ready to attack, crouched on the floor beside him.

"I'm guessing you're not here to offer me my old job," Joshua said.

"No," Cork said. "I'm here to destroy you the way you destroyed me."

CHAPTER FORTY-EIGHT

Molly looked at Joshua. "You were right when you said you couldn't trust anyone connected with the Hollister Expedition."

Joshua did not take his eyes off Cork. "Who discovered that cache of Alien artifacts in the Glass House sector? It couldn't have been you. The publicity department of Cork and Ferris does a good job of making you look like you are an expert in Underworld exploration work, but we both know that's not true. It was your partner, Ferris, who provided those skills. You're the business and marketing guy."

"A wildcat miner named Doncaster found the cache a few months ago, before anyone had filed a claim on the Glass House sector," Cork said. "Glass House was still just a legend in the mining world. Doncaster and Ferris worked together in the old days. They trusted each other. Doncaster knew he was going to need help dealing with the legal side of staking a claim on the artifacts. Getting lucky can be dangerous down in the Underworld."

"Deadly in Ferris's case, apparently," Joshua said. "You murdered him, didn't you? Doncaster, too, no doubt."

"I had no choice. Ferris went down to take a look at the site. When he returned, he told me about the cache. Said it was special. Objects of power. Maybe weapons. Whatever they were, he said, they were dangerous and they had to be reported to the authorities."

"All of which would make them worth a fortune on the black market," Joshua said.

"Ferris said he was going to advise Doncaster to contact the Bureau of Antiquities. I argued with him, but he insisted the discovery had to be registered."

"The last thing you wanted was for the authorities to get involved," Joshua said. "So you murdered Ferris and Doncaster and took control of the site. You never filed a claim because you didn't want to draw attention to it."

"Ferris may have been a legend in the mining world," Cork said. "His name certainly opened doors and brought in clients. But he never did have a head for business. I knew there would be headlines when he died, so I made sure it looked like an accident. As for Doncaster, like most wildcatters, he was a loner. No one even noticed when he disappeared."

"You had control of the site but you had a problem," Joshua said. "You needed to set up an off-the-books operation. Business of any kind, legal or otherwise, requires staff. It wasn't difficult to hire the muscle you needed to clear out the energy ghosts and traps and handle security. There are a lot of ex-hunters on the streets looking for work, no questions asked. But you needed professional para-archaeologists to evaluate and test the artifacts."

"You knew you could not risk trying to hire that kind of talent through legal channels," Molly said. "So you arranged the ambush and kidnapped an entire team, including my sister."

Joshua watched Cork closely. "You must have been shocked when I made it back to the surface."

"You were supposed to die down there in those tunnels," Cork said, his voice shaking with anger. "They ambushed you with two ghosts and took your amber while you were semiconscious. They were going to finish you off with their flamers, but you came around long enough to make it into a hot room. They told me they couldn't follow you because a gate closed right behind you. Harkins tried to open it, but it was too complicated for him. But they were sure you wouldn't survive. *There was no fucking way you could have made it back to the surface.* How did you do it?"

"Navigator's luck," Joshua said.

"You're lying."

"When you realized I had returned and checked myself into a parapsych hospital and that the media was paying a lot of attention, you couldn't make me disappear, at least not right away."

"Don't think I didn't try," Cork said. "But I couldn't even get close to you because the security in that hospital was airtight. They put you in a fucking locked ward. You were under surveillance at all times. I figured as long as you were there, you couldn't do much damage. I decided to wait. Then you escaped the hospital."

"I needed time to recover my senses and try to find the Hollister team," Joshua said. "The only lead I had was this house. I had to come back here. Turns out that worked well for me, at least for a while."

"It has a lot of built-in security," Molly said. "The mansion is a fortress."

"I figured it was the last place anyone would look for me," Joshua said. "But I was wrong. Griffin Investigations managed to track me down. It took them a while, though. You, on the other hand, showed up out here in the middle of nowhere the day after Molly arrived. You said your in-house security people had located me, but that's not true, is it? How did you find me, Cork?"

JAYNE CASTLE

"It doesn't matter," Cork said.

"It matters," Joshua said. "Because I'm pretty sure it explains the murder of the cat burglar in Molly's shop."

"What?" Molly gasped.

"He was watching you, Molly." Joshua did not take his attention off Cork. "Leona and the others had locked themselves inside the pyramid. Cork planned to use you as a hostage to force the members of the Hollister Expedition to come out. He went to Illusion Town because he intended to kidnap you."

"I didn't have a choice," Cork said. "The Griffin bitch and her pals thought that all they had to do was sit tight until someone rescued them."

"It wasn't like they had a choice," Molly said. "They were getting close to finishing their analysis of the relics. They knew that you would kill them once you didn't need them anymore."

"Well, this does settle one question," Joshua said. He looked at Cork. "You're the one who murdered the thief who tried to steal Molly's crystals."

"That poor man," Molly whispered. "Mr. Invisible was in the wrong place at the wrong time."

Joshua and Cork glanced at her in disbelief and then immediately went back to focusing on each other. She and Newton seemed to have been relegated to the status of bystanders. That might prove useful, she decided.

"You were the other intruder in Singing Crystals that night, Cork," Joshua said. "The thief was already inside. You were in the alley and saw him enter. You must have guessed that he was after some of the crystals. Why murder him? Why not wait until he left?"

"Because he saw me," Cork said, his voice tight. "I was on the sidewalk in front of the shop. I knew he had probably recognized me. Who wouldn't? My face has been in the media almost as much as yours during the past month. I didn't realize he was in the neighborhood to steal any-

280

thing, and he had no way of knowing I was there to grab Molly Griffin, but when he disappeared into an alley, I followed him. The next thing I knew, he was breaking into the shop."

"You panicked and shot him because you knew that after you grabbed Molly, a lot of people, including the police, would start looking for her. The thief was the one person who could put you at the scene of the kidnapping."

"Then you realized I wasn't even home at the time," Molly said.

"I had no way of knowing when you would return, so I decided to pick you up the next night," Cork said. The unstable vibe in his voice was very audible now. *"But the next morning you left town.* By the time I realized you were not coming back, it was too late to follow you. I phoned your shop. Said I wanted to speak to you about a contract. Your assistant told me that you were away and would be gone for a while because you were driving to a desert town called Outpost."

"I think that answers most of the questions," Joshua said. "You can do your little party trick anytime now, Molly. We really need to get on the road if we're going to get back to Illusion Town in time for dinner."

"You two aren't going anywhere," Cork shouted. "You're both dead."

Molly touched the crystal at her throat and pulled hard on her talent. The effect was immediate. Lightning blazed in the hallway and danced wildly in the looking glasses. Several of the crystal faces of the nearby mirrors cracked and fractured. The wall sconces went dark.

"What the fuck?" Cork gasped. There was a series of increasingly desperate clicks as he tried again and again to rez the trigger of the gun.

"You're wasting your time," Joshua said. He moved forward and snapped the weapon out of Cork's hand, then tossed it on the floor. "All the amber and crystal in a radius of about twenty feet just went dead, including the amber in your mag-rez."

"Fuck you, Knight," Cork screamed.

With a roar of primal fury, he launched himself at Joshua. Molly was shocked by the sickening thud as the two men landed on the unforgiving fireglass floor.

Newton growled.

Molly spotted the gun and scooped it up. She straightened and turned quickly. Joshua and Cork were locked in mortal combat. In the weak daylight slanting through the doorway, she could see Newton dashing around the pair, searching for an opening. She did the same. She had just de-rezzed all of the tuning in the amber and crystal-based tech in the immediate vicinity, but she could still use the gun as a club.

There was no way to get close to the two men. It was not like watching a dramatically staged movie fight. There was nothing slick or choreographed about it, just a lot of thuds and grunts. She had never witnessed such violence.

It was clear that Newton wasn't having any emotional problems with the violence, but like her, he could not find a way to effectively intervene on Joshua's side.

The battle ended as abruptly as it had begun. Cork went limp. Newton chortled, fluffed out, and closed his hunting eyes.

Joshua got slowly to his feet. He had his back to her.

"Are you okay?" she whispered.

Under the circumstances it sounded like a dumb question, but it was the only thing that came to mind.

He turned to face her. He was sucking in great gulps of air, and blood dripped from his lip and his nose, but when he looked at Molly his eyes were fever-hot.

"Never better," he said.

Chapter Forty-Nine

"Unfortunately, now we have to deal with Cork," Joshua said.

On the floor, Cork groaned. He did not open his eyes.

Molly took some deep breaths and tried to pull her thoughts together. She was feeling strangely lightheaded. Maybe that was because she had never before used her third talent on such a dramatic scale. Or maybe it was the sight of all the blood. There seemed to be a lot of it. Some was dripping from Joshua. Some was coming from Cork.

"We need to turn him over to the police," she said.

"I'd like to dump him in Outpost, but the local authorities aren't prepared to handle a situation like this." Joshua wiped his bloody mouth with the back of his sleeve. "Looks like we'll have a passenger on the drive back to Illusion Town. I'll use some of the drapery pulls to tie his hands."

"I'll get some damp towels," Molly said. "We need to get you cleaned up."

The lights were still on in the rest of the house, so she hurried upstairs to the nearest bath, grabbed a towel and some washcloths, dampened the lot, and headed back downstairs.

Halfway down the stairs it occurred to her that the house energy was getting hotter again. She would be very glad to see the mansion in the rearview mirror.

When she returned to the front hall, she saw Joshua crouched on the floor knotting a length of tasseled drapery cord around Cork's wrists. Newton watched with great interest.

Joshua got to his feet and took one of the wet washcloths. "Thanks." He wiped away some of the blood, dropped the washcloth on the floor, and looked at Molly. "How's that?"

"Not great. Here, let me try."

She used another washcloth to erase more blood, dropped it on the floor, and handed him a third washcloth. "Press it to your mouth and nose."

He took the washcloth. "Give me a minute to get my former boss into the car. Then we'll be on our way."

"Where are you going to put him?" Molly asked.

"Plenty of space in the cargo area now that we're not taking a couple cases of energy drinks and snack bars back to Illusion Town," Joshua said. He leaned down and hauled a groaning Cork upright. "Give me that towel. I don't want him bleeding all over the back of my car."

Without a word Molly handed over the towel. Joshua tossed it over his shoulder and then half dragged, half steered Cork out the door. Newton fluttered after them.

Molly hesitated, wondering what to do with the bloody washcloths on the floor. She decided they were not her problem. The real estate agent could deal with them. The scene in the front hall combined with the trashed living room would add a few more interesting details to the legend of the Funhouse.

She turned to leave but stopped when one of the cracked mirrors suddenly blazed with silver fire. The fractured looking glass on the opposite side of the hall reflected the wild energy, setting up a chain reaction that traveled swiftly down the hallway into the main part of the house.

Understanding struck. She had flatlined the tuning in the nearby mirrors as well as the amber in the mag-rez when she had wielded her third talent. But nothing she or any other human being could generate was capable of de-rezzing the raw power stored in the looking glasses or in the fireglass stone of the house itself.

"Oh, shit."

She raced outside. Joshua had just finished closing the cargo bay door. He came around the SUV, a damp washcloth pressed to his mouth. The front of his blue button-down shirt was stained with blood.

"Got another washcloth?" he asked.

"No, get in the car. I'll drive." She yanked open the driver's side door. "Hurry. Newton? Where are you?"

Newton appeared, ears perked. He bounded up into the front seat. She got in after him, sliding behind the wheel.

"What's going on?" Joshua said.

"Just get in the damned car," she said.

She slammed her door and rezzed the engine. Joshua got in on the passenger side.

"Hang on," she said.

She floored the accelerator. The SUV shot out of the circular driveway and flew down the road. Thrilled, Newton hopped up onto his favorite perch, the back of the passenger seat, and chortled encouragement.

Joshua grabbed his seat belt. "Mind telling me what's going on?"

"It's a little hard to explain."

The explosion was loud enough to awaken any Alien Sleepers who happened to be wandering around the basement. The roar thundered across the desert. The currents of energy released by the blast acted like storm winds on the SUV, shoving it from side to side. Molly fought to maintain control.

Enthralled, Newton leaped onto the back of the rear seat to watch the scene through the cargo bay window.

Joshua twisted around to get a better view. "Wow. Just wow."

"How bad is it?" Molly asked, afraid to take her attention off the narrow strip of pavement.

"Oh, it's bad," Joshua said. "Spectacular. But I think the worst is over. Stop the car. Newton and I want to watch."

CHAPTER FIFTY

Reluctantly Molly took her foot off the accelerator and gently tapped the brakes. The SUV slowed to a stop. She cranked the wheel and turned the vehicle around on the empty road so that it was facing the scene of the exploding house.

She watched, mesmerized, as the mansion continued to shatter in a series of brilliant flashes of light and energy.

"Sort of like watching fireworks," Joshua said.

"More like a volcano," Molly whispered.

"I think some of the fireglass is actually melting," Joshua observed. He leaned over the back seat and retrieved a bag of Zing Chips. "Impressive."

A wave of guilt washed through Molly. "It's my fault. I apologize for destroying your house."

Joshua ripped open the bag and held it out to Molly. "How is the explosion your fault?"

Numb with shock, she took a couple of chips, stuffed them into her mouth, and munched mechanically. "The house was still very, very hot. When I used my crystal to de-rez all the tuned stones in the vicinity, I sent out a blast of strong, hot energy. It was just one hit too many for the house. I think I overloaded it. Or something. I don't know. I'm not an engineer. I'm an artist, damn it."

"Interesting," Joshua said. "Logical." He gave Newton a couple of chips and then popped some into his own mouth.

"Shit," he muttered.

"I know," Molly said. "It was a horrible house, but it was a solid financial asset. Now there's nothing left to sell except the property, and no one is going to want to buy a chunk of empty desert out here in the middle of nowhere."

"I wasn't swearing because the house is gone," Joshua said. "I said shit because the salt on the Zing Chips stings."

"Oh." She glanced at him and winced as he cautiously dabbed his damaged mouth with the bloody washcloth. "Salt on an open wound. Yeah, that's gotta hurt. Are you okay?"

"Yep." Cautiously, he tried another chip. When it went down without incident, he grinned. "See? All good."

Molly studied him for a moment. Then she smiled faintly. "You are really buzzed, aren't you?"

"Oh, yeah."

"Probably the adrenaline." She put the SUV in gear and turned the vehicle so that it was once again headed in the direction of Illusion Town. This time she accelerated sedately. "I wonder why the inventor who built the Funhouse went to all the trouble in the first place."

"I've got a theory," Joshua said. "We know that the mirror chamber in the Underworld has probably been putting out a lot of energy for eons. It is, effectively, a generator."

"Agreed. So?"

"I'll bet it was discovered by the inventor who later built the mansion. He used fireglass as his construction material and then filled the house with crystal and mirrors because he intended for the entire structure to function as a giant battery."

"A battery to store the power it absorbed from the mirror chamber?"

"Right."

"For what purpose?" Molly asked. "Okay, so power accumulated in the house. What good is a charged battery if you don't have a means of transmitting the energy to a machine or a device?"

"Ah, but he did make use of it. That's how he kept the house going. Think about it—the lights, the kitchen appliances, the water system, the heating and air-conditioning—all operated on an endless flow of power generated by the mirror chamber."

Molly considered briefly. "That's why all of the crystals in the mirrors were tuned. He used them to transmit and focus the power that operated the appliances and the lights and everything else."

"He conducted one hell of an impressive experiment, but it was a DIY job. He apparently kept the results to himself. Maybe he planned to tell the world someday and achieve fame and glory, but he died before he could file any patents. Now there's no way to know how he tuned the mirrors to control the Alien power source he had tapped."

"I'm not so sure it would have done much good if he had tried to explain how he did it," Molly said. "His talent must have been very unique. I doubt there are many talents around who could tune mirrors to store and transmit the power that was flowing into the house from that mirror chamber."

Joshua glanced back through the rear window. "Probably not a great idea anyway, given what just happened to my house."

She checked the rearview mirror. There was nothing to be seen now but empty desert and a small mountain of fireglass rubble in the distance. She shivered. "Probably not."

Joshua munched a couple more chips. "Think you could do it?"

She shot him a quick, wary glance and then concentrated on the road. "Maybe. But I don't plan to try, and I would appreciate it if you would not mention the possibility to anyone."

"No problem. I'll keep your secrets. All of them, even that cool party trick that just saved our lives."

She smiled. "I know."

"Just one question. How long does our dating relationship phase have to last before we can talk about marriage?"

Stunned, she braked to a screeching stop. Newton tumbled into the front seat. He chortled madly, evidently concluding they were playing a new game.

Joshua was thrown against the seat belt.

"Ouch," he said. He used the washcloth to dab his mouth. "You know, if this is an example of your driving style, I'm going to be in bad shape by the time we get to Illusion Town."

Molly twisted around to confront him.

"What did you say?" she said.

"You heard me—I'm going to be a little battered by the time we get home."

"Not that. The marriage stuff."

"Right," Joshua said. "The marriage stuff. I admit I'd rather not drag out the process, but if you need time to make you feel more comfortable and satisfy your mothers' concerns, so be it."

"I don't do Marriages of Convenience."

"Neither do I."

"You're talking about a real marriage? A CM?"

"I'm not interested in any other kind," he said quietly.

She closed her eyes and took a deep, steadying breath. Maybe she was hallucinating. The exploding house had unleashed a lot of strong energy.

When she opened her eyes, she saw that Joshua was watching her with a steady, intent gaze that belied the casual tone of his voice.

Newton chortled, urging her to get the car moving again. She ignored him and fixed her attention on Joshua.

"I'm a triple talent," she reminded him. "What's more, I didn't come by my psychic abilities the natural, normal way. I was *engineered* to be a triple."

"You were not engineered; you were born, just like everyone else. Your mother got a dose of unknown paranormal radiation while you were in the womb. Hardly the first time that's happened here on Harmony. There is unknown radiation all over this world. As for the injection of a mysterious formula, big deal. People have been experimenting with drugs designed to promote psychic talents since back before the Curtain opened on the Old World. And as for you being a triple, I don't think that's an accurate assessment of your abilities."

"Excuse me?"

"It's obvious you're a very powerful talent," Joshua said. "Off the charts, for sure. Like me. But all of your abilities are related to tuning, one way or another. Right? You said it yourself. It always comes down to tuning."

She hesitated and then shook her head. "Maybe you can make that case for my crystal work and expand it to include my dream-walking, but how do you explain my ability to melt tuned amber and shatter crystals?"

"Easy. They say every talent has a dark side. You can tune crystals and amber, so it isn't much of a stretch to discover that, being such a powerful talent, you can reverse the process."

"That's not what people mean when they talk about the negative aspects of a talent. The idea is that your greatest strength is always the source of your greatest weakness."

Joshua ate another chip. "You want armchair philosophy? Try this.

Talent is talent. It is ethically and morally neutral. What matters is what you do with it. The power to create is always the flip side of the power to destroy. I could go on, but I think you get the point."

"You're saying you don't have a problem with my talent."

"That's exactly what I'm saying."

"Or my weird origin story."

"Or that," he said. "I fell in love with you the day you and the dust bunny forced your way into my one and only real estate asset. Today you destroyed that real estate asset, and I am still in love with you. If that's not love, I don't know what is."

"Huh." A thrill of joy sparkled through her. "Neither do I."

"Do you think there's a chance that you can learn to love me?"

"Looking back, I knew I was in love with you the first time we kissed and you fainted."

"I did not faint," Joshua said. "I was rendered unconscious due to a lot of blunt force psychic trauma and a severe lack of sleep. My senses were temporarily overloaded."

She smiled. "You fainted. In a weird way, it was romantic."

"You know, if it wasn't for this lip, I'd kiss you right now. But I don't think it would go well for either of us."

"Probably not. Let's go home."

"Good plan."

She took her foot off the brake and stomped on the accelerator. The SUV surged forward, forcing Joshua deep into the seat. Newton chortled the dust bunny version of a cheer.

"Upon reflection," Molly said, "I don't think we need to wait long before we discuss the possibility of marriage."

"That's great." Joshua dabbed his cut mouth again. "Because I'd really like to get that side of my life squared away so that I'll be free to focus on building my business. Priorities, right?"

"One more word about getting marriage out of the way so that you can concentrate on your business priorities, and I will stop this car and kick you to the side of the road. You can hitchhike home."

"Understood."

She shot him a suspicious glance. "You were trying to make a joke, weren't you?"

"I believe I was."

"You failed."

"I'll practice." He held out the chip bag. "Another Zing?"

"Thanks."

CHAPTER FIFTY-ONE

The following morning they gathered in the offices of Griffin Investigations. Charlotte, styled in one of her signature Amery Ames business suits—violet this time—sat in the chair behind her desk. Eugenie, wearing her customary faded denim jeans, white shirt, and amber-studded belt, had angled herself on a corner of the desk.

Molly and Leona occupied the two client chairs. Joshua lounged, arms folded, one shoulder propped against the wall. Newton was on top of a file cabinet, the small mirror in one paw.

"Reed left town yesterday?" Molly looked first at Charlotte and then at Eugenie, flummoxed. "Are you serious? He just closed Resonant Crystals and took off?"

She and Joshua had been delayed on the long drive home, first by a road closure and then by the process of getting Cork arrested and taken into police custody. Fortunately Guild security had already uncovered evidence of Cork's involvement in the illegal excavation scheme. That had come, as it so often did, in the form of a seemingly innocuous piece of paper. In Cork's case it was a receipt found in a crate of toilet paper in the pirates' outhouse. There was nothing like a solid paper trail.

By the time they had walked into the little apartment above Singing Crystals, she and Joshua had been ready to drop. They had gone straight to bed and straight to sleep. Even Newton had called it an early night. He had flopped down on the foot of the bed.

"Reed had a ticket on the noon train out of Illusion Town," Leona said. "The moms went to the station to make sure he was on board."

"I waved to him as the train pulled out of the station," Eugenie said.

Joshua chuckled appreciatively. "Griffin Investigations scared the ghost shit out of Latimer."

"On the contrary," Leona said smoothly. "They did him a very big favor by warning him that some people here in town were upset because they thought he might have been the individual who shot Mr. Invisible."

"Got it," Joshua said. "Griffin Investigations gave Latimer the impression there might be a contract out on him."

Molly shuddered. "That was . . . diabolical."

"He should not have messed with the Griffin family," Charlotte said.

"Damn right," Eugenie said.

"By now he will have heard the news that Cork has been arrested on a variety of charges, including the murder of Mr. Invisible," Molly pointed out. "He'll know he's in the clear."

"He may no longer be in fear of his life," Charlotte said, "but he won't be returning to Illusion Town, because the word went out that he's the person who arranged to hire the thief. If he turns up, the police will want to have a chat with him. That would not be good for his reputation as a crystal artist."

Eugenie smiled, satisfied. "He'll realize he's had a very close call. He'll choose another location for his business."

"He really is a very good crystal artist," Molly said.

"He's a lying, cheating asshat," Leona said.

"That, too," Molly agreed.

"Congratulations on the slick handling of the Latimer situation," Joshua said. "As far as I can tell, most of the loose ends have been cleaned up, but there is one very interesting question left."

"Yes," Molly said. "Who was the anonymous client who wanted Reed to find a consultant who could tune a crystal that appears to be similar to the stones Leona and I wear?"

Charlotte shook her head. "We don't know. Yet. I got into Latimer's phone records, but whoever sent the text messages to him is very, very good with tech. We've got one thin lead, thanks to some text messages, but that's it."

Joshua straightened away from the wall. "What's the lead?"

"Early on, Latimer insisted on viewing the crystal in person before he would agree to take the commission," Charlotte said. "He was probably assuming he could handle the job. He was sent to a hotel room at the Amber Palace here in Illusion Town."

Joshua went still. "He met the collector?"

"No," Eugenie said. "The viewing was overseen by an exclusive private security firm that specializes in handling those kinds of arrangements in the rare and exotic crystal world."

Molly got the whisper of intuition that told her something was off. "The collector was there. I know that type. They don't let the objects of their obsessions out of their control. If the crystal was transported to a hotel room here in town and shown to a stranger, you can bet the collector was watching from somewhere nearby. Maybe posing as one of the security people or in a connecting room watching a camera feed."

Joshua looked thoughtful. "I think you're right."

"I agree," Leona said. "I've dealt with a few collectors. They are intense, to say the least. And they don't trust anyone."

"Regardless, it's the only lead we've got, so we'll keep looking," Charlotte said. She relaxed. "Meanwhile, we've got lots of reasons to celebrate. Leona is home, safe and sound, Molly is being hailed as the best crystal artist in town, Latimer has left the building *and* the city, and Cork is sitting in jail."

"Case closed," Eugenie said. "Who's up for drinks and dinner, Griffin Investigations' treat?"

"Excellent idea," Leona said.

"Count Joshua and me in," Molly added. She steadied her nerves to deliver the news. "We've got an additional reason to celebrate. Joshua and I are getting married."

There was a short, stunned silence, and then Charlotte and Eugenie exchanged enigmatic looks.

Leona glanced at Joshua and turned to Molly. "You told him the family secret?"

"Yes," Molly said. "He knows the Griffin family secret and he didn't run, screaming, in the opposite direction."

Leona's smile was as bright as the desert sunlight streaming through the window. She jumped to her feet, pulled Molly out of the chair, and hugged her.

"I told you so," she said. "I knew the minute I saw the two of you together that this time would be different."

"*Different* is one word for our relationship," Joshua said. But laughter heated his eyes.

"That is ... very exciting news," Charlotte said. "Congratulations."

"We'll order a bottle of champagne at dinner to drink a toast to the two of you," Eugenie added.

Their voices were warm and the sentiments genuine, but Molly sensed the concern beneath the surface. Still, neither mom had fainted in shock. That was a good sign.

Leona smiled at Molly. "When did you know for sure?"

"Gee, what woman could forget the most romantic moment of her life?" Molly said in a dreamy voice. "The Funhouse had just exploded. We had barely escaped with our lives. Cork was tied up in the rear of the SUV. Newton and Joshua were buzzed on adrenaline. Joshua was dripping blood down the front of his shirt. We were eating Zing Chips. That's when Joshua popped the question."

"There's nothing like a road trip to bring two people together," Leona said.

CHAPTER FIFTY-TWO

Melody Palantine wanted to scream. She had to fight the urge to pick up the fist-sized chunk of yellow crystal and hurl it through her office window. Weeks of planning had come to nothing. Yes, she had managed to track down the two women who were the living, breathing results of the old experiment, but the project had failed.

In hindsight it had been a mistake to try to work through Reed Latimer. But she had been reluctant to approach Molly Griffin in a more direct way. It would have been too risky. Nor was it her style. She had a talent for manipulating people, but she preferred to maintain a very low profile when she did so. She was the woman in the room that no one noticed, the unseen texter, the person orchestrating your computer searches without your knowledge.

She was currently running the new edition of the company that had formerly been known as Spooner Technologies. Taggert Spooner, the disgraced and recently fired CEO, was locked up in a para-psych hospital for the criminally insane. She was not responsible for his insanity—he had brought that on by conducting experiments with the Vortex machine on himself—but she had been instrumental in orchestrating his downfall and arrest. She had done so while working as his administrative assistant, the woman no one noticed.

Her first move had been to manipulate the board of directors into appointing Walter Willoughby as CEO. The bewildered Willoughby was still trying to adjust to his abrupt upgrade from mid-level management in Shipping & Receiving to the C-suite. He relied on Melody to guide his every move.

Thanks to her talent for strategy, she was now, for all intents and purposes, in charge of one of the most advanced tech companies in the four city-states. She had access to the firm's cutting-edge labs and researchers. She was in the process of establishing a top secret, black-box department so that research on the Vortex machine could resume.

She should never have allowed herself to get distracted by her aunt's diary. Until a couple of months ago she had not even been aware of it, but then, she had barely been aware of her aunt. Agnes Willard had been institutionalized in an asylum when she was in her early twenties. She had died recently, quietly and out of sight, forgotten by most of the family. Her affairs had been handled by a disinterested, court-appointed executor who had sent the diary, along with a few other odds and ends, including a certain yellow crystal, to the only heir who could be found—Melody Palantine.

For the most part the diary had proved boring reading. Page after page was crammed with records of hallucinations and detailed dream reports. But the notes relating to the experiments carried out by her eccentric brother, Nigel Willard, were now causing Melody a lot of sleepless nights.

Nigel had been dead for some time, but intuition had compelled her to track down the two infants whose mothers had been subjected to the experiment. She had finally located the adult Griffin sisters and was stunned to discover they were not only alive, they were obviously stable.

To Melody's relief, there was no outward indication Molly and Leona Griffin had developed multiple talents, but she had wanted to make certain the old experiments had not been successful. There was a lot at stake.

She herself was one of the vanishingly small number of triples who could handle their multiple talents. She had been hiding two of her three abilities ever since she had come into her psychic senses as a teen. She was as stable as her notorious ancestor, Vincent Lee Vance, the powerful triple who, a hundred years earlier, had led the one and only armed insurrection on Harmony.

Vance had been convinced that he was destined to command the four city-states. Things had not gone well for him. In the end, he and his cult of followers had been crushed by a combination of the Ghost Hunters Guild and a pissed-off citizenry that had not shared his vision.

Vance had failed because he had not understood that true power lay in controlling the technology and vital resources that enabled modern civilization to exist. You didn't need guns and soldiers to accomplish that goal. Okay, occasionally a mag-rez came in handy. But, generally speaking, she preferred to rely on manipulation and strategy.

She had a destiny and she was determined to fulfill it. But while she was working toward her goal, she intended to make certain she did not have any serious competition. If Willard's experiments on the Griffin sisters had been successful—if his protocol had produced strong, stable dual or even triple talents—she needed to know.

She was fully invested in her own enhancement research, which focused on the old Vortex machine. Unfortunately, Vortex still produced serious and dangerous side effects. She needed to know if Willard had been onto something she could use to enhance stability. Currently Vortex produced unstable monsters that had to be destroyed if they did not self-destruct like her former boss.

She got to her feet, picked up the yellow crystal, and went to stand at the window of her office. Twilight had settled on the city of Frequency. The lights were coming on. In the center of the modern, urban landscape, the massive walls and towering spires of the ancient Dead City were starting to glow.

It was time to go home to her apartment. She would pick up takeout and pour herself a couple glasses of wine. But after she had decompressed, she would go back to work. She had to make new plans.

Molly was probably a double talent at most, but not a particularly strong one. She was just another crystal tuner who did a little dream therapy on the side. Since she used crystals in her dream work, her ability to do the therapy might simply be a side effect of her core talent. Even if she was a double, that did not make her unique. Doubles were not common, but they weren't all that rare, either.

That left questions about the sister.

Melody closed the door of her office and walked toward the elevators. Leona Griffin might be an ordinary para-archaeologist with an ordinary talent. Or not. The question required an answer.

When you have a destiny to fulfill, you have to destroy the competition before it gets traction.

CHAPTER FIFTY-THREE

Molly's phone rang, bringing her awake on a shivering jolt of energy. Late-night phone calls tended to fall into one of two categories: youth shelter emergencies or family disasters. The news that the Hollister Expedition had been lost had come at night.

She grabbed the phone and checked the screen. *Charlotte*. At one o'clock in the morning.

Joshua stirred and propped himself on an elbow. He waited for her to take the call, saying nothing, but his concern was evident.

She gripped the phone and put it on speaker. "What's wrong, Mom?"

"Eugenie and I are calling to give you the good news. We knew you would not want us to wait until morning."

Molly went blank. "What good news? Who gets good news at this hour?"

"We all do. While you were busy, Charlotte and I registered you and Joshua at the Banks matchmaking agency," Eugenie said.

"You did what?"

"The agency is something of a start-up. It caters to a niche market, namely difficult-to-match talents. We filled out the questionnaires on behalf of each of you, and guess what? You two are a wonderful match."

Molly flopped back down on the pillows, stunned. "I can't believe this."

"We knew you and Joshua would be thrilled," Charlotte added.

"I don't know what to say," Molly said. "I think I'm in shock."

Eugenie spoke from the other end of the connection. "We're delighted for you two."

Molly stared at the phone. Joshua took it out of her hand. "Molly is speechless, but rest assured we are both excited to get the good news. Not that we had any doubts, but we know this provides reassurance to the two of you."

"Yes, it does," Charlotte said. "We really are very happy for both of you. Congratulations."

"Thanks," Joshua said. "Molly and I are going to say good night now."

He ended the call, tossed the phone onto the end table, and leaned over Molly. "They meant well. They're parents. They love you."

Molly groaned. "I know. But what if the report from the Banks agency had been negative?"

"There was never a chance of that."

She smiled and wrapped her arms around his neck. "What makes you so sure?"

"I've got a talent for navigation, remember? I know when I'm going in the right direction. You will always be my true north. I love you, Molly. Now and forever."

Joy whispered through her. "I love you," she said. "Now and forever."

Joshua lowered his mouth to hers in a kiss that sealed the vow.

The future looked very, very good. It looked right.

CHAPTER FIFTY-FOUR

Two cases of Zing Chips were delivered to Singing Crystals the following day. Newton was on the sales counter playing with his mirror. When he saw the familiar yellow-and-orange logo on the cartons, he chortled and bounced so hard he nearly fell off the counter.

"I'll take these upstairs to your apartment for you, boss," Clement called to Molly.

She came out from behind the counter to examine the cases. "There must be some mistake. Who would send us two cases of Zing Chips?"

"There's a note." Clement handed it to her.

Molly opened the envelope and read the message aloud.

Dear Ms. Griffin:

On behalf of Zing, Inc., I am delighted to present you with two cases of our Original Zesty Flavor Zing Chips as a thank-you for the attention that Newton, the heroic dust bunny, brought to our product recently. The photos and videos of him munching Zing Chips as a band of pirates was arrested by the Illusion Town Guild and the local police went viral. The result has been a boom in new orders.

We sincerely hope that Newton will get his very own social media channel. He is endowed with the charm and charisma it takes to attract a large following. Clearly he has a bright future as an influencer. We here at Zing, Inc., are excited to be a part of his success.

Our marketing department will be in touch soon to discuss future collaborations.

Sincerely,
Charles G. Bristow
President and CEO, Zing, Inc.

The two cases of Zing Chips were waiting in the alley behind Singing Crystals. Newton's guests arrived shortly before midnight. Each dust bunny got an individual-portion-sized package of chips. Within twenty minutes the hors d'oeuvres had been consumed, leaving nothing but chip crumbs and empty bags.

When they were finished, the dust bunnies took off in search of games and thrills in the Underworld. The party was just getting started. On Harmony the real excitement came after dark.

ANOTHER NOTE FROM JAYNE

Thanks for joining me on another adventure in my Jayneverse. I hope you had as much fun reading *People in Glass Houses* as I did writing it. Leona's story will be next.

If you are curious about the "wedding of the season," the marriage of Gabriel Jones and Lucy Bell, I invite you to read their story in *Guild Boss* (by Jayne Castle). Yes, there is another dust bunny in that one.

Waving from Seattle,
JAYNE